T0194991

JOHN MARK

Born in Africa—Martyred in Africa

JOHN MENCH

WESTBOW
PRESS*
A DIVISION OF THOMAS NELSON
& ZONDERVAN

Scriptures taken from the Holy Bible, New International Version®, NIV®. Copyright © 1973, 1978, 1984, 2011 by Biblica, Inc.™ Used by permission of Zondervan. All rights reserved worldwide. www.zondervan.com The "NIV" and "New International Version" are trademarks registered in the United States Patent and Trademark Office by Biblica, Inc.™

WestBow Press books may be ordered through booksellers or by contacting:

WestBow Press
A Division of Thomas Nelson & Zondervan
1663 Liberty Drive
Bloomington, IN 47403
www.westbowpress.com
1 (866) 928-1240

Because of the dynamic nature of the Internet, any web addresses or links contained in this book may have changed since publication and may no longer be valid. The views expressed in this work are solely those of the author and do not necessarily reflect the views of the publisher, and the publisher hereby disclaims any responsibility for them.

Any people depicted in stock imagery provided by Getty Images are models, and such images are being used for illustrative purposes only.
Certain stock imagery © Getty Images.

ISBN: 978-1-9736-3705-9 (sc)
ISBN: 978-1-9736-3707-3 (hc)
ISBN: 978-1-9736-3706-6 (e)

Library of Congress Control Number: 2018909769

Print information available on the last page.

WestBow Press rev. date: 10/10/2018

DEDICATION

Dedicated to my wife, Rose, who for thirty-four years, focused our lives around Jesus' message and to my second wife, Ann, who encouraged me for the last twenty years. Her illness provided me with the time to write and her love of life encouraged me to tell my stories. God's grace be with both of you.

CONTENTS

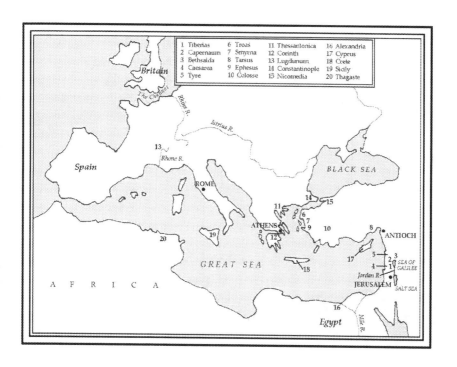

1 Tiberias	6 Troas	11 Thessanlonica	16 Alexandria
2 Capernaum	7 Smyrna	12 Corinth	17 Cyprus
3 Bethsaida	8 Tarsus	13 Lugdunum	18 Crete
4 Caesarea	9 Ephesus	14 Constantinople	19 Sicily
5 Tyre	10 Colosse	15 Nicomedia	20 Thagaste

INTRODUCTION

The Foundation of Christianity

In an effort to stimulate your imagination, I have written several books concerning the formation of the Christian Church.

Our understanding of Christianity was probably formed when we attended Sunday school. Hopefully, what we learned was based on an interpretation of the principles of the Bible. The Bible's New Testament provides us with a disjointed series of stories about Jesus. The stories are incomplete and have caused me to be concerned about the incidents not preserved in history. Some will say they are a figment of my imagination.

After reading the book, I encourage you to form and record your imagination about the unrecorded events.

My books are written as fiction related to history. In my opinion, history concerning any specific topic in ancient times is fiction. The amount of written history that is accurate is pure speculation. The amount of fiction that is contained in written history is based on several items:

1. elapsed time (from event to now)
2. government influence (the winners of war write history)
3. greed (writing to make money)
4. perspective (being human)

When you read a history book, you are reading a written perspective that has been deemed acceptable by your generation and your environment. Most history books are the perspective of well-paid victors.

INTRODUCTION

John Mark was born John and became the Christian Mark. He was related to several early Christians including Barnabas and Peter. He traveled on missions with both and recorded Peter's lessons concerning Jesus. He was educated and lived in Jerusalem where as a young man he saw Jesus on several occasions. After Jesus was crucified, he met with the resurrected Christ and became a dedicated missionary and teacher. He was a scribe for Paul and became known as the author of the second gospel which is a record of Peter's lessons and memories of Jesus. He spent his last years in Alexandria teaching Jesus' message and expanding the influence of the Christian Church.

CHAPTER 1

BORN IN NORTHERN AFRICA

John Mark was born in Northern Africa near the town of Cyrene. The area was represented by a Roman senator who was a relative of John's father. Cyrene was located in the Roman providence of Cyrenaica. It was a relatively small, peaceful town surrounded by small family farms. John and his family lived on a small farm. His father worked at their market in Cyrene where he sold vegetables that he and his family grew.

After Emperor Augustus' grandsons died, Augustus adopted Tiberius and groomed him for his position. At the age of fifty-nine, Tiberius became the emperor of the Roman Empire. He was an uneager ruler who wished the senate would make all the necessary decisions for him to manage the country. The military controlled those who invaded the empire; the senate ruled the people.

John was born twenty-three years after Jesus. He was the second son and the youngest child in his family. His father, Aristopolus, was considered a good Roman citizen, and when he was younger, had served in the Roman army. Mary was John's mother. Aristopolus gave both of his sons Hebrew names. John's older brother, by twelve years, was Joseph. Ester, who was five years older than John, was his sister. The family regularly attended services at the local synagogue where they were members in good standing. Mary spent many hours trying to teach Latin and religion to Joseph who preferred spending his time playing outside. As John matured, he became very interested in reading. In the evenings, Mary enjoyed sharing scripture lessons with her children.

"When our nation was threatened with destruction by invasion, the prophet Isaiah told us about a great man who was coming to lead us to freedom," she said. "We have suffered since then, but we are still free. God is good to us."

"Mother, please tell us another story," John said. "I want to hear another."

"No, son," she said. "It is your bedtime. My attendant will help all of you get ready for bed."

The children reluctantly followed their mother's attendant to their rooms and were soon asleep. Aristopolus and Mary relaxed in the living area and drank wine.

A few days later, when Aristopolus arrived home from work, he smiled as he told his wife about his day.

"It was a good day at the market," he said. "I sold everything that I brought with me. Our vegetables are very large this year."

Mary nodded and smiled.

"We do have very nice crops this season. You can take another wagon load tomorrow. I am saving the largest vegetables for their seeds to plant next year."

Aristopolus gave Mary a kiss.

"You are a great wife and mother. We make a good team. Next year's vegetables will be even better."

Then he reached into his pack, slowly pulled out his hand, and opened his fingers.

Mary saw a hand full of silver coins that he had earned that day. She took a large silver coin from his palm.

"May I keep this one? I will save it for a rainy day."

She put it in a jar in the kitchen.

"Joseph and I will work in the field tomorrow," she said. "Joseph thinks working in the field is fun."

"It is fun for him now while he plays," he said. "Eventually when he has to work to help us, he will not find it so much fun."

"You are probably correct, but he enjoys being outside," she said.

After dinner one evening, while Aristopolus and Mary were quietly relaxing in the living room, John burst in and ran up to his mother.

"I would like to learn to read more scrolls!" he exclaimed.

"I have taught you how to read all the scrolls we have," she said. "Reread the scroll written by the rabbi."

"Does the rabbi have scrolls?" John asked, suddenly more excited. "Maybe he will teach me how to read the scrolls he has."

"John, please don't bother your mother," Aristopolus interjected. "She worked many hours in the field today. I will talk to the rabbi myself."

Pleased, John smiled and then disappeared as quickly as he had appeared.

The next Sabbath after the service, Aristopolus talked with the rabbi while the family waited outside.

"Do you teach young boys how to read scrolls?" he asked. "My son, John, wants to learn to read other material than what I have at home."

"I am too busy at the synagogue to teach children," he said. "However, Rabbi Joel, my assistant, might be free to teach your son. Could you pay him a fee?"

His assistant overheard the conversation and approached them.

"I could give you a few vegetables," Aristopolus said to the young rabbi. "I have a small farm."

"Food is as good, maybe better than money," Rabbi Joel said. "I will be pleased to work with him one day a week. You can bring him with you in the morning and leave him with me."

"John would like that," he said. "When would you like to start?"

"Mid-week," Joel said. "By midweek, I have all of my regular duties completed."

Aristopolus thanked the rabbi and took the family home.

"I saw you talking with the rabbi," Mary said. "Will he teach John to read their scrolls?"

"Yes," Aristopolus said. "He is willing to work with John one day a week. I promised to provide them with some vegetables."

"That sounds like a good arrangement for both of us," she said. "I will separate a few vegetables just for them."

Mary explained to John that he would be going with his father one day a week and Joel, the Rabbi's assistant, would be teaching him how to read the scrolls at the synagogue.

"I hope they have many, many scrolls," John said. "I know I will enjoy reading them."

"I know they have several scrolls that tell the story of our religion," Mary said. "And I have seen a room full of scrolls."

John envisioned a large room filled with scrolls and all for him to read. He smiled to himself.

The following week, John's grandfather came to visit the family.

"I wanted to see you before your grandmother and I move to Rome," Anthony said. "I have been confirmed by the new senate and expect we'll be in Rome for a long time."

"I will miss you, Grandfather," John said. "I hope grandmother likes Rome. I am learning how to read Greek."

"Learning how to read Greek is a very good idea," he said. "Who is your teacher?"

"Rabbi Joel,' he said. "I spend one day a week with him."

Anthony smiled at his grandson.

"We have already found a new house in the city," he said. "And there is a synagogue close by where we can worship."

Aristopolus looked at his father.

"You were fortunate to find one near you," Aristopolus said. "I didn't know we had many synagogues in Rome."

"There are about twenty temples for every synagogue," Anthony said. "The emperor isn't in favor of synagogues, but he allows them."

"I sold our house here to a local government official," he continued. "He is taking the job I used to have."

"He is lucky to have your house," Aristopolus said. "Maybe, I will see him at the market."

"Someday we will visit you in Rome, grandfather," Joseph said. "I would like to see the city."

Mary was quiet. She knew she would never see Rome.

Early one morning, after Aristopolus loaded the wagon with vegetables, he and John went to town. When they arrived at the synagogue, Rabbi Joel was waiting for them.

"My wife has separated your vegetables from the others," Aristopolus said. "She picked the very best for you."

Joel looked over the assortment of vegetables in the basket.

"These are wonderful, thank you," he said. "Today, I will be discussing many things with John. We will see you this afternoon."

Aristopolus spent the rest of the day at the market. He was very pleased that it was turning out to be such a busy day. A customer approached him.

"Do you have any more of these?" the customer asked. "I am going to my relatives for dinner tomorrow. I could use about twenty of them."

He held up an orange root. Aristopolus politely smiled.

"I can have them for you tomorrow," he said. "My wife is harvesting them as we speak. I will bring twenty extra just for you."

"That will be good," he said. "I will tell my wife. She will probably purchase several other items from you."

"I will take two of those," another customer said. "Give me one large and one small."

After a very successful day, only two root vegetables were left in the basket. Aristopolus took them to a man who was leaning on a cart at the edge of the market area.

"Are you hungry, sir?" he asked. "You look like you would enjoy a good root."

The man shyly looked at the two large vegetables that Aristopolus held in his hand.

"I can't afford to buy those," he said, his eyes lowered. "I don't have any money. I was going to clean the area after everyone went home. Sometimes I find a few root vegetables and take them home to my family."

Aristopolus handed the roots to him.

"Take these to your family. Be at my stand in the morning. You can help me unload my wagon. I will give you a few root vegetables as payment."

"Thank you, sir," he replied, standing up straight. "I will see you in the morning."

Aristopolus unknowingly had just hired a dependable part-time employee.

After he finished at the market, Aristopolus went to the synagogue to meet John.

"Your son is very smart," Joel said. "Your wife has taught him well. I plan to teach him Greek and more details about our religion."

"Father, I had a good time, and I learned many new things," John said. "Thank you Rabbi Joel. I will see you next week."

As they drove home, John told his father everything he had learned that day.

When they arrived at the farm, they found the rest of the family working in the field.

"Everyone, go inside and get ready for dinner," Aristopolus said. "I want to talk with your mother."

The children ran into the house while the slaves carried the newly harvested vegetables to the wagon for the next day's trip to the market.

"Rabbi Joel said that he thought John would be a good student. He complimented you for doing a fine job teaching him stories about our religion."

Mary smiled and took his hand.

"I have told John a story almost every day," she said, humbly. "I am glad he remembers some of them."

They walked hand in hand to the house.

After enjoying a nourishing meal of vegetables, they settled in the living room. Joseph was quiet for a moment and then looked at his father.

"Father, I want to work on our neighbor's farm," he said. "He grows grain for the Roman government and employs several people. He said he has seen me working with mother in our field and has offered me a job."

Aristopolus was surprised.

"Are you certain you want to be a farmer?" he asked. "It is hard work."

"Yes, I have thought about it," Joseph said. "I don't enjoy studying, but I do like to be outside. I have always helped mother in the field. She has encouraged me to develop good work habits."

Aristopolus discussed Joseph's request with Mary. They decided to allow him to work for the neighbor.

"You have to start working someday," Aristopolus said. "If you work for our neighbor, at least you will be home in the evenings."

"Actually, I plan to live on the farm," Joseph said. "I will have one day a week away from work, and I will go to the synagogue with you."

Aristopolus looked at Mary as she began to frown. The tears flowed down her face, but her head nodded in the affirmative.

"We will expect to see you every week," Mary said as she wiped the tears away. "You have grown to be a young man. I must acknowledge that you are no longer my little boy."

Joseph gave his mother a kiss. Two days later, he moved to the neighbor's farm.

The morning of the next Sabbath, Joseph appeared at the door while the family was finishing breakfast.

"I am here to go to the synagogue," he said. "I have all day away from work."

"How was your first week?" Aristopolus asked. "What did you do?"

"I worked very hard," Joseph said. "He gave me the responsibility of caring for all the animals. I get up very early in the morning, prepare the horses to work in the fields, and milk the goats."

"It must be a long day for you," he said. "Do you bed down the animals at the end of the day as well?"

"Yes, that is all part of my job," he said. "I eat breakfast after the workers go to the fields, and I eat dinner after I clean, feed, and bed the animals."

"That is a very long day," Mary said.

"Well, I don't have to work after breakfast. I rest until noon. Then I clean the barn."

"Everyone has a first job," Aristopolus said. "My first real job was as a soldier. At least you don't have to march!"

Father and son laughed.

John excused himself from the table and thought, 'I don't want to be a farmer. Maybe, I will be a rabbi.'

After the service, Aristopolus told Rabbi Joel about his son's new job. Then the family boarded their carriage and started for home. The weather was muggy and still. The warm breeze felt good as the carriage picked up speed. The horse held his head high, his nostrils opened wide.

After lunch, the family sat outside on the porch.

"Do you see the large field of grain?" Joseph asked, pointing out in the distance. "It belongs to the Roman government. The grain will be shipped to Rome."

"Why don't they grow their own grain?" John asked.

"So many people live in the city that they must import their grain," Aristopolus said. "It takes a lot of grain to make enough bread for a city."

The family stayed in the shade of the porch and visited together the remainder of the day. The brothers talked about how John was now the oldest son at home. Late in the afternoon, Joseph said goodbye and started back to the neighbor's farm.

A few months later, Joseph told his mother that he liked the farmer's daughter.

"Do you think you earn enough money to support a wife?" she asked. "You are quite young to shoulder the responsibility of a family."

Joseph paused for a moment.

"Sarah thinks her father will give us a piece of land," he said. "If I have a farm, we will have plenty of money."

Mary was concerned, but quietly happy.

She thought, 'If you lived on a piece of their farm, you and Sarah would live next door to us.'

"Talk to your father," Mary said. "We have been married for many years. He can tell you what it is like to be married."

Joseph went to his father. Aristopolus told him that he should wait a few years.

"We don't want to wait," Joseph said. "We want to get married. She is the same age as me."

Aristopolus could see that his son had already made up his mind. He decided to help him.

"You owe it to her father to talk with him," Aristopolus said. "Does he know you are in love with his daughter?"

"I didn't think about that," Joseph said. "No, I don't think he has any idea. He treats Sarah as property."

Joseph went back to the farm later that day and found Sarah.

"My father thinks I should talk with your father," he said. "I guess that is the proper thing to do."

Sarah became a little nervous.

"My father probably wants me to marry an older man who already has a large farm," she said. "When we go to the synagogue, he only introduces me to the older men."

Joseph's eyes opened wide.

"He introduces you to men? I guess he does want you to get married."

"He wants me to marry the son of one of his friends," she said. "I don't think he cares which one."

"I will talk with him," he said. "I hope he understands."

That evening, Joseph went to speak with Sarah's father.

"Good evening, sir," he said.

"What can I do for you, Joseph?" Sarah's father, Claudius, asked.

Joseph clenched his fists at his side and took a deep breath.

"Your daughter and I are in love and want to get married," Joseph announced. "I would like your approval to marry her."

Claudius' face suddenly turned red. He jumped to his feet and began yelling.

"You are just a hired hand! No! My daughter will only marry a land owner!"

He called for Sarah. She came into the room and quickly realized that her father wasn't happy.

"Joseph just told me that he wants to marry you," he said. "Do you really want to marry a lowly farm hand?"

She looked directly at her father.

"Yes, father," Sarah said. "We love each other very much."

"Haven't I made it clear to you that I expect you to marry an older man who owns a lot of land?" he asked. "I can't allow my daughter to marry a hired hand."

"Yes, you have introduced me to several of those men," she said. "They scare me. I don't like the way they look at me."

Claudius was taken back, not believing what he heard. He chastised her.

"You will not marry, Joseph," he said firmly. "Never, you deserve a rich man. My daughter will marry a rich man."

Sarah cried out and ran from the room. Claudius turned to Joseph.

"You, Joseph, are no longer welcome on my farm," he said. "Pack your belonging and go home."

Joseph was stunned at Claudius' outburst. He immediately went to his quarters and packed his bag. As he slowly walked home, he looked up at the night sky.

"It is normal to want to marry," he said out loud. "I don't understand. I don't want to hurt anyone. God, give me direction."

When he arrived at his father's house, Joseph knocked on the door.

"Why are you knocking?" Mary asked when she opened the door. "Come in; you are always welcome."

His mother immediately sensed something was wrong.

"Let me get your father," she said.

Mary returned with Aristopolus and they both sat down, waiting patiently for Joseph to break the silence.

"I should have listened to you," Joseph said. "Sarah's father called me a hired hand and told me to leave his farm."

Aristopolus became disturbed.

"He shouldn't have done that," he said. "I can understand that he didn't what you to marry his daughter, but he didn't need to be cruel."

"What does Sarah think?" Mary asked. "She might still want to marry you."

Aristopolus looked at Mary.

"I don't know," Joseph said. "Sarah was crying when her father told me to leave."

His mother grasped Joseph's hand.

"I think John moved into your old room," she said. "You may have his old room."

Sadly, Joseph took his belongings and walked slowly to his room.

"She will be here tomorrow," Mary said to Aristopolus. "We are going to have to decide what we are going to do."

Aristopolus didn't believe her.

"We will never see her again," he said. "Her father is an important farmer in the community. He wants her to marry a man of means."

Mary just shook her finger slowly at her husband.

After Aristopolus had gone to work the next day, Mary sat on the porch. She puzzled about Joseph and Sarah. As she thought, she noticed a figure coming down the road. It was Sarah carrying a pack over her shoulder.

"I told my father I was going to marry Joseph," she said. "He told me to get out of his house. I don't know what to do. He scared me. I've never seen him so mad. Is Joseph home?"

Mary took Sarah by the hand.

"What does your mother think about you wanting to marry Joseph?" she asked.

"My mother just wants me to be happy," she said. "She loves me, but she will never question any decision of my father's."

Mary hugged her.

"Sit down," she said. "You are welcome to stay with us."

Mary told her attendant to get Joseph. When he arrived to speak with his mother, he saw Sarah.

"What are you doing here?" he asked. "I didn't expect to see you. I was trying to think of how I was going to get to see you."

"Father threw me out of his house," she said. "Do you still want to marry me?"

"Certainly," he said. "We have a lot of planning to do."

"When your father gets home, we will talk with him," Mary said. "He will help you."

When Ester appeared on the porch, Joseph turned to her.

"Ester, meet my future wife, Sarah," he said.

Ester was so shocked she couldn't speak.

"I think you surprised your sister," Mary said. "She will understand in a few moments."

"No one ever tells me anything," Ester said. "Does father know you are planning to be married?"

"We are going to talk with father this evening," Mary said. "I think you are old enough to sit quietly and listen to our discussion. One day, you will want to marry."

When Aristopolus and John arrived home, John didn't notice Sarah. He ran past her and tugged on his mother's arm.

"I had a really good day at the synagogue," he said. "Rabbi Joel started to teach me the Greek alphabet."

Finally, John noticed Sarah.

"Who is she?" he asked his mother. "What is she doing here?"

"You will learn more about her tomorrow," Mary said. "Dinner will be served in a few moments."

John sensed something was wrong, but didn't ask any more questions. After dinner, Mary's attendant took John for a walk. The rest of the family moved to the living room.

"We have something to discuss with you, Aristopolus," Mary said. "Do you remember Joseph telling us about Sarah?"

"I remember vividly," he said. "I am still not happy about the situation."

Mary explained the new situation to Aristopolus. He looked at Sarah.

"I didn't expect to see you, Sarah," he said. "You must really love our son."

"Yes," she said. "Yes, I do."

Aristopolus thought for a few moments.

"My brother, Barnabas, might have a job for Joseph," he said. "He has a large vineyard and produces wine. He also grows vegetables and sells them in bulk."

"He lives on Cyprus, doesn't he?" Joseph asked.

"Yes," Aristopolus said. "My other brother, Jonas, is a fisherman in Capernaum. I'm afraid we don't have a lot of choices."

Joseph looked out the window.

"I don't want to be a fisherman," he said. "But, I could work for Uncle Barnabas. I like him and I know about vegetables. How would we get to Cyprus?"

"By ship," Aristopolus said. "I will give you a little money to help both of you."

He smiled at his son.

"Sarah, would you like to live on Cyprus?" Joseph asked.

"I will live anywhere," she said. "As long as I am with you, I will be happy."

She took Joseph's hand.

"Your mother and I have to talk about how to do this," he said. "Don't worry, we are family. We will take care of you."

The next Sabbath, Aristopolus talked with Rabbi Joel about the sudden turn of events in his family. Joseph and Sarah were quickly married at the synagogue that afternoon and then began planning their departure for Cyprus.

A few days later, Mary took Joseph and Sarah to the port. It turned out to be a bright, brisk, sunny day. The sun's image twinkled on the water. Joseph hugged his mother.

"Tell father we appreciate all of his help," Joseph said. "We will make you proud of us."

"We are proud of you," Mary said. "I will miss you. I hope I can visit you next year."

Joseph kissed his mother goodbye.

Her son and new daughter boarded the ship, and Mary watched as it sailed out of sight. Her heart was heavy, but she was pleased that they were able to marry before leaving for Cyprus. She was proud of her husband. The driver saw that Mary had started to cry.

"They will be fine," he assured her. "They are facing a new adventure. I am certain Barnabas will take good care of them."

"I know," she said. "I just have to worry about my children. Just like your mother worried about you."

He smiled.

"She still worries about me," he said.

A few days later, Sarah's father came to see Aristopolus.

"I have come to take my daughter home," he said. "I know that I over-reacted. I do want her to be happy."

Aristopolus looked at him.

"Sarah isn't here," he said. "She and Joseph were married and have moved."

Claudius became agitated.

"She got married?" he asked. "I have made a grave mistake. Who married them?"

"Rabbi Joel," he said. "I know him very well. He is tutoring my son, John."

"Where have they moved?" he asked.

"I won't tell you that," Aristopolus said. "If she wants you to know, she will contact you."

Claudius mumbled a few words and departed.

After six months, John started to read simple Greek sentences. Mary had taught Ester how to manage the servants, and Aristopolus had hired an attendant for his daughter.

"I want to go to see Joseph," Mary announced. "He has been gone six months."

"I can't go," Aristopolus said. "We are too busy with the farm and at the market."

Mary sat very still.

"When can I visit him?" she asked. "After the growing season, we won't be so busy."

"Maybe after the season," he said.

"That means I won't have seen him for almost a year," she said. "Aristopolus, will you come with us?"

"No, I need to stay and work," he said. "I will send the three of you and two attendants."

"Do you think we will need them?" she asked.

"You will be gone for at least a month," he said. "I think you will have fewer problems if five of you travel together."

Mary thought for a few moments.

"Ester and John have been looking forward to traveling," she said. "I don't know about sailing on a ship."

"You will be fine," he said. "Ships are so large; it is like being on land."

Mary thought about the ship that took Joseph and Sarah to Cyprus.

Aristopolus was very successful at selling all of his produce that season, and the family prospered.

"I have purchased another wagon," he said. "One of the servants will help me load the wagons in the mornings."

"I am so pleased that you are doing well," Mary said.

A year passed before Mary spoke of their trip again with Aristopolus.

"Ester and I would like to have some new clothes for our trip," she said.

"That is fine," he said. "But the more you spend on clothes; the less you will have to give to Joseph and Sarah."

Mary thought for a few moments.

"We will be careful," she said. "It will be nice to help them out."

When Mary and Ester went into town, they stopped by the market to say hello to Aristopolus. He was so busy that he didn't have time to talk with them.

"Now that you have two wagons of vegetables to sell, you might consider hiring another person to help you," Mary said. "I am certain you would be able to find someone you can trust."

Aristopolus considered Mary's suggestion and soon hired a young man named Markus.

With the extra help, Aristopolus' days became shorter. He was home at the same time as before when he only sold one wagon load of vegetables each day.

CHAPTER 2

A Trip to Cyprus

The Roman Empire experienced a somewhat normal, peaceful coexistence with those of the Jewish faith. Emperor Tiberius was now allowing the senate and the military to control the decisions required to manage the empire. He occasionally went to work, but he lived a semi-retired life.

Things were well with Aristopolus. His business prospered and grew. He was able to afford two employees, one full-time and one part-time, at the produce market in town and maintained a large staff for his farm and home. His family was about to leave on a journey to visit his oldest son, Joseph.

The family arose early, and Aristopolus loaded their travel packs into the carriage, while the driver hitched the horses. It was a pleasant ride to the harbor. John always enjoyed watching the fish, birds, and ships. Today, he was focused on one specific ship, the "Wind." They found it tied to the dock. The dock reminded John of a beehive. Everywhere he looked dock workers were loading cargo. He noted only a few passengers being escorted to their cabins.

A mate noticed Aristopolus' family.
"This way, I will help you to your cabin."
The mate carried most of the packs. The attendants carried the remainder. Aristopolus stood on the dock and watched. Soon, his family

stood at the ship's rail and waved to him. He stayed until the ship sailed away.

"I hope they have a safe journey," the driver said. "I will miss taking care of them."

"I will try to find something for you to do," Aristopolus said.

He looked at his driver and smiled.

When the men arrived home, two wagons loaded with vegetables stood ready to go to market. Aristopolus boarded one, the driver boarded the other, and the two headed to town. Soon, the wagons were unloaded and Markus began selling vegetables to customers who had patiently waited for the delivery.

"If you didn't have the best vegetables, I would purchase mine at a different market," a customer said. "I guess I can wait occasionally for the best vegetables in Cyrene."

"I shall give you a few fresh dates, because you had to wait for the produce to be delivered," Markus said. "I'll see you tomorrow."

The customer enjoyed the dates and waved goodbye.

"I hope your family likes traveling by ship," Markus said. "The weather is fine today."

As he counted vegetables for a customer, Aristopolus thought about their ship sailing towards the horizon.

The day was warm and a steady wind prevailed. John heard the waves lapping against the hull of the ship, it sounded as if a giant was slapping the ship at the waterline, as it bounced towards Cyprus.

"We are making very good time," a mate announced. "If you are going to stand on the main deck, you should hold onto the railings."

Mary didn't like the motion of the ship and stayed in her cabin with her attendant.

The children stood at the rail and watched the ocean.

"This is exciting," Ester said. "I hope mother feels better before dinner."

A few sailors watched Ester with great interest.

"If you put your arm over the side, you can feel the mist," John said. "I am enjoying this trip more than I thought I would."

Ester didn't want to attract any more attention from the sailors.

"Come on John," she said, pulling his arm. "We should go to our cabin."

John reluctantly went with her.

When it was time for dinner, Mary took John by the hand and followed a mate to the galley.

"What is for dinner?" John asked. "I am hungry."

"I haven't looked," the mate said. "It will be some variety of fish."

He looked at Ester. Soon, another mate brought fives bowls of fish soup to the table.

"We also have warm bread," he said.

John grabbed a chuck of bread and dipped it into his soup. As he cobbled the bread, soup trickled down his face.

"Not bad," he said.

He dunked another piece of bread and looked at his mother.

"I think you will like the soup, mother." He mumbled with his mouth full of bread.

He wiped his mouth with the back of his hand. Mary looked at him sternly.

"Mind your table manners," she reminded him.

Then she focused on her soup and tasted it. John was the only one who asked for a second serving.

That evening, the family listened as the sailors played music and sang songs. Many passengers sat on the deck with them, watching the stars and enjoying the moment.

After a few days, John saw land in the distance.

"We are approaching Cyprus," the mate said. "We have made very good time. We don't always have such a good tail wind."

"I am ready to be on land," Mary said.

"I will help you and your family with your packs," he said. "And I will look for you when you return."

Mary nodded. She knew he was trying to impress Ester.

After their packs were on the dock, Mary talked with a driver.

"Our relative, Barnabas, owns a large vineyard near here," she said. "I have a silver Roman coin. If I give this coin to you, will you take us to the vineyard?"

"I know Barnabas," he said. "I will be glad to drive you there. I can't take that much money from you. I will give you several bronze coins in change."

Mary thanked him, and they boarded his carriage. After a short ride, they arrived at the vineyard. The driver knocked on the door and a large, burly gentleman answered it.

"I have visitors," the driver announced. "They are related to you."

Barnabas looked past the driver and saw Mary in the carriage.

"Mary, it is good to see you," he called out, waving to her. "I will have the servants take your packs."

He tried to pay the driver.

"The lady has already paid me, sir," he said.

"Mary is my brother's wife," Barnabas said. "Her oldest son manages my vegetable business."

The attention caused Mary to feel self-conscious. They proceeded into the very large house, and Barnabas escorted them into the very large living area.

"Did you say that Joseph is managing your vegetable outlet at the market?" she asked. "He helped us for many years."

"He convinced me to sell my vegetables at my own market stand," he said. "It has been very profitable for us."

"You will have to show me the market," she said. "I grow many vegetables in my field."

"Joseph has done very well, and I have made him my partner in the business," Barnabas said. "I pay him half the profits. He sells all the vegetables I can grow."

"Where does he live?" Mary asked. "Here in this large house?"

"No," he said. "He has his own house. I gave him a small piece of land, and he had a small house build on the land. It is just across the field from here."

"He must be doing very well," she said. "I can't believe he already has his own home. How is his wife?"

"I will invite them for dinner, and you can see for yourself," Barnabas said. "Unpack and rest this afternoon. I will see you and your family for dinner."

Mary went to her room and told John and Ester about their brother.

After a few hours, a servant knocked on the door and announced dinner. Mary, Ester, and John made their way to the dining area where Joseph waited for them. He went directly to his mother and hugged her. Then Sarah arrived holding a swaddled bundle.

"Is Sarah holding a baby?" Mary asked.

She was in a mild state of shock. Her eyes weren't focused and all she could do at the moment was smile.

"This is your grandson, Joseph," he said. "We didn't know what to name him, so we named him after me."

Sarah showed her son to Mary.

"You are a father," Mary said to Joseph, slowly realizing that her son was all grown up. "I'm a grandmother."

She looked at John with tears of joy in her eyes.

"The baby is your nephew," she said. "He looks just like your father."

John looked at the baby.

"He looks like a baby to me," he said. "When he grows a little, he might look like father."

The servants served dinner.

"John, please bless our meal," Mary said.

John blessed the dinner and thanked God for his new nephew. After dinner, they moved to the living room and enjoyed wine.

"You are lucky to have an attendant to help you," Mary said to Sarah. "You and my son have been greatly blessed."

"We do feel blessed," she said. "Joseph sells many vegetables. Not many people have a place at the market. Barnabas grows more vegetables than anyone in the area."

"I have several slaves who work for me and tend to the fields," Joseph said. "On an average day, I can sell five wagon loads of vegetables. I plan to grow more next year."

"Barnabas told me that you have your own house," she said as she proudly beamed.

"Yes, we do," he said. "Barnabas gave me a small piece of land and had his workers help me build a house. We have enough land to expand the house when our family gets larger, and we have a nice garden."

She walked to little Joseph and kissed his forehead.

"While I am at the market, you should visit with Sarah," Joseph said. "She would enjoy the company."

"Barnabas promised to take me to town tomorrow," Mary said. "I want to visit your market."

"Then I will see you tomorrow," he said. "Please excuse us. We need to get the baby home, and I need to get to bed. I get up very early in the mornings."

Mary hugged her son and daughter-in-law.

The next morning, Mary and her family met Barnabas on the porch.

"I have assigned a driver to you," he said. "He will take you wherever you want to go. I will be in the fields today. I will see you at dinner."

Mary leaned over the porch rail and looked up at the beautiful, clear, blue sky.

"Good morning, Miss Mary," the driver said. "I have the carriage ready to take you and your family to town."

They boarded the carriage.

"This is my son, John," Mary said. "And this is my daughter, Ester. The two ladies are our attendants."

"Yes Miss Mary," he said. "It certainly is a beautiful day for a ride."

The weather was warm, but occasionally, the passengers experienced a gentle sea breeze.

Soon, they arrived in town.

"First, I would like to go to the market," Mary said. "My son, Joseph, manages a vegetable stand."

"I know your son," the driver said. "Everyone knows him. The business has greatly increased since he has been with us. We have a much larger staff and many new slaves. We old timers have been given better jobs."

Mary felt good that Joseph was contributing to the success of Barnabas' business.

"Here we are," the driver said. "I will be at the end of the market waiting for you. Take as long as you like."

Mary immediately saw Joseph. He was placing vegetables on the stands. He looked up and noticed her.

"It is busy today," he said. "We have five stands open. Four of my employees serve the customers and three keep the stands filled with produce."

"This is a big business," she said. "You must get up really early."

"Yes," he said. "When I get up, the slaves have already loaded the wagons, and all of us bring the produce to the market. They help unload the wagons and go home to prepare for tomorrow."

"Will you be able to have lunch with us today?" she asked. "I would like to eat at the dock. John likes to see the ships and feed the fish."

"Certainly," Joseph said. "I brought an extra person with me today, so I could have lunch with you."

Mary and her group walked through the market. They entered a small clothing shop.

"I want to bring a present home for your father," she said. "I am sad that he wasn't able to travel with us."

"He stayed home so he could run the business," John said. "I think he likes it. I can see that Joseph likes running Barnabas' business."

"Yes, John, that's right," Mary said.

Joseph met his family at lunch time, and the driver took them to the harbor.

"Stop here," Joseph said. "I have eaten at this restaurant with Barnabas. I think it is his favorite restaurant."

The server saw the carriage and hurried outside. He escorted Mary to a table.

"We have some fine fresh fish," he said. "We also serve some of Barnabas' root vegetables."

Mary realized he recognized Joseph.

"I want some of Barnabas' vegetables," Mary said. "My son works for Barnabas."

She pointed to Joseph.

The server addressed Joseph, "You probably know my cook. He purchases produce from Barnabas every morning."

"He probably purchases them from me," Joseph said. "I'll have the fresh fish."

When the server looked at John, he said. "I want bread to feed the fish."

"What would you like to eat?" he asked. "I could serve you a smaller portion of fish."

John nodded. After John had finished his lunch, Mary escorted him to the edge of the dock. He handed his mother a crumbled piece of bread and fed the fish.

"I have to go back to work," Joseph said. "I will walk. I will see you at the house."

The next day, Mary, Ester, and John visited with Sarah. They spent the day playing with baby Joseph and walking in Sarah's field. Mary was impressed with their home. When dinner time arrived, they all went to the main house.

"Mary, tomorrow I want to talk with you," Barnabas said. "I will see you after breakfast. We will take a ride through the vineyards."

"I would enjoy that," she said. "Can I bring John?"

"No," he said. "I would rather it be just you and me."

Mary smiled curiously and agreed.

The following morning, they boarded the carriage and the driver slowly headed to the vineyards.

"We grow red grapes that are made into our most popular wine," Barnabas began. "The dark grapes are made into the wine we serve with lamb. The white grapes seem to be very popular with fish. We have three buildings to keep the different grape varieties separated. It is a complicated business."

Mary was impressed with the size and organization of the operation. Everywhere she looked, she saw workers handling grape vines. Barnabas turned to her.

"I wanted to talk to you about Jerusalem," he said. "I think you and Aristopolus should take your family there. The city is being rebuilt and is growing rapidly. The opportunity to provide food to the new city is great."

Mary listened carefully.

"I can't make a decision like that," she said. "Aristopolus is doing very well at home."

"He would do much better in Jerusalem," Barnabas said. "I could be a partner and supply wine for him to sell."

"I will tell him about your offer," she said. "We have always wanted to live in Jerusalem."

They continued their tour of the vineyards and at noon returned to the main house.

The following evening, Joseph and his family joined them for a lamb dinner.

"This wine is one of our better sellers," Barnabas said as he raised his glass. "It goes very well with lamb. The flavors complement each other."

Mary took a sip of the dark red wine.

"I have never tasted anything like it," she said. "Is it expensive?"

"Yes," he said. "I hope you like it."

John looked at Barnabas.

"I forgot that this is a vineyard," he said. "May I taste the wine?"

Barnabas looked at Mary and waited for her approval. She nodded to him.

"You probably won't like the taste," he said. "After you have a taste, I will give you some grape juice."

"Just a small amount," Mary said. "You can give him a large cup of juice."

John took the small glass and held it at arm's length as he had seen Barnabas do on several occasions. He drank the wine and his face turned bright red. He coughed and sputtered. He quickly drank a large swallow of juice.

"I like the juice better," he said. "May I have some lamb?"

Everyone laughed.

After two weeks, it was time for Mary and her family to return to Africa. Barnabas had arranged for a better cabin and food service for their trip home. Barnabas and Joseph took them to the ship.

After a few days, the ship approached their port.

Aristopolus was at the dock waiting for them. Today was Markus' first day to manage the market without Aristopolus' help. It was a big day for both of them. Aristopolus saw Mary and the family as they walked down the ramp to the dock. A mate carried their packs.

"I see you have help," he said. "I hope you had an enjoyable visit. I hope you all learned a lot of new things."

"I learned a lot," John said. "I don't like wine, but I do like grape juice."

Aristopolus looked at him.

"You will probably learn to like the taste of wine," he said. "It is an acquired taste."

John made a funny face and ran towards their carriage.

"Your brother is doing very well," Mary said. "He purchased first class passage for our return trip."

Aristopolus didn't say anything.

"I will talk with you later this evening," she said. "Little Joseph is also doing very well. We are grandparents."

Aristopolus hesitated while he processed what Mary said.

"I have a grandson?" he asked. "Where do they live?"

"I will tell you all about Joseph and Sarah and the baby," she said.

They held hands as they walked to the carriage. John talked all the way home.

"Joseph has a baby," he said. "They have a nice house and field."

Aristopolus was focused on Mary and didn't hear what John said. When they arrived home, John ran into the field and stared at the vegetables. The others in the group unloaded their packs.

After the children went to bed, Aristopolus and Mary sat in the living room and talked.

"Barnabas thinks we should move to Jerusalem," Mary said. "He wants to be your business partner. He said that Herod has rebuilt the city and many opportunities are available."

"I have always dreamed of living in Jerusalem," he said.

Mary was a little surprised at his willingness to move.

"Barnabas said that the city is growing to the north," she said. "He has visited and found that land is very reasonably priced in that area. He has purchased land just outside the wall."

"You said he wants to be my partner?" Aristopolus asked. "What did he mean?"

"He would fund the costs of our move and give us the land," she said. "He would expect you to run an outlet in the market. You would grow and sell vegetables, and he would send you wine to sell. You would share in the profits."

Aristopolus looked at Mary.

"Would you like to live in Jerusalem?" he asked. "I think it would be good to be near the great temple."

"I will have to think about it for a while," she said. "I need to talk with Ester and my attendant."

Several days later, Mary was ready to discuss a move.

"I have talked with Ester, and she is willing to move," she said. "John is very excited about life in general and is willing to do almost anything."

"And your attendant?" he asked. "I know you depend on her."

"I have talked with her, and she isn't sure what to do," Mary said. "She is going to talk with her family."

"I haven't talked with the staff yet," he said. "We have plenty of time."

"I think you should go to Cyprus and see your brother," she said. "This is a very important decision that will influence the lives of many people."

"I just can't leave the market," Aristopolus said. "I am needed there."

"What is going to happen if we move?" she asked. "You won't be there if they ask questions."

"I guess you are correct," he said. "Maybe Markus will manage the market while I'm visiting Barnabas."

Aristopolus planned a trip to Cyprus.

First, he talked with Markus, "I would like to visit my brother. I will be absent for about one month."

Markus looked at Aristopolus. He realized he was waiting for an answer.

"I could manage the market for you," he said. "I know your family would ensure the produce arrived at the market each morning."

Aristopolus hesitated. He hadn't thought the situation completely through. He hadn't talked to Mary and his foreman about the farm.

"Good," Aristopolus said. "I knew I could count on you."

"It would be good experience for me," Markus said. "When you are older, maybe you will even want a partner."

Aristopolus looked at him. He was surprised and pleased that Markus was interested in being his partner. When Aristopolus arrived home, he told Mary about their conversation.

Plans for Aristopolus' trip were finalized the following week.

"I will bring the vegetables to the market every morning," Ester said. "I will work with Markus. Mother will manage the farm."

"That sounds like a good plan," Aristopolus said. "I will leave for Cyprus in two weeks."

Aristopolus reviewed every detail with Markus and his family many times over during those two weeks. Then his driver took him to the harbor.

"Don't worry, Mr. Aristopolus," the driver said. "Everything will be just fine. God will continue to care for us."

A few days passed before Aristopolus arrived at Barnabas' vineyard. They greeted each other.

"I have been waiting for you to visit," Barnabas said. "The sooner you move to Jerusalem, the sooner we can start our business."

"I am excited, but apprehensive," Aristopolus said. "I have a nice business at home. We are doing fine."

"You could have a large successful business in Jerusalem," he said. "I already own the land, and a house is being built for you. You will own three fields behind your house. I paid a lot extra for the land because it has a spring on it. The spring will provide the water you'll need to grow your vegetables. I talked with several people about the stream. It has been there for as long as anyone can remember."

"I thought Jerusalem had aqueducts," Aristopolus said.

"Aqueducts do exist," he said. "It is a long walk to the aqueduct from the house. The tunnel has not been expanded to the newest area of town yet. When it arrives, the land will be too expensive to purchase."

Barnabas drew Aristopolus a map showing the location and extent of his land.

"I am ready to start sending wine to Jerusalem," he said. "I will send it in barrels, and you could sell it in smaller portions."

"Are you certain they will like your wine?" he asked. "Give me a sample."

Aristopolus had a glass of one of Barnabas' wines.

"This is very good," he said.

"That is my average wine," he said. "The wines that I would be sending to you are better. When I was in Jerusalem, I couldn't believe the poor quality of wine being sold."

Aristopolus raised his glass of wine and said, "Then I guess we will be moving to Jerusalem; I have to sell my business first."

"I am going to send my foreman to Jerusalem," Barnabas said. "He will have everything ready for you. He has agreed to stay there and help you manage the business. He knows all about my operation."

"I would like to meet him," he said.

They went into the field. Aristopolus saw a tall, muscular man instructing the workers.

"His name is Able," Barnabas said. "He is a good worker, and he knows our religion. His mother taught him well."

He signaled for Able to come over to their carriage.

"I want you to meet my brother, Aristopolus," he said. "You will be working for him in Jerusalem."

"Good day, sir," Able said. "I am looking forward to having everything ready for your arrival. We will have a great business in Jerusalem."

Barnabas and Aristopolus returned to the house.

"Joseph and his family will be dining with us this evening," Barnabas said. "He is doing a great job for me."

"He has always been a good worker," Aristopolus said. "He did a fine job for me. Then he went to work for our neighbor and fell in love with Sarah, his daughter."

"Yes," he said. "He told me the story. I am pleased you sent him to work for me."

"I am going out on the porch to enjoy the breeze," Aristopolus said. "I will see you at dinner."

Aristopolus became comfortable on the porch and soon fell asleep. Visions of Jerusalem filled his subconscious.

When Joseph arrived for dinner, he saw his father asleep on the porch.

"Hello, father," he said. "Would you like to meet your grandson?"

Aristopolus woke up and rubbed his eyes.

"I guess I fell asleep," he said. "Certainly, I want to see him. How is Sarah? Barnabas told me you are doing well."

Joseph handed little Joseph to Aristopolus and made a rocking motion. Little Joseph looked up at his grandfather and smiled.

"He likes you," Sarah said. "Will you be moving to Jerusalem?"

"Yes," he said. "It sounds like a very good situation for Mary and me."

"We will come and visit you," she said. "I have always wanted to see the temple."

"We will show you all the great sites of the city," Aristopolus said. "The Romans have built several complexes."

"I hope mother will like Jerusalem," Joseph said. "I am certain you have talked with her."

"Yes, I have," he said. "The family is ready to relocate."

The time had arrived for Aristopolus to return to Africa. Barnabas took him to the port and said goodbye. The weather was warm and the breeze was steady.

When he arrived at the harbor, he went directly home. Mary saw a carriage arrive.

"Your father is home," she said. "Ester, get your brother."

They went outside and met Aristopolus. When John saw his father, he ran to him.

"Hello, father," he said. "When are we leaving for Jerusalem?"

His father looked at him.

"When do you want to leave?" he asked.

"I am ready," he said. "Mother told us all about your new job."

"I guess I will have to talk to your mother," he said.

Mary gave Aristopolus a hug. They walked hand-in-hand into the house.

Mary told her attendant to take John outside. Ester excused herself. She understood her mother and father had important things to discuss.

"I had a very good discussion with Barnabas," he said. "I will talk with Markus about purchasing the business. Our new house is probably completely built."

"I guess he was certain we would move," she said.

"I have a feeling that even if we didn't go to Jerusalem, he would still start a new business," he said. "His foreman, Able, is on his way there," Aristopolus said. "He will have everything prepared for our arrival."

They went into the living area and drank wine.

"Wine will never be the same for me," he said. "It is all Barnabas thinks about."

Mary snuggled up to him.

The next morning, Aristopolus drove a wagon loaded with vegetables to town. When he arrived at the market, Markus was busy cleaning the area.

"Give us a hand with the vegetables," Aristopolus said. 'It is good to be home. How was business while I was in Cyprus?"

"It was fine," Markus said. "Ester and the driver brought the vegetables each morning. She stayed and worked with me. I think we might have gained a few male customers."

He looked at Aristopolus and laughed.

"I have decided to move to Jerusalem," Aristopolus announced. "Would you like to purchase the business?"

Marcus never hesitated.

"Certainly," he said. "The problem is I don't have a lot of money. I have been saving to purchase a house."

"I will sell you my house and my slaves," he said. "A few members of my staff might want to relocate with us. I don't plan to tell them until I find a buyer."

"I could give you the money I have saved," Markus said. "I would have to pay the remainder over the next seven years."

"Correct," Aristopolus said. "Our religion requires us to forget all debt every seven years. You could pay me half of the profits from the business for the next seven years."

Markus thought for a few moments.

"I guess that would be a good deal for both of us," he said. "I would have a house, fields, and a market."

Aristopolus looked at him.

"I would have some money to sustain us until my new business is profitable," he said. "I anticipate that won't take a long time."

"I will tell my wife," Markus said. "She has wanted a house for several years."

"I will tell my wife," Aristopolus said. "She will have to make arrangements to relocate. I will provide some furniture with the house."

"We have furniture, but some new furniture would be appreciated."

Aristopolus went to a law office and ordered contracts to be created. When he returned, he was told everything would be finalized in one week.

"Bring your wife and visit us on the Sabbath," Aristopolus said. "You can survey the grounds, and your wife can look at the house with Mary. By then, I will know who is going with me to Jerusalem."

"We will be there," he said. "We have a business to run for a few more days."

"You will need to hire a helper," he said. "I am certain the slave who brings the vegetables to market everyday will stay with you. He has family here."

Aristopolus boarded his wagon and went home.

When he arrived, Mary was waiting.

"Was Markus interested in purchasing the business?" she nervously inquired. "Does he have any money?"

"Yes, he does," Aristopolus said. "He has been saving to purchase a house for himself."

"He should pay you more than the house costs," Mary said. "He is going to get much more than just a house."

"Don't worry," he said. "I will make the financial arrangements. You need to make arrangements to get our belongings to Jerusalem."

She stared at Aristopolus and walked back into the house.

After dinner that evening, the family, staff, and slaves assembled in the living room.

"I want to inform all of you that my family is relocating to Jerusalem," Aristopolus said. "If you want to come with us, I must know very soon."

"What are you doing with the farm and business?" a worker asked. "Are we going to lose our jobs?"

"No," he said. "I am selling the house, field, and market business to my employee at the market. He will be the new employer, and his family will live in this house. Some of you have met him when you went to the market with me."

"Will you allow us a few days to decide?" he asked. "It is a big decision. What are you going to do in Jerusalem?"

Aristopolus looked at the worker.

"I am going to manage a business," he said. "It will involve growing and selling vegetables. I will own three fields. The business will be much larger. Markus is going to visit us on the Sabbath. You can talk with him."

Cheese, bread, and wine were served to everyone. They talked for several hours.

On the Sabbath, Markus and his wife met the family's staff and slaves. Most of them had decided to remain in Africa. Mary's attendant and one older slave family, who worked in the house, decided to move to Jerusalem with the family.

CHAPTER 3

JOHN'S PARENTS RELOCATE TO JERUSALEM

The staff built storage boxes and prepared the family's personal belongings for shipment to Jerusalem. The legal documents for the transfer of the market business to Markus were signed, and Aristopolus no longer went into town every day. The shipping manager from the dock came to see Mary.

"I need to inspect the materials that you will be shipping," he said. "I have to arrange for the proper storage."

He carefully inspected the two boxes that had been packed.

"You are doing a fine job," he said. "When you and your husband are ready to travel, contact me."

"My husband is traveling in a few days," Mary said. "My family and I will be following at a later time."

"Contact me two days before your ship sails," he said. "I will personally supervise the loading of your belongings."

A few days later, Aristopolus departed on his new adventure. When he arrived in Caesarea, he hired a carriage and driver to take him to Jerusalem. Able greeted him when he arrived at the new house.

"Everything is ready for you," he said. "I already have planted one field and have arranged for two workers to help me. Tomorrow, you and I will go to the market and acquire an outlet for our goods."

Aristopolus looked at the front of the house and then walked inside.

It was quite large with seven rooms and a separate kitchen. Behind the house was a large stable.

"I will want to purchase a carriage and horses," he said. "My family will be arriving in a week."

"I already have purchased four horses and a wagon," he said. "We will look for a carriage. Barnabas has taken care of every contingency."

Aristopolus placed his pack in a room and went to the stable.

"Which of the horses will I be using?" he asked.

"You can choose," Able said. "They are all young and strong. I haven't noticed much difference."

"Where do you stay?" Aristopolus asked.

"I own the next house over," he said. "I am your neighbor. I will supervise loading of the produce every morning before it is delivered to the market."

"It will take a while to grow vegetables," he said. "What are we going to sell?"

"I have already received two shipments of wine and small items from Barnabas," Able said. "As soon as we decide on the location of our outlet, I will start selling those items. It's been arranged for me to receive a shipment from Cyprus every other week."

"Next week's shipment is my family," Aristopolus said. "I already miss having them with me."

Able grinned at him.

"Are you ready for dinner?" he asked. "I am hungry."

"Yes,' he said. "I am so excited; I didn't realize the day is almost gone."

They walked toward the gate in the wall that surrounded the city.

"Do you think they will build another wall around the new part of the city?" Aristopolus asked. "It feels like we live in the country."

"I don't know," he said. "The restaurant is just before the gate. If you go through the gate, past the arch, and continue down Tyropoeon Street you will see the temple complex."

They were seated in the restaurant, and a server approached them.

"I would like some fresh vegetables," Able said. "We are hungry."

"I would also like some fresh vegetables," the restaurateur said. "It is difficult for us to purchase vegetables."

"Give us your best vegetables and a glass of your best wine," he said.

They were served their meals.

"I see why Barnabas was so certain of our success," Aristopolus said. "These vegetables were picked a week ago. I don't know much about wine, but this wine is of poor quality."

"I will provide good wine at a very competitive price," Able said. "That is why I want to get started as soon as possible. I plan to make the owner of this restaurant my first customer."

After dinner, they returned to Able's house. Aristopolus decided that he wanted to have company and stayed with Able until his family arrived the following week.

The next morning, the two men went to the market. It was located within the older wall that surrounded the city. Most of the vendors sold small crafts and religious items. Finally, they found a vendor selling dried dates.

"Good morning," Able said. "I haven't seen any fresh vegetables. Do you know where I can purchase vegetables?"

"I sell vegetables, but I don't display them," he said. "I have a few customers who I sell a bag of fruit and vegetables to every day."

"I am also thinking of selling vegetables," Able said. "But, I won't be selling any fruit."

"Where can you get fresh vegetables?" he asked. "It is difficult to find a sufficient quantity to make it a profitable business."

"I plan to grow them," he said. "We live north just outside the second gate."

"If you don't sell fruit, I will gladly introduce you to my customers," he said. "You can sell them vegetables. Are you planning on selling anything else?"

"Yes," he said. "I am planning to sell wine and whatever small items I can find."

"You should do very well," he said. "I will introduce you to the owner of the market. I would like your stand next to mine. Your vegetables will allow me to sell more fruit and that is what I grow."

The three men walked to the end of the stalls where Able talked with the owner of the market.

"I am interested in purchasing two stalls adjacent to each other," Able said. "I plan to sell vegetables and wine."

"I will be happy to sell you two spots," he said. "My friend here said you want them next to him."

"That is correct, our products complement one another," he said. "We think we can share customers."

"I will be pleased to finally have a vendor who sells good vegetables," he said. "From whom are you purchasing your wine?"

"His brother, Barnabas," Able said, pointing to Aristopolus. "He has the largest and best vineyard on Cyprus."

"I think I tasted his wine on my last trip to Cyprus," he said. "You will do a very good business."

They purchased two spaces and spent the next few days installing stands to display their goods.

Three days later, they were in the market business. One of Able's workers tended the outlet during the day while Able managed the workers in the fields.

He planned to have two fields planted at all times. The other field would be resting. Barnabas developed a field rotation system for him to follow. Business at the market was very slow the first day. When Able and Aristopolus visited their outlet, Able made a suggestion to their worker.

"Give everyone a free small sample of our wines," Able said. "After they have tasted our wine, I know many will become our customers."

It wasn't difficult to give away free wine.

"Barnabas told me to give away free wine," he said to Aristopolus. "He assured me business would increase dramatically."

Barnabas was correct. Their business grew quickly.

"I came to see you for my free sample of wine," a customer said. "I will try the white wine. Yesterday, I purchased a red wine."

He was given a sample of white wine. Soon, many of the vendors drank samples and purchased a bottle or more of wine every morning.

After a week, Aristopolus drove the carriage and followed Able, who was in the wagon, to Caesarea. When the ship arrived, Aristopolus saw his family on the deck. John saw his father and ran to him. Aristopolus took the family to an inn for the night. He returned to the harbor and helped, Able, load the wagon.

"We will stay in Sychar tomorrow evening," Aristopolus said. "We'll be in Jerusalem in two days."

"By then we will have everything arranged in the house for you," Able said. "It was good to meet Mary. You have a nice family."

"We have been married for many years," he said. "I think she is looking forward to being near the temple. I hope John and Ester find many new friends."

Soon, Able had loaded the wagon departed for Jerusalem.

The next day, Aristopolus and his family stopped at the inn at Sychar. When he entered the inn, he was greeted by Abraham.

"Good day, sir," he said. "How many rooms do you need for the evening?"

"I need two rooms," he said. "I would like one room for my wife and me. The second room is for my son and daughter, and our attendants. I will also need our horses stabled, cleaned, and fed."

"Very good, sir," Abraham said.

Aristopolus informed Abraham that they would be departing early in the morning and would appreciate an early breakfast.

"I will make certain you are awake and that breakfast is ready for your family," he said. "I'll have your carriage prepared and loaded for you."

The next morning, they found everything ready for their departure. After breakfast, the family started towards Jerusalem. It was quite late when they arrived at their house.

"Hello, Mary," Able said. "Welcome to Jerusalem. The house is prepared for you and your family."

"I will take care of the horses for you," he said to Aristopolus. "My cook has prepared dinner for all of us. When you are ready, please come to my house."

The family went into the house. After Aristopolus gave them a tour,

Mary expressed her joy. While humming a psalm, she rearranged a few small items. Aristopolus smiled at her.

"I am hungry," he said. "Let's go to Able's."

They walked to the house next door.

"I would like you to meet my girlfriend, Martha," Able said. "We have been seeing each other for a few weeks. She will take us to the synagogue on the Sabbath."

The family greeted Martha, and then enjoyed a grand dinner.

"Is this Barnabas' wine?" Mary said. "Before I visited Cyprus, I had never tasted such good wine."

"It is wine from the vineyard," he said. "I am selling it at our market outlet."

They sat and talked for a short time. Then Aristopolus yawned, mentioned that it was late, and excused the family.

The next morning, Aristopolus and Able went to the market. The remainder of the family went shopping at a clothing outlet and then stopped by the market.

"Hello, Aristopolus," Mary said. "You don't have many vegetables. It looks like you could use some help."

"Able planted vegetables when he first arrived, but they aren't ready to be harvested," he said. "We are selling what we can find that is of good quality."

"You certainly have a nice selection of wine," she said. "You should do well with the vegetables. I haven't seen anyone here with good quality vegetables. Your neighbor has a nice fruit selection."

"Yes, he is our friend," Able said. "He is the main reason we are in this spot. He sells fruit, and we will sell vegetables."

Mary hugged her husband.

"You will do well," she assured him. "We are going home. We have the carriage loaded with items for the house."

Aristopolus gave her a kiss on the forehead.

Two weeks later, Mary went into the field to inspect the vegetables. She was stopped by a field hand. He didn't know her, and he thought she might be looking to help herself to a few vegetables.

"This is a private field," he said. "Please leave."

His voice was gruff and intimidated Mary.

"My husband owns this field," she said, holding her ground. "I can be in this field whenever I desire."

The worker didn't believe her and insisted that she leave.

"Able owns this field," he said. "He isn't married."

Frustrated, Mary went back to the house.

When Aristopolus came home that evening, she explained what had happened.

"He was just doing his job," he said. "He didn't know you. I will make certain this doesn't happen again."

Later, Aristopolus talked with Able. They decided to have a meeting that evening with Mary and the field workers. After dinner, Able and the workers came to Aristopolus' house. He introduced the field workers to Aristopolus and the family. He also explained to them that he worked for Aristopolus.

"My wife and daughter have always worked in the field," Aristopolus said. "They will pick vegetables to be sold at the market each morning."

He looked at the field workers.

"You will do all the other work, including loading and delivering the vegetables to market," he continued. "I recommend that you are very thorough at removing the weeds. Mary has on occasion sent me back to redo my weeding."

He laughed. The workers weren't certain if he was joking. The field hand looked at Mary.

"I am sorry if I dishonored you Miss Mary," he said. "I was just trying to do my job properly."

Mary ensured him that she understood and wouldn't interfere with his work. After another glass of wine, Able and his workers departed.

Two weeks passed before any vegetables were ready for market. Mary and Ester went into the fields and began harvesting vegetables. They placed them in the foot path between each row. The field hand approached Mary.

"You have a very good eye, Miss Mary," he said. "Thank you for helping us. I will load the vegetables into the wagon and take them to Aristopolus. He will be pleased to start selling vegetables."

When the wagon was loaded, Mary watched as they headed to market. 'They will be the best vegetables sold at the market today,' she thought. She smiled to herself as the wagon disappeared out of sight.

When Aristopolus saw the wagon arrive loaded with vegetables, he cheered. He helped unload it and placed the produce. He called to his friend.

"I am finally in the vegetable business," he said. "Look at these. My wife won't send me anything but the best. Our customers should be pleased."

When the first customers arrived, they were astounded by the freshness and quality of the vegetables.

"Where did you get these vegetables?" a customer asked. "We've never seen produce this nice."

"I grew them myself," Aristopolus said proudly. "You will have vegetables like these available to you every day. My wife gets up early to harvest them."

"These vegetables were picked fresh this morning?" she asked. "I think I will take a root to my neighbor."

Aristopolus sold all the vegetables that day.

One evening when Aristopolus arrived home, Mary announced, "I have found a tutor for John."

Aristopolus took off his coat and sat down.

"That is very good," he said. "Will he be coming to the house?"

"No," she said. "John will be going to the temple."

"What is his tutor's name?" he asked.

"He is a rabbi," she said. "I think he said his name is Moses. He will teach John to speak and write Greek."

"How did you learn about him?" he asked. "I have been so busy that I forgot about John's education."

"The ladies at the synagogue told me about him," she said. "He is tutoring the son of a friend."

"Thank you, Mary," he said. "You are a great help to me."

He walked over to her and kissed her. She blushed and looked at the floor.

Aristopolus' business grew quickly. He became known for the best produce and wine throughout the city. He was also faithful and helped support the functions at the synagogue. The rabbi noted Aristopolus' success.

A month had passed; John was at the temple and talked to Rabbi Moses about his father.

"My father sells vegetables at the market," he said. "We once lived in Africa, and he sold vegetables there."

"How long have you lived here in Jerusalem?" Moses asked.

"One year. My father has always wanted to be in Jerusalem."

"I have a friend, Paul, who is a Rabbi," Moses said. "His father, Omar, also has an outlet at the market. His sister, Yona, manages the outlet for him."

Moses paused and thought for a moment.

"You know, I think my mother buys produce from your father," he said. "Does he sell wine, too?"

"Yes, he does," John said. "His brother, Barnabas, has a large vineyard on Cyprus. He was the one who encouraged us to move to Jerusalem. He gave us a house and fields north of the city."

"My family lives in the older section of town," Moses said. "They are close to the temple."

When John returned home that evening, he told his parents about his conversation with Moses.

One day at the market, Able confided in Aristopolus about marriage.

"I would like to marry," he said. "Martha and I have known each other for over a year, and we want to start a family."

Aristopolus listened while he rearranged a display of herbs.

"I will talk to one of the rabbi at the synagogue," Aristopolus said.

"Thank you," he said. "Martha will be very pleased."

Aristopolus spoke to the rabbi and arranged for a wedding and a feast at the temple. Able and Aristopolus decided to invite all their employees and their best customers.

On the day of the wedding, their slaves gave away free vegetables at the market.

"How much do I owe you?" a customer asked. "Where is Aristopolus and Able?"

"Able is getting married today," the slave said. "They told us to give away free vegetables today. You don't own us any money."

The customer was delighted.

"Please tell Able that I wish him the best," she said. "I will see him tomorrow."

She took her vegetables and told all of her friends about the free food.

The wedding ceremony was a somber affair, but the feast was boisterous and joyous. Moses and other rabbi attended.

"This is very good wine," one rabbi said.

He nudged Moses.

"You should try the white wine and some cheese," he said.

"They sell this wine at the market," Moses said.

"Did you say you know Able?" he asked.

"I know the son of Able's employer," Moses said.

"We should consider purchasing wine from him for the temple," he said. "It is much better than what we serve."

"The wine comes from Cyprus, but I am certain he would be pleased to provide wine to the temple," he said. "I will talk with him."

A few days later, Moses went to see Able at the market. Able agreed to sell wine to the temple for the same price they paid for the inferior wine they had been purchasing. After Able received the first payment, he visited with the head rabbi.

"I can't charge you that much," Able said. "I don't charge that much at the market for even small quantities of wine."

The rabbi considered Able's offer.

"You are an honest man, Able," he said. "Tell me what I should pay you. The rabbi-in-training enjoy your wine with their dinner each evening."

They agreed on a price, and both were pleased.

Ester had become very good friends with Martha. They often visited during the day. On occasion, they would take Mary and go to lunch. Their attendants and staff also became friends.

One day, while John was being tutored at the temple, Moses told him that he was going to visit Rabbi Paul's brother, Hezekiah, in Tyre.

"I will be gone for about two weeks," he said. "I will give you some assignments to complete while I am away."

"I will tell my parents that I won't need to come to the temple for the next two weeks," John said.

"Don't forget to come on the Sabbath," Moses said.

John looked at him and explained he meant except for on the Sabbath days.

"I am going to purchase some wine at the market tonight to take to Hezekiah," he said. "He has an outlet in Tyre. He might want to sell some of your uncle's wine."

The first night, Moses stayed at the inn in Sychar. He gave Abraham a jug of wine.

"I would like this wine served with my dinner," he said. "It is very good with lamb."

Abraham felt insulted.

"My wine isn't good enough for you?" he asked.

"Pour yourself a glass, and then tell me how good your wine is," Moses said.

He handed Abraham the bottle. Abraham poured a glass full of wine and returned the bottle to Moses' table.

After dinner, Abraham approached Moses.

"That is the best wine I have ever had with lamb," he said. "Where did you buy it?"

"It is produced on Cyprus," he said. "I purchase it at the market in Jerusalem."

"I wonder if they would sell wine to me." Abraham asked. "I would sell it by the glass at the inn and by the jug in my outlet."

Moses told him about Able and his outlet at the market in Jerusalem.

The following week, Abraham traveled to Jerusalem and negotiated an agreement with Able to have extra wine shipped from Cyprus and delivered to Sychar.

Moses continued to Tyre. Hezekiah's family enjoyed the wine he had brought to them. From then on, whenever Moses visited Hezekiah, he would bring a case of wine to him.

Although the two weeks passed very quickly, John thought Rabbi Moses' absence would never end. He completed his assignments early and then waited eagerly to see his teacher. When it was time for John to go to the temple, Able drove him.

"Welcome home, Moses," Able said. "I have received a nice standing order of wine from Abraham in Sychar."

Moses was surprised Abraham had acted so quickly.

"He is a good business man," he said. "He manages the very popular inn at Sychar. He should be a very good customer."

"I have brought you two things," Able said. "A jug of wine and a young man excited to study."

"This will be a good day," Moses said. "Not everyone will receive two such good gifts today."

John ran to the study area, excited to see Moses. After Moses reviewed John's assignments, he told him he was disappointed with the work. He looked sternly at John.

"I expected you to complete your assignments thoroughly," he said. "Instead, you rushed through them. Your father will not be pleased."

"I like it better when you are here to work with me," John said. "Do you have to tell my father?"

Moses thought quickly and then smiled at John.

"That depends on the quality of the assignments you complete during the next week," he said.

John became a very serious and studied his lessons diligently.

After leaving John at the temple, Able returned home. The workers were in the fields, using donkeys to carry packs of vegetables to the wagon. He went to the foreman.

"It is time for us to turn under field number one," he said. "It will remain fallow for the next growing season."

"Why don't we plant all three fields?" a worker asked. "You could sell more vegetables."

"No, I am not interested in selling the most vegetables," Able said. "We are interested in giving our customers the best vegetables. We will always have one field resting. This way we will always have large, high quality vegetables."

"The man I used to work for grew grain every season," he said. "He sold a lot of grain."

"What does he do now?" Able asked.

"His field stopped producing good grain and there wasn't enough work for me," he said. "I don't know what he does."

"If we allow our fields to rest," he said. "You will always have a job."

The worker scratched his head. Then he grabbed his tool and turned the old crop under the soil. Field two produced vegetables and field number three grew plants that would soon produce product.

One evening after dinner, Mary's attendant answered the door.

"Barnabas is here," she announced to the family.

He and another man entered the living room.

"Good evening, everyone," he said. "I would like to stay with you for a week. The man with me will be staying on and working for you, managing the field workers. I want Able to sell more wine."

Barnabas was so excited and spoke so fast that Aristopolus had a difficult time taking in all that he had said. Finally, he stood and walked over to his brother and greeted him.

"Where is my nephew?" Barnabas asked.

"John is already in bed," Mary said. "He gets up early to go to the temple. He studies with a tutor."

"That is good," he said. "He is a smart, young man. I am pleased that you are able to provide him with a tutor."

"Thanks to you, we are doing very well," Aristopolus said. "You and I can visit with Able at the market tomorrow."

Early the next morning, Barnabas was dressed and ready to leave for the market.

"How far is it to the market?" He asked.

"The market is a short ride," Aristopolus said. "I usually walk and get there before the vegetables are delivered."

The brothers decided to walk to the market. Aristopolus introduced Barnabas to his friend who sold fruit.

"When will Able arrive?" Barnabas asked, impatiently. "I want to talk with him."

"He is probably on his way," Aristopolus said. "He brings a wagon load of wine every morning and follows with the wagon of vegetables."

Able finally arrived. He saw Barnabas and they embraced each other.

"We have made good progress since you were last in Jerusalem," Able said. "Selling wine and produce has been successful."

"That is why I came to see you," Barnabas said. "I want you to do more managing and a little traveling for me."

"I am already very busy here," he said. "Where do you want me to visit?"

"First, why do you store the wine at your house?" Barnabas asked. "If you stored it at the market, you would only have to move it once."

"I have to store it in the barn," Able said. "It is much safer there. No one leaves products in the market overnight."

Barnabas nodded slowly.

"I guess you know what you are doing," he said. "I brought a trained worker to you. He will oversee your fields and workers for you."

Able became a little concerned about what Barnabas had in mind for him.

"I plan to open an outlet in Tyre, and in six months, an outlet in Caesarea," Barnabas continued. "I want you to manage them for me. I will give you a nice salary increase. Your new wife should like that. You can hire an attendant for her and start having sons."

Able was quiet, still digesting what Barnabas told him.

"She would travel with you on occasion," he said. "She might like to see other places."

"Yes, sir," Able said. "I will talk with her this evening."

"Why don't we have dinner at our house this evening?" Aristopolus asked. "After I am finished here, I will go home and tell the staff to prepare a celebratory dinner."

They agreed to dine together.

"I thought about having Joseph manage the outlet in Tyre," Barnabas said. "He is managing the vineyard while I am away. But, I decided to keep him in Cyprus, and I would do a little traveling."

Aristopolus was pleased to hear that his son was doing well.

"Could he visit us sometime?" Aristopolus asked. "It's been a while since his mother has seen him."

"They have two children," Barnabas said. "Their names are Little Joseph and Barnabas. Barnabas was born a year ago. We love those children as if they were our own."

"I am certain they all love you," Aristopolus said. "You have been very generous to my family."

After his tasks were finished, Aristopolus went home. Barnabas stayed with Able and they talked business the remainder of the day.

That evening, Able and Barnabas walked to Aristopolus' house.

"I smelled the lamb cooking before we arrived," Barnabas said when they walked in. "I can't wait to taste it."

"Everything will be ready shortly," Mary said. "Have a seat in the living room. We will bring you a glass of wine."

"I thought I might look at the fields," Barnabas said. "I'll enjoy the walk."

"Have a glass of wine," Mary said. "I will show you the fields in the morning."

Barnabas turned to Aristopolus.

"Does she still work in the fields?" he asked. "She is the owner's wife."

"She may be the owner's wife, but she will always be a farm girl," Aristopolus said.

"It is understood among the field workers that she picks the vegetables to be sold each day," Able said. "She allows them to do all the other chores. She is doing fine."

Barnabas smiled at Aristopolus and then laughed.

"I bet they understand her," he said. "She has made a few things understood to all of us."

Dinner was announced. As soon as Barnabas entered the dining room, he noticed the dark red wine from his vineyard on the table. He was pleased. Then, John blessed the meal and they began passing platters of food between themselves.

"I love lamb," John said. "Someday, I will be old enough to drink wine."

He looked at his mother.

"Mary, you serve the best dinner," Barnabas said. "Everything is just perfect."

Mary blushed and gave credit to Ester and the staff. After dinner, they all moved to the living area. Barnabas turned to Martha.

"Able told me today that he is going to hire an attendant for you," he said. "Then he wants a house full of boys."

He laughed.

"I am going to have a few rooms added to the house for you," Barnabas said.

Martha looked at Able who was smiling and nodding. Mary thought she should say something.

"You know, they haven't been married very long," she said. "Give them some time. Martha has been helping me with John."

"Able and I are going to visit Tyre on my way back to Cyprus," Barnabas said.

"We can stay at the inn in Sychar," Able said. "He is a good customer."

"I have never been to Tyre," Martha said. "Someday, I would like to travel."

'It might be sooner than later,' Barnabas thought.

Two days passed before they headed to Tyre. The first evening, they stayed at the inn. Able introduced Abraham to Barnabas.

"You have a very nice inn," Barnabas said. "I see you also have a sales outlet."

"Yes, I sell things delivered from my friend's son in Tyre," Abraham said. "I sell many different items."

"I see that you are selling jugs of my wine," Barnabas said. "I plan to open an outlet in Tyre. It will make it easier to service customers in that area."

"You should do very well," he said. "I get to Tyre on occasion. Many people from that area stay with me on their journey to and from Jerusalem. The temple is a great draw during the holidays."

The next morning, the two men continued on to Tyre where they found a location for a wine outlet. After Barnabas was satisfied with their new endeavor in Tyre, Able escorted him to his ship. The following day, he returned home.

The head rabbi approached Aristopolus on the next Sabbath.

"We would like you to join several other influential merchants who advise us on the physical aspects concerning the temple," he said. "We count on our members to maintain the complex."

Aristopolus agreed. Soon, he became an important member of the temple's advisory board.

CHAPTER 4

JOHN MEETS PETER

The son of Emperor Tiberius died in the year twenty-three. Soon after his son died, the Emperor became a recluse uninterested in ruling. He was referred to as the gloomiest of men. He gave the Praetorian Prefects the powers to govern the country, and he spent most of his time away from Rome.

Life was good for Aristopolus and his family. They quickly adapted to life in Jerusalem. John studied geography, history, religion, and the Greek language with his tutor, Moses, at the great temple. He noted that Moses traveled and quickly became interested in visiting the Sea of Galilee.

"Mother, Moses has been teaching me about the Sea of Galilee," he said. "I have learned about a new Roman fortification, called Tiberius, located along the west bank of the Jordan River."

Seeking her praise, he looked at his mother.

"You know more about the area than I," she replied.

"I would like to visit the Sea of Galilee someday," he said. "Maybe, I could take a ride in a boat."

Mary didn't want to make any promises she couldn't keep.

"We will talk with your father," she said. "Remind me to talk with him this evening after dinner."

John was satisfied with her response. He was fairly certain that his father would allow him to travel for educational purposes.

That evening, the family was together in the living room.

"Mother, you have something to talk with father about," John whispered in her ear. She smiled at her son.

"We would like a glass of wine," Mary said to her attendant.

John went to his room. When the attendant returned, Mary took a sip of wine and turned to Aristopolus.

"John told me he has been studying the Sea of Galilee," she said. "He would like to visit the area. Maybe, he could take his tutor along."

Aristopolus thought for a few moments. He raised his glass of wine and looked through it to watch a candle flicker, and then he ran his fingers through his dark hair.

"It is good that he is interested in his studies," he said. "Do you think Rabbi Moses would be willing to take him if I paid his way?"

Mary was pleased with Aristopolus' answer. She didn't want to seem overly aggressive, so she paused for a moment.

"I'll have John ask him. We can discuss this again."

Ester sat next to her mother, listening carefully. She was impressed with how her mother handled the situation.

The next day, Mary talked with John.

"If Rabbi Moses is willing to travel with you, your father will take care of the arrangements," she said.

John was elated.

"I will ask him when I see him tomorrow," he said. "Rabbi Moses enjoys traveling. If father pays all the expenses, he may be willing to accompany me on an educational outing."

He ran outside to play. He saw the workers in the field and watched them weed. He noted they were being especially diligent in their work.

"I know how to pull weeds," he said. "You must get the roots. My mother taught me all about good gardening."

A weary worker looked at John and smiled.

"Your mother is a very knowledgeable," the worker said. "I am glad she is busy at the synagogue."

John carefully pulled a weed and placed it in the worker's sack. Then he ran toward the stable.

The following day, John talked with Moses.

"I am sorry, John," he said. "I can't leave. I like to travel, but when I do, someone else must do my work. I have to plan these things in advance."

John was disappointed, but understood. He told his mother that Moses won't be traveling with him. She was disappointed for John.

"I will talk with your father again," she said. "Maybe, I can think of something. I haven't seen the Sea of Galilee. Don't say anything. After dinner, I will talk with him."

Mary had the staff prepare a wonderful dinner served with the best wine. When Aristopolus saw the great arrangement of food, he became suspicious of Mary's motive.

"This certainly is a very grand meal," he said to Mary. "Do you have any news for me this evening?"

"Everything is fine. I just thought that after a long hard day at the market, you might enjoy a good dinner."

"I will enjoy it," he said. "Pour me another glass of wine. Whatever it is, it can wait until after we eat."

He savored the meal.

"Things are good at the market," he said. "We stay busy all day and usually have a line of customers waiting to pay. You grow excellent vegetables, Mary."

Aristopolus' praise brought a smile to her face.

After dinner, they moved to the living room. Aristopolus was seated in his favorite chair.

"John talked to Moses today," Mary said. "Unfortunately, Moses is too busy to travel with him."

Aristopolus now understood the reason for the special dinner. John left the room quietly.

"That is too bad," Aristopolus said. "It would have been a very good learning experience for John."

"Why don't you go with him?" she asked. "I could manage the market for a week or two."

"It is a very busy time of year," he said. "I can't afford to leave. I know you would do a fine job keeping things running, but I wouldn't have any fun. I would be thinking of the market the whole time I was away."

Mary's large, dark eyes filled with tears.

"I guess I will have to tell John," she said, sadly.

Aristopolus changed the subject and began talking about the fields and the new donkey that he had just purchased.

"He is very strong," he said, proud of his investment. "The workers use him in the field, and then he pulls the wagon to the market."

Mary wasn't very excited about a new donkey.

The next morning, Mary talked with John before he left for the temple.

"Your father is too busy to take you traveling," she said. "You will have to wait."

She watched as John's lower lip protruded from his jaw.

"You could take me and Ester to see the sea," he said. "Father could stay home and work all day. That way everyone would be happy."

Mary considered John's comment for a moment and then turned to Ester.

"Ester, would you like to see the Sea of Galilee?" she asked.

Ester answered immediately.

"I would love to travel," she said. "Many of the young women at the temple talk of traveling all the time. I can only tell them about Cyprus and Africa."

A smile appeared on Mary's face.

"I think I will have another discussion with your father," she said. "This might work to your advantage, John."

Excited, John ran to the carriage and headed to the temple. He waved as he disappeared from sight.

That evening, Mary talked with Aristopolus again.

"Ester would also like to do some traveling," she said. "And I have never seen the Sea of Galilee."

Aristopolus clearly understood that John was going to visit the sea. He decided he would stop opposing the trip and help make it enjoyable for everyone.

"My brother, Jonas and his family live in Capernaum," he said. "He is married to Ruth, and they have two sons, Andrew and Peter. Jonas and the boys fish on the sea. You could visit them."

Mary looked skyward and clapped her hands.

"John will be very pleased," she said. "I will break the news when he gets home. We will plan to be gone for two weeks."

The next day, Mary told Ester and John that their father had agreed to a two-week trip to visit their uncle and his family in Capernaum.

"Thank you, mother," John said. "I am finally going to get to see the Sea of Galilee. I will tell Rabbi Moses that I will be away for a few weeks. When do we leave?"

"In about three days," she said. "I have to make the final arrangements with our driver."

Aristopolus had already instructed the driver to hire a helper for two weeks. He wanted two men to travel with the family. When Mary approached the driver, he was prepared for her questions.

"I need a driver for two weeks to take the family to Capernaum," she said. "When can you be ready?"

"We are ready," he said. "I have checked and cleaned the carriage. I will be taking a helper with me."

"I will have to ask my husband about that," she said.

A puzzled look appeared on the driver's face.

"Your husband told me to hire a large man to travel with us," he said. "I hired a friend of mine."

"Yes, that is fine," she said.

Two days later, they loaded the carriage and headed north to Sychar. When they arrived at the inn, Mary went inside and talked with Abraham.

"I have a case of wine in the carriage for you," she said. "It is a gift from my husband. I need two rooms and accommodations for my two escorts."

"Thank you for the wine," Abraham said. "I will take care of the horses and your escorts."

He motioned to a woman who was standing near him.

"My wife will escort you to your rooms," he said.

Mary and the children were taken to their rooms. The helper carried the wine into the inn for Abraham. Abraham was a large man himself, but he only came up to the helper's shoulders. He looked at him.

"You are a large man," he said. "I have good accommodations arranged for you and the driver."

The helper smiled at him.

"Thank you, sir," he said. "I eat a lot."

"Mary has arranged for you to have all the food you would like," Abraham said. "It is our pleasure to serve Mary and her group."

Early the next morning, the group continued on their journey. When they approached the military fortification at Tiberius, two soldiers on horseback rode up next to the carriage.

They looked in at the family and then noticed their two large escorts.

"Is everything satisfactory?" a soldier asked.

Mary looked out at them. "We are fine," she said. "We are going to Capernaum. My son, John, wanted to see the sea."

"Have a good day," he said.

"They named that fortification after the emperor," John told his mother and sister. "His friend, Herod, is our ruler."

"What about Pilate?" Ester asked.

"He works for Herod," he said. "The government employs many people to ensure our safety and well-being."

The family continued north. That evening, they stayed at an inn on the outskirts of Capernaum.

The next morning, they found Jonas' house.

"Ester, go and knock on the door," Mary instructed.

Ester gently knocked, and a young man answered.

"Hello, my name is Ester," she said. "Is Jonas home? He is my uncle."

"Please have your family come inside," he said. "My name is Peter. I will help stable the horses."

The family went inside the house and Mary recognized her brother-in-law.

"You look just like my Aristopolus," she said.

Jonas introduced his brother's family to Andrew and Ruth.

"We were just getting ready to go to work," Jonas said. "We are fisherman. We will return this afternoon. You can spend the day with my wife. She will take you to town."

"Can I go fishing with you?" John excitedly asked.

"No, son," Jonas said. "It is dangerous and hard work. Later, I will have Peter take you for a boat ride while Andrew and I prepare the fish for market."

John went to his mother's side and grasped her hand. She looked into his sad face.

"Your uncle said you are going to get a boat ride. Peter will show you the Sea of Galilee."

She brushed a wisp of hair from John's forehead. He tried to smile. The family sat and talked with Ruth a while. Mary noticed that the house was small.

"I should start lunch," Ruth said. "Today is my day to cook for Peter's mother-in-law. Peter's wife lives with her and takes care of her. Peter doesn't see much of his wife."

Mary listened and tried to understand the situation.

"Would you like me to make lunch for your family?" she asked.

"No, no," Mary said. "But, we would like to go with you to see Peter's mother-in-law. After we visit, I will take everyone to lunch."

Ruth took Mary's hand.

"That would be nice," she said. "I haven't been to a restaurant in a long time. Ever since Jonas purchased the boat from his friend, Zebedee, we haven't had a lot of extra money. But, it is a very nice boat."

Mary tried to change the subject.

"We will be staying at the inn for two days," she said. "I want the children to see the area."

"How large is the boat, can it hold four men?" John asked.

"It will easily hold four men," Ruth said. "Our friends, who moved to Bethsaida, built it for us."

"That is what I call a good friend," John said.

"He owns a fishing business and builds boats," she said. "He is a very wealthy man. He owns a very large piece of land and many slaves."

"Did you have to pay for the boat?" John asked.

Mary motioned at John. He shrugged.

"John, mind your manners," she said. "Boats are not free."

Ruth looked at Mary.

"When Jonas' boss found out he was purchasing his own boat, he terminated his employment," she said. "Zebedee gave Jonas the boat. We are paying him for the boat as the men fish and earn money."

"That is a good friend," Mary said. "We have a few good friends like that."

They walked to visit Peter's mother-in-law. She was so weak that she couldn't get out of bed. Afterwards, Mary and the group were taken to the inn. Mary arranged for everyone to have a large meal. Ruth ate three different root vegetables for lunch.

"Tonight, Peter is taking John for a boat ride," Mary said. "But, tomorrow evening, I want to treat your family to dinner here at the inn."

"That is very generous," Ruth said. "I will have to convince Jonas."

"Tell Jonas that his brother instructed me to do so," she said. "I can't disappoint my husband."

That afternoon, Peter returned to the house to get John.

"Are you ready for a boat ride?" he asked. "I have cleaned the boat and it is ready to sail."

John jumped to his feet and ran to Peter.

"I am ready," he said. "I have never been in a small boat. I have only sailed on ships."

"Well, I have never sailed on a ship," Peter said. "We are lucky. We have a very nice boat."

When they reached the sea, John spotted the boat and ran to it.

"This is actually a large boat," he said. "I thought it would be small."

He admired the beautiful wood and the curved planks.

"It must have required a great amount of skill to build this boat," John said.

"They are always working on boats," Peter said. "They keep two boats on the water every day."

John climbed into the boat, and Peter pushed it away from the shore. The momentum was just sufficient, so that when he put his hand into the water, he was able to maneuver it. Then he let John help him raise the sail. The wind quickly filled the sail, and they moved further out into the open sea. After an hour, Peter turned the boat around.

"It's time to head back," he said. "They will be expecting us."

John wanted to continue sailing, but he didn't complain.

"Andrew and I have been going to hear a minister on the Sabbath," Peter said. "They call him John the Baptist. He preaches about repentance and how baptism can cleanse you of your sins."

"Why doesn't he use the synagogue for that?" John asked.

"He talks about the lack of morals shown by our Roman leaders," Peter said. "He doesn't want to be thought of as a rabbi or associated with a synagogue."

"The Romans probably wouldn't like him," John said.

"I wish you could hear him talk about the coming messiah some time," he said. "He is a great teacher."

Peter and John continued their discussion about the teacher until they reached the shore.

"Thank you for taking the time away from your work to give me a ride in the boat," John said, remembering his manners.

"I enjoyed it," Peter replied. "I had almost forgotten how much fun sailing is. When it involves work, you don't take time to enjoy it."

They pulled the boat onto the shore, secured it, and then returned to the house.

Soon, Mary, Ester, and John headed to Sychar. Ester turned to her brother.

"Tell me about your boat ride," she inquired enthusiastically.

John responded quickly.

"Well, the workmanship on the boat was excellent."

"How far did you go?"

"I'm not sure," John said. "The sea is large. All I saw was water in every direction."

"Did you see Andrew?" she asked. "He seems like a fine fellow."

Mary listened to their conversation.

"No," he said, a little annoyed at his sister. "It was just Peter and me."

John proceeded to ignore his sister's probing and fell asleep before they arrived at the inn. He decided not to mention John the Baptist to his mother. He was certain she wouldn't approve of the teacher's accusations against the empire.

The following morning, Abraham approached Mary.

"Tell Able that I will be in Jerusalem toward the end of the week," he said. "I would like to purchase at least twelve jugs of wine from him."

"I am certain he will have plenty of wine for you," she said. "He stores a month's supply in the barn and takes several jugs to market each day."

"And how is the family?" he asked.

"We have been visiting with my husband's brother," she said. "My son, John, went for a boat ride on the Sea of Galilee."

John smiled at Abraham.

"I really liked it," he said. "But, I don't want to be a fisherman. The odor of dead fish is not very pleasant."

John clasped his nose with his fingers and made a low noise.

"I don't blame you," Abraham said. "What do you want to be when you are older?"

"I think I would like to be a rabbi," John said. "My tutor is a rabbi. I think I would like a job like his."

Abraham nodded. Soon, Mary and the children boarded the carriage and departed.

When they arrived in Jerusalem, Aristopolus was waiting for them at the front door. He hurried to Mary and hugged her. Ester and John kissed their father.

"If you ever need any help, I would be honored to work for you again," the escort said. "Thank you for the opportunity."

Aristopolus had already paid the escort in advance, but after Mary talked to him about how well he treated her and the family, he gave him an extra silver coin.

John went to the temple the next day and discussed John the Baptist with Moses. Moses wasn't familiar with his ministry.

"He should be very careful," Moses said. "We have an unwritten agreement with the Roman government. We don't condemn what they do, and they allow us to worship our God."

"I didn't know that," John said. "Is that agreement satisfactory with God?"

"I doubt it," he said. "The agreement was made so we could coexist with the pagans."

John wasn't sure what all that meant.

"Let's go and talk with Rabbi Paul," Moses said.

They walked to another office.

"No," Paul said. "I have never met him, but I have heard about him. He is more of a threat to the Romans than to us. Yet, many synagogues have distanced themselves from him."

John and Moses returned to the office and talked about John's trip.

"I went for a boat ride on the Sea of Galilee," John said. "It is a very large sea. My cousin, Peter, is a good fisherman."

The following week, Abraham visited Jerusalem and purchased a carriage load of wine.

"People in the area have started to dine with me just to imbibe this wine," he said. "This is a good arrangement."

"My vintner is opening an outlet in Tyre this week," Able said. "We will have a better supply of wine to sell to you when you need it."

A few months passed before Jonas and his family traveled to Jerusalem during a religious feast.

"Come in, Jonas," Mary said when she opened the door. "We have plenty of room for your family. Aristopolus will be pleased to see you. He should be home from the market very soon."

Just then, John walked through the door. He saw Peter and ran to him.

"Welcome," he said. "I can take you to the temple. I know several rabbis."

"We have been to Jerusalem several times," Peter said. "I am familiar with the city, but I would like to see your market."

Later that evening, the adults sat in the living room and talked while the younger members of both families sat on the porch. Peter and Andrew talked about John the Baptist and his problems.

"He is in prison," Peter said. "They will release him this time, but he must respect the authorities."

"I don't think he will do that," Andrew said. "I am afraid he is destined to be killed."

"Why don't you talk with him?" John asked.

"I talk with him several times a week," Peter said. "He is not afraid of death. He wants the people to understand the immorality of our Roman leaders."

"He talks of repentance, baptism for the washing away of sins, and has identified a man named, Jesus, as our coming messiah," Andrew said. "John the Baptist said he was preparing the way for Jesus."

"We may be joining Jesus and traveling with him," Peter announced.

John and Ester listened carefully.

"I hope Jesus doesn't speak against the Roman government," John said. "Tell me more about him."

"We haven't spent much time with Jesus," Peter said. "He will be in Capernaum in a few weeks, and we are going to listen to him."

Mary's attendant walked out to the porch and told them it was time to go to bed.

After the religious holidays, Jonas and his family returned to Capernaum. When John resumed his tutoring at the temple, he told Moses about John the Baptist. Moses insisted that he tell Paul.

"Yes, he has aroused many citizens against our rulers," Paul said. "He is very radical. I don't think he will live long. As soon as the government can find a suitable excuse to kill him, he will be thrown in prison."

John became very concerned about Peter's friend.

That evening, John told his mother about John the Baptist. Then he told her about the new messiah, Jesus.

"Peter heard him say that Jesus is our new messiah?" she asked. "I thought Peter was busy fishing."

"Yes, he heard him," John said. "Peter and Andrew are planning to spend time traveling with Jesus."

Mary's own interest in Jesus grew and she often questioned John about him.

"I would like to see Peter again," John said.

"I don't know if your father will allow us to visit them again," she said. "I think Able has established a customer in Capernaum."

Mary was trying to develop a plan for another trip that Aristopolus might approve.

Mary talked with Able.

"I am going to send a wagon loaded with wine to Sychar and then on to Capernaum," he said. "Your driver could follow my wagon and help deliver the wine."

It was exactly what Mary wanted to hear. That evening, Mary approached Aristopolus.

"John wants to visit with Jonas and Peter again," she said. "He learned a great deal on his last trip."

"I guess he enjoyed his boat ride," Aristopolus said. "Your trip doesn't have anything to do with Jesus, does it?"

Mary was taken back. She had no idea Aristopolus knew anything about Jesus.

"How do you know about Jesus?" she asked. "John would like to go with Peter and Andrew to listen to him."

"I do talk about more things than maintaining the temple when I'm there," he said. "Religion is one of those subjects. I guess it won't hurt John to attend one of Jesus' sermons."

Mary explained to her husband that they would travel at the same time Able's driver who was scheduled to deliver an order of wine to that area. He agreed that was a good plan.

When the day came for the family to travel to Sychar, they boarded the carriage and went to Able's house. Mary noted the driver of Able's wagon was the man who was her escort on their last trip.

"Good morning, Miss Mary," he said. "I am working full time for Able. We do a lot of traveling. It is my pleasure to have you travel with me. I know your driver very well."

Able wished them well and they started north.

The trip to Sychar was slower than normal. The loaded wagon set the pace. When they reached the inn, the wagon driver parked it at the delivery door of the outlet. Abraham saw the wagon and went outside. He recognized Mary's carriage.

"What a pleasant surprise," he said. "I have received a load of fine wine and a fine lady with her family as guests at my inn."

Mary blushed and went inside. Abraham's wife showed them to their room. About one third of the wine was stored in the outlet. The wagon was secured in the stable and the horses bedded down for the evening.

The next morning, they headed to Capernaum. When they arrived, they went to the inn. The wagon went on to transport the remaining wine to the new outlet. After they secured lodging, Mary's family made their way to Jonas' house. Ruth greeted them.

"Peter and Andrew have told Jonas that they are going to leave home and follow Jesus," Ruth said. "Jonas isn't happy. Now, he is going to have to hire day-workers to help him fish."

Mary was shocked by the news.

She questioned Ruth, "Why do they want to follow Jesus?"

"When Jesus was here a few months ago, he healed a boy who was near death," Ruth said. "Peter hasn't been the same since that incident."

Mary suddenly became concerned about what Peter would tell John.

"I have a present for you," she said, changing the subject for a moment. "Aristopolus sent you a large jug of wine."

"Jonas will especially appreciate that," she said. "It will be later this afternoon before he and the boys arrive home."

"Would you like to dine at the inn this evening?" Mary asked. "I would love to treat you and your family."

"Certainly," she said. "I enjoyed our meal very much the last time you visited us."

They talked for a while and then Mary and her family returned to the inn.

Later that evening, Jonas and his family dined with Mary and her family.

"The lamb is delicious," Ruth said. "I didn't realize until I ate with you in Jerusalem that root vegetables, when prepared properly, can be very tasty."

"The vegetables you had with us were picked that same day," Mary said. "If you eat them the day they are picked, they taste much better. That is why we sell so much fresh produce."

"I am going to see Peter's mother-in-law tomorrow," Ruth said. "Would you like to come with me? She enjoyed meeting you."

Soon, after dinner, Jonas excused himself and the family.

"I need to go home," he said. "We will be fishing tomorrow."

John said goodbye to Peter and Andrew.

"I will see you on the Sabbath," John said. "I am looking forward to listening to Jesus with you."

"We will see you then," Peter said. "Tomorrow we will slay the fish."

Peter laughed and then left with his family.

The next morning, the driver took Mary and Ester to visit with Ruth. They walked to visit Peter's mother-in-law. The driver took John to the Sea of Galilee.

Peter's wife greeted them.

"She is much better today," she said. "She is sitting in a chair in her bedroom."

She brought the women to the room.

"I am feeling better," Peter's mother-in-law said. "Peter has been saying a lot of prayers for me. I think it is helping. He is telling me about a new rabbi who is preaching in the area."

"I am pleased that you are feeling better," Mary said. "We will be attending the synagogue on the Sabbath. Peter, Andrew and my son, John, are going to listen to Jesus."

"I am happy that you will be staying a few days," she said. "Please say a prayer for me."

The women walked back to Ruth's house.

"I am a little worried about Jonas," Ruth said. "He is not happy with our sons. He thought they would become fishermen. He purchased the boat so they could eventually have their own business."

"I understand," Mary said. "John has decided that he is not going to sell produce. I don't know what Aristopolus has planned for the business."

Ester took her mother's arm.

"Maybe, I will marry a man who will manage the market," she said. "That way the business will remain in the family."

"Do you have someone?" Ruth asked.

"Not yet," she said. "But, I have met several men at the temple."

"I guess you will have many men from which to choose," she said. "Jerusalem is much larger than Capernaum."

Mary listened to their conservation with great interest. When they returned to the inn, the very large driver of the wagon greeted them.

"I have delivered all my wine," he said. "I have arranged to take John fishing on the sea tomorrow."

"That is great," Mary said. "We will just visit with Ruth. The next day is the Sabbath. The following day, we will start home. Thank you for waiting for us."

After dinner, Mary, Ester, and John relaxed close to the fireplace in the parlor of the inn. The radiant heat warmed the family.

"So, you have been meeting men at the temple," Mary said. "I did see you talking with a few young fellows."

"Yes," Ester said. "Joshua is especially nice."

"Why don't you invite him to dinner?" Mary said. "Your father would probably like to meet him."

"Is that satisfactory with you?" she asked. "I don't want to upset father."

"Yes, dear," she said. "I was a young lady once upon a time."

Ester blushed while John grinned from ear to ear.

"Ester, are you really going to get married?" John asked. "I am never going to marry."

"Yes, your sister will get married someday," Mary said. "All young ladies want to be married and raise a family."

"I like Joshua," he said. "And I know his younger brother."

John finished his grape juice and went to bed.

CHAPTER 5

JOHN MEETS JESUS

On the morning of the Sabbath day, Mary and Ester joined Jonas and Ruth as they walked to the synagogue. Peter and Andrew met John at the inn, and the driver took them just south of Capernaum to a site where a large crowd had gathered. Peter left the group to find Jesus. Eventually, he returned, explaining that Jesus was preparing to speak.

"Do you know where he will stand?" John asked. "I want to be close to him, so I can see him."

"People tend to crowd around him, so he tries to stand on the highest ground," Peter said. "But, I'll be able to see him."

Soon, Jesus started to speak.

John could hear Jesus' voice now and again, but he couldn't see him. His driver picked John up and put him on his shoulders.

"Can you see him now?" he asked.

"Yes, I think so," John said. "Does he have reddish colored hair and a beard?"

"That is him," Peter said. "I met his family in Cana a month ago. Some of his relatives are quite light in color and have blue eyes."

"I see him," John said. "He certainly draws a large crowd."

The driver was getting tired of holding John and put him on the ground.

"I can't see him from here," he said.

Peter grabbed John and put him on his shoulders.

"Quiet," he said. "Some of us are interested in what he is saying."

Jesus talked about repentance, and then asked the crowd to pray with him.

"Bow your head," Peter whispered to John. "We are going to pray."

John looked down at Peter.

"What do I say?" he asked.

"Listen to me then repeat what I say," Peter instructed.

John nodded.

After the prayer, Peter put John on the ground and grabbed his arm.

"Follow me," he said.

The three of them walked up the hill as the crowd dispersed.

"He has finished his message for the morning," Andrew said. "He will probably speak again this afternoon. He gives people time to go home to eat."

Peter led them to Jesus.

"Jesus, I would like you to meet my friend, John," he said.

Jesus moved close to John and put his hand on his shoulder. John was humbled to be in Jesus' presence. He exchanged greeting with Jesus, and then he looked at Peter and the three of them talked for a few moments, before Jesus excused himself to pray.

"Thank you for bring me to see Jesus," John said. "I didn't know you knew him personally."

"We have become friends," Peter said. "I have helped him with the crowd and other small items. Sometimes he just needs someone to talk with him."

John was very impressed.

Early the next morning, Mary and her family traveled south towards Jerusalem.

They arrived home the following evening. Aristopolus was waiting for them. He saw the carriage and jumped to his feet. He ran outside to greet his family. John saw him coming and ran to him.

"Father, I talked with Jesus," John said. "He was a very special person."

Aristopolus hugged Mary.

"Did you hear me?" John asked. "I said I saw Jesus."

"I heard you son," he said. "That is very nice. I would like to talk with your mother."

Ester took John inside.

"We had a wonderful trip," Mary said, putting down her things.

"I think Able has a new customer in Capernaum," he said. "Whenever you want to visit Ruth again, you can check Able's delivery schedule."

In an effort to show her appreciation, Mary hugged Aristopolus.

"Thank you, dear. And how are the fields?" she asked. "I missed them."

Aristopolus gave her a little smirk.

"You can check them in the morning," he said. "They are exactly where they were when you left."

"Very funny," she said.

"The donkey has significantly reduced the amount of time it takes to harvest the vegetables," Aristopolus said. "The workers don't have to walk to the wagon every time they pick a few vegetables. They secure packs across the donkey's sides and put the vegetables in them. They harvest until the packs are full. Then one worker takes the packs to the wagon."

They sat in the living room, sipped wine, and talked for the remainder of the evening.

Early the next morning, Mary went out into the fields. She put her hands in the soil and pulled a few weeds. Then she said a short prayer. She smelled breakfast and heard John. When she went back inside, Aristopolus and John were at the table.

"Did you see the wagon being loaded for the market?" Aristopolus asked. "I am almost ready to go."

"Yes," she said. "They are waiting for you."

Aristopolus gave Mary a kiss and waved to John.

"Mother, you can tell the driver I am ready to go to the temple," John said. "I don't want to be late."

"Moses will still be at his morning prayers," she said. "Our driver won't forget you."

When John finished breakfast, he hurried to gather his bags and ran out onto the porch. A few moments later, the carriage appeared.

"Come on, John," the driver said. "Are you ready?"

"I sure am," he said as he jumped into the carriage.

When he arrived at the temple, John leapt from it and ran to the room where Moses waited for him. John was very excited to see him.

"I talked with Jesus," he said, out of breath.

"Who is Jesus?" Moses asked. "Is he a new rabbi?"

"Yes, I think so. He is the one John the Baptist talked about. Jesus travels around the Sea of Galilee talking about God and encouraging people to love and care for each other."

Moses took John to Paul's office. John told Paul about Jesus.

"I have heard of him," Paul said. "Now that John the Baptist is in jail, Jesus is teaching the people. Many of those that listened to John now listen to Jesus."

"My friend, Peter, used to listen to John, and now he listens to Jesus," John said. "He and his brother spend most of their time with Jesus."

Paul was mildly concerned with what John was saying and how enthused he was about Jesus.

That afternoon, Martha went to see Mary and Ester. She acted coy, and Mary guessed her news. Martha beamed.

"I am going to have a baby," she announced. "Able wants a boy. I am hoping for a boy. I don't want to disappoint him."

She placed her hand on her stomach.

"You can't control that," Mary said.

"Did Aristopolus want a boy?" she asked.

"I think all men want a boy for their first child," she said. "We hoped for a boy for our second child, and Ester was born. We love her."

"Maybe, I will have all boys for Able," she said. "He will teach them the family business."

Mary looked at her and smiled.

She thought 'she certainly has a lot to learn.'

"By the third child, we just wanted it to be healthy," she said. "I gave birth to John. He has always been different from our other children. He is very inquisitive."

"I am really looking forward to having our baby," Martha said. "It will make my days more enjoyable."

"More enjoyable and much more active," Mary said. "Infants require a lot of attention."

She was happy for Martha.

When Aristopolus came home that evening, he told Mary that Able was going to have a son.

"You mean Able and Martha are going to have a child," she said. "And it might be a girl."

"Yes," he said. "That is exactly what I meant. Martha must have visited you today."

"We had a nice chat," she said. "She is very excited about their future. Please ask Able not to pressure her about a boy. God will determine whether their child is a boy or girl."

"Yes dear," he said. "He is also excited."

Jesus' ministry grew quickly as people became aware of his healing powers. Peter and Andrew traveled with him everywhere.

Late one afternoon, Peter and Andrew appeared at the door of Mary's house. She was startled, but greeted them.

Peter spoke, "Jesus went to the temple, so we thought we would stop in and visit. Where is John?"

"He is at the temple studying with his tutor," she said. "He will be home soon. Please don't encourage him to follow Jesus. He is too young and needs to continue his education."

Peter and Andrew promised to encourage John to continue his studies. They also promised to return for dinner. When John came home, his mother told him Peter and Andrew were going to dine with them that evening.

"Is Jesus in Jerusalem?" he asked.

"Yes," she said. "He is visiting the temple. You can tell Moses about Peter and Andrew tomorrow."

Eventually, Aristopolus came home from the market and noticed that the staff had prepared two extra places at the dinner table.

"Are Able and Mary joining us for dinner?" he asked.

"No," Mary said. "I have a surprise for you, but you will have to wait. They should be here soon."

They waited several hours. Finally, Mary told Aristopolus that she was expecting Peter and Andrew.

"I think they are with Jesus," she said. "We should eat."

"If they said they were going to be here, they will," he said. "It isn't like them not to be where they are expected."

Peter and Andrew never arrived that evening, and John became concerned for his friends.

When John arrived at the temple the next morning, it was a hub of activity. John went directly to his work area.

"Didn't you tell me you listened to that Rabbi named, Jesus?" Moses asked. "He visited with us last evening. We are still trying to clean up the mess he made."

John was startled. He looked at Moses.

"What did he do?" he asked. "He seemed like a very mild mannered man."

"He yelled and screamed at the money changers," he said. "Then he overturned their work tables and the money went all over the floor. We will never get it all back into the treasury."

"What made him so upset?" John asked.

"He said the money changers were cheating the poor people," Moses said. "He was out of control. We chased him, but he and his followers headed north."

John didn't say anything about Peter and Andrew, but he understood why they hadn't come to dinner. John completed a few study assignments, before Moses was called into a meeting.

After John walked home, he talked with his mother.

"I know why Peter and Andrew didn't come to dinner," he said. "Jesus had a problem with the money changers and made a hasty exit going north. I am certain that is where Peter and Andrew are located."

Mary listened very carefully. She didn't ask any questions. She didn't want to upset John any more than his current state. When Aristopolus came home, she explained the situation to him. He had heard a rumor at the market about a crazy man in the temple.

Several months passed before Ester asked her mother if she could have Joshua to dinner.

"He has been very nice to me," she said. "I would like to introduce him to you and father."

"We know who he is," Mary said, washing vegetables with John. "I have talked with his mother a few times, although I don't think she knows I am your mother."

Mary remained quiet as she continued to sort produce. Ester waited patiently for her answer.

"Yes, you can ask him to dine with us," Mary said, finally. "I will inform your father."

"What if Joshua turns me down?" she asked. "Do you have to tell father now?"

"No," she said. "I will wait until you know. I am certain he won't turn down your invitation."

John looked at Ester.

"I would turn you down," he said, making a face.

He ran out of the house.

"Close the door!" Mary hollered. "Be nice to your sister."

John was out of sight.

"He is still a child," Ester said, annoyed at her little brother. "Someday, he will grow into a man."

At the temple on the next Sabbath, Ester asked Joshua to dinner. While her family walked home, she talked with her mother.

"Joshua said that he can dine with us the day before the next Sabbath," Ester said. "He will be at the university studying the entire week."

"I didn't know he went to the university," Mary said. "What is he studying?"

"He is studying governmental policy and law."

Mary was pleased and was certain Aristopolus would be impressed. When he came home, she talked to him.

"Joshua is going to dine with us at the end of the week," she said. "Ester met him at the temple."

Aristopolus thought 'it is about time'.

"Yes, I know Joshua's father," he said. "He and I talked several months ago. Joshua has been interested in Ester for some time."

"What do you think of him?" Mary asked. "Do you know that he attends the university?"

"I like him," he said. "He has been working with the town council and studying about the government. I think he will finish his studies this year. I am certain the council will hire him."

Mary realized that Aristopolus had already looked into Joshua's background and was pleased with him and his family. She didn't mention any details of their conversation to Ester.

When Joshua arrived, he was clean shaven and wore very nice clothes and new shoes.

"You look nicer than on the Sabbath," John said when he answered the door.

Joshua looked at him.

"Good evening, John," he said. "Is your sister at home?"

"She might be," he said. "She has been waiting for you all week,"

"That is enough, John," Mary said, coming to the door. "Go and tell Ester that Joshua is here."

She led him to the living room. A few minutes later, Ester entered the room wearing a new dress.

"You look very nice, Ester," he said. "Your brother is quite a fellow."

"I guess you could say that," Ester said, dryly. "Do you know him?"

"He knows my younger brother," he said. "My brother thinks he is quite smart."

Ester wasn't particularly interested in talking about John at that moment and took a seat next to Joshua. Later, Aristopolus arrived.

"Welcome to our home," he said. "I am pleased to see you."

Ester was delighted with her father's greeting. They talked for a few moments before dinner was announced. Joshua exhibited perfect table manners and didn't speak unless he was spoken to. After dinner, he took Ester for a carriage ride. Mary turned to Aristopolus.

"Do you think he will ask her to marry him?" she asked. "They make a wonderful couple."

"It's hard to say," he said. "He is still a student. Maybe after he graduates, he will want to get married."

"I hope so. Ester likes him very much," she said.

"She shouldn't get too excited," he said. "He has to find a job and earn some money first. I don't think he is in a hurry to get married."

"You never know," she said. "Ester might change his mind."

She looked at Aristopolus and batted her eyes. When they returned from their ride, Joshua went home, and Ester came into the house.

"Did you have an enjoyable ride?" Mary asked. "I think he is a nice young man."

"I had a good time," she said. "But, I'm not certain about Joshua. He was very formal."

Mary took Ester into the next room and had a quiet mother-daughter talk with her.

Time passed slowly for her daughter. After a few months, Mary decided she wanted to visit Ruth in Capernaum. She talked with Aristopolus and then checked Able's wine delivery schedule. The following week, Mary, her attendant, Ester, and John boarded the carriage. They followed the wagon, loaded with wine, to Sychar. The wagon driver unloaded part of his wine. They stayed at the inn overnight and went to Capernaum the next day. The inn at Capernaum became a customer of Able's. The next morning, the family went to Jonas' house. They greeted each other.

"Peter's mother-in-law is doing very well," Ruth said. "Peter took Jesus to see her, and he healed her."

Mary was stunned. She was unable to think of anything to say.

"We can go see her," Ruth said. "She will tell you about it. She is completely healed. It was a miracle."

John went to his mother's side.

"I would like to see Peter," he said. "Where is he?"

Ruth looked at John.

"I don't know," she said. "He and Andrew are somewhere with Jesus. I haven't seen him for a few weeks."

"John, why don't you go to the sea with our driver?" Mary suggested. "You can drop us at Peter's mother-in-law's house first. Then pick us up this afternoon."

John was at the sea when he heard some people talking.

"A few weeks ago, Jesus and some of his followers were in a boat and a storm came upon them," a man said. "His travelers became afraid, so he calmed the storm. I heard that he made the wind stop and the waves subside almost at once."

"Many members of our synagogue have joined with him," another man said. "He is really gaining in popularity. Our rabbi is very concerned about the loss of members."

John listened intently.

After a few days, it was time to return to Jerusalem. Everyone, especially John, was disappointed that they weren't able to see Peter.

When they arrived home, Aristopolus greeted them.

"Joshua is graduating next weekend. He came to see you, Ester, but you weren't home. He left a message for you."

"Where is my message," she asked.

Aristopolus took the opportunity to have a little fun with his daughter.

"I can't remember where I put it."

He paused for a few moments and then reached into his pocket.

"Maybe this is it," he said.

He handed the message to Ester. She took the message and read it. Tears welled up in her eyes.

"What is wrong?" Mary asked. "Is it bad news?"

Ester wiped her face.

"He accepted a job in Caesarea," she said. "I thought he was going to work here with the town council."

"He will come see you," Mary said.

Joshua didn't visit Ester until after graduation.

"I have been so busy preparing to move, I haven't had time to do what I want," he said. "I was given a very good position. I will be working with the provincial government as a lawyer-in-training."

Ester looked down.

"I will miss you," she said. "I thought you would be staying here."

"When I get settled, I would like you, your mother, and John to visit me," he said.

"I will have two days a week away from work."

Ester was visibly very disappointed.

"I don't know," she said, glumly. "I will need to talk with my mother."

She ran to her room and left Joshua to see himself out.

One day the following week when John returned home from the temple, he announced, "John the Baptist has been killed."

Ester turned from the table.

"What happened?" she asked.

"He insulted Herod," John said. "Moses told me that the Romans had planned to do away with him, and after he insulted Herod, it was just a matter of time."

"Did he tell you anything else?" Mary asked. "Did he mention Jesus?"

"Moses said that the rabbis are concerned about him. Jesus is taking a lot of members from the synagogues. He is very careful not to upset the Roman officials. They don't believe that he really heals people. I didn't tell them that we are friends with Peter and Andrew."

"Good," Mary said. "It is better that way."

When Aristopolus returned home, Mary updated him with the news.

After a Sabbath service several months later, Joshua's father approached Aristopolus.

"We visited Joshua," he said. "He is very concerned that he hasn't heard from Ester. He wants your wife and Ester to visit him."

Aristopolus was surprised.

"Ester thinks he lost interest in her," he said. "She will be pleased to know that that is not the case. I will arrange for her to go to Caesarea."

"Joshua will like that," he said. "He has rented a modest home. He has a good position. He is a very lucky, young man."

On the way home, Aristopolus talked quietly to Mary. He wanted Mary to tell Ester that Joshua missed her. Mary spoke with Ester that evening.

"When can we go to Caesarea?" Ester asked. "I thought I had lost him."

"I will check Able's delivery schedule," she said.

The following day, she talked with Able.

"My wagon driver will be going that direction next week," he said.

"He is on the road three weeks a month. I may have to hire another driver. Business is good."

"We will plan to follow him," she said. "Ester is very excited."

The following week, they headed to Caesarea.

"Will we stay in Sychar for the night?" Mary asked.

"Not on this trip to Caesarea," the driver said. "We will stop there on our return."

"Where will we stop then?" she asked. "It will take two days to get to Caesarea. Aristopolus told me to be prepared to stay overnight."

"We will stop in Joppa," he said. "The innkeeper is a very good customer."

Late the second day, they arrived in Caesarea. The manager of the wine outlet knew Joshua and directed the group to his house.

Mary knocked on the door. When Joshua answered it, he was very surprised.

"Come in, come in" he said. "I will tell my staff you will be staying with me. I have plenty of room."

"I brought someone to see you," Mary said.

Ester moved closer to Joshua.

"John and my attendant are here as well" she said.

Joshua hesitated.

"I don't want you to have to stay in the inn," he said. "If the women can share a room, John can stay with me."

Mary and the family agreed to stay with Joshua. They all had an enjoyable visit, and the following week, they returned home.

When Aristopolus came home from work, Mary brought him into the living room.

"Joshua asked me to marry him," Ester said. "I was very surprised. He missed me as much as I missed him."

Mary hugged her.

"My sister is going to get married!" John exclaimed. "I guess it is time. You are getting old."

"Your sister is just the proper age to be married," Aristopolus said. "I strongly recommend you be nice to her."

John noted a threat in his father's tone.

"Yes, sir," he said. "I am pleased for her."

The families planned a large wedding at the temple two weeks before the Passover holiday.

One day, there was a knock at the door. Mary heard her attendant answer it.

"May I help you, sir?" she asked.

"My name is Simon. I was a neighbor of Aristopolus in Cyrene," he said. "Please tell him I would like to stay with him during Passover."

Mary went to the door.

"Come in," she said. "You are just in time for my daughter's wedding."

They hugged each other.

"I had a pleasant journey from Paraetonium," he said. "The weather couldn't have been better."

"I am so pleased that you came to see us," she said. "Aristopolus will be surprised. He is at the market and should be home late this afternoon."

That evening, Aristopolus and Simon drank wine and reminisced. Mary told him all about the upcoming wedding.

The wedding took place that weekend. It was splendid. When Mary saw Ester in her flowing, white wedding dress, she cried. Aristopolus held her hand. The feast was held at Joshua's home and lasted two days. When the day came for Joshua to return to Caesarea, Ester was with him. Mary suddenly felt the pain of losing her daughter, and she became very melancholy. John sensed his mother's sadness.

"Mother, don't be sad. You still have me. Father and I love you."

Mary started to regain her composure. She hugged John.

"Yes," she said. "I still have my two men."

"We can visit Joshua and Ester," John said. "I liked the harbor in Caesarea."

It took some time, but eventually, the family adapted to Ester being gone.

John told Simon about the Jewish messiah named Jesus. Simon was very interested in his ministry.

"Jesus mostly stays north along the Sea of Galilee," John said. "He does come to Jerusalem, occasionally. Our friend, Peter travels with him."

Simon was particularly interested in Jesus' ability to heal people.

"Has Peter witnessed him heal anyone?" he asked. "If you can heal people, you are certainly going to be popular."

"Yes," John said. "Peter has been with Jesus when God healed the sick. Peter believes that God does the healing because Jesus prayed with the sick."

Simon noted that Peter gave all the credit for healing to God.

One evening as Passover approached, Aristopolus heard a knock on the door.

Mary's attendant answered the door. It was Peter.

"Good evening," he said. "Jesus and his disciples are coming to Jerusalem for the Passover Feast."

"Please be careful. Don't cause any disturbances," Aristopolus said. "The rabbis are a little nervous about Jesus' success."

They talked for a few moments, and then Peter went outside with Aristopolus. He spoke quietly with him.

"I may need to use your donkey," Peter said. "Please don't ask questions. Just tie him to the post at your house for me."

"I will be glad to," he said. "We won't need him until after Passover."

He wondered why Peter needed a donkey, but didn't ask any questions. Peter disappeared into the night. Aristopolus didn't tell Mary all of the details of Peter's visit. They didn't mention Peter's visit with John.

It was while John was studying at the temple that he heard Jesus planned to visit and would be arriving the following day. When he came home, John talked with his mother.

"I want to watch Jesus and his followers enter the city," John said. "I don't know what is going on, but the rabbis are concerned. They will all be watching for him at the gate."

"Ask for your father's permission," she said. "I will take you if he approves."

"Why are the rabbis so concerned?" John asked.

"I don't know what they are anticipating," she said. "I hope Jesus just wants to celebrate Passover in Jerusalem."

John talked with his father. He gave John permission to go with his mother, but told him to stand near the rabbis. John spoke with his mother.

"I will take you," she said. "But, I want you to stay with me."

"I will stand right next to you," he said. "It should be an enjoyable day."

The following day, they found a place in the crowd that had lined the street. The crowd placed palm branches on the street. Jesus appeared riding a donkey. It wasn't unusual for Kings to ride a donkey. When he passed Mary, she turned to John.

"That donkey looks like ours," she whispered. "Do you think that could be our donkey?"

John was certain that it was their donkey, but he didn't know what he should tell his mother. He didn't say anything.

After Jesus passed, Mary and John returned home. Mary checked the barn and saw that the donkey wasn't there. Mary quizzed Aristopolus when he arrived home.

"Did you loan Peter our donkey?" she asked. "The donkey that Jesus rode into the city looked a lot like ours."

"Yes, I did," he said. "He didn't tell me why he wanted it, and I didn't ask."

Mary looked at him.

"That could be dangerous," she said. "Jesus isn't popular with the rabbis. I hope they don't figure out that the donkey was ours."

When Aristopolus went out to the barn, the donkey was there, eating grain. Aristopolus became puzzled about what happened.

When Jesus went into the temple and began teaching his lesson, he healed several in the audience who came to him. When he was about to leave, he noticed people selling doves for sacrifice. He became upset at the high price they charged for the birds and forced them to stop selling. Suddenly, he overturned the money changers' tables and left. Money was scattered all over the floor and a mob formed as people began rushing to fill their pockets. The rabbis yelled at them to stop, but no one listened. Finally, all the money and the people disappeared.

Peter ran to Aristopolus' house.

"I might need a place for Andrew and me to hide," he said. "Jesus has predicted his death and isn't being cautious. We don't know what is going to happen."

Aristopolus sensed fear in his voice.

"You can stay with us," he said. "We will take care of you."

Peter shook his head.

"No," Peter said. "I can't be associated with you. They know I am with Jesus, and I don't want harm to come to you or your family."

"Then you can stay in the room upstairs in the barn at Able's house next door," he said. "No one would look there. The barn is full of wine, and no one knows about the extra room."

Peter thanked Aristopolus and ran out into the night.

The next day, the rabbi found Jesus teaching in the temple again. He was surrounded by a large crowd. Many children had gathered close to him. A rabbi moved up to the front.

"By what authority do you do these things?" (Matthew, 21, 23, NIV) he asked.

Jesus paused. He knew if he said his authority came from God they would have him arrested for blasphemy, so he deflected their questions and put them on the defensive. They became irritated with Jesus manner and after a while they departed.

Two days later, Judas, one of Jesus' followers, went to the chief-priest. He negotiated a deal to turn Jesus over to their guards. For thirty silver coins, he promised to clearly identify Jesus to Roman soldiers.

That evening, Jesus and his closest followers went to the upstairs room of Able's barn and ate their last supper. They had wine and bread.

"And while they were eating," he said "Truly I tell you, one of you will betray me." (Matthew, 26, 21, NIV)

Peter couldn't believe that someone sitting at the table with him would betray Jesus.

"I would never betray you," Peter said. "I would kill anyone who tries to harm you."

Jesus cautioned Peter to be careful about what he said. He expected Peter to deny knowing him, but Peter expressed his love for Jesus. The disciples didn't understand what Jesus was telling them. Later, Peter and his friends chanted a hymn, said a prayer, and went to the olive grove.

The next morning at the table, John spoke with his father.

"I saw a group of men go into Able's barn last night," he said. "Do you know what they were doing?"

"No," Aristopolus said. "I didn't notice anything. They probably wanted to purchase wine from Able."

It was clear to John that his father was not in the mood for discussion. He quietly ate his breakfast.

Jesus and his disciples went to Gethsemane. Jesus talked with Peter then Judah approached Jesus and kissed him on the cheek. It was the agreed upon signal that this man was Jesus. Roman soldiers seized Jesus and arrested him. Peter tried to fight off the troops. He clenched the handle of his knife. He was so upset, his lips trembled. Jesus looked at Peter and encouraged him to be at peace. Peter couldn't believe what had just happened.

All the disciples scattered, and Peter and Andrew fled to Able's barn. They hid in the upper room. When Aristopolus arrived home, they asked for food. He brought bread and wine to them.

"They took Jesus before the high-priest," Peter said. "They are going to take him to the governor. This is not good."

"Herod, who is a Jew, appointed Pilate," Aristopolus said. "I don't think he will take drastic action against your friend."

The next day, Jesus was condemned to death. Saddened by the news, Aristopolus, Mary, John, and Simon stood in the crowd to witness his crucifixion. They grieved as they watched him drag his cross. Mary took John by the hand and the three went home. Simon remained. Jesus, who was carrying his cross, crawled past Simon and fell to the ground. Simon called out to the Roman soldier who was walking with Jesus.

"I will carry Jesus' cross," he said. "He is too weak to carry it."

Jesus looked at Simon. He was too weak to speak.

A strange feeling of satisfaction came upon Simon, and he picked up Jesus' cross and slowly walked behind Jesus as they made their way to the execution site.

When Simon returned to Aristopolus' house, he told him what had happened.

"He was an innocent man," Aristopolus said. "Yes, he did things differently than we are accustomed, but he lived to help people."

John and Mary cried and embraced each other.

"I will be returning to Cyrene," Simon said. "I don't want to cause you any harm."

The following week, the disciples and Aristopolus' family met in the upper room of Able's barn. The group talked about what Jesus' followers were going to do. Suddenly, Jesus appeared to them. All saw him. A few touched him. Everyone there believed in his resurrection. Jesus commissioned them to teach his message.

The disciples decided to meet in the cenacle until they could find a new meeting place that was not connected to Aristopolus and his family.

"We will be safe here for a while," Peter said. "But, I want to find us a new location."

"Do not worry," Aristopolus said. "Our family's routine will not change. I will work at the market, Mary will be at home, and John will continue his studies at the temple."

"I don't think they will bother us," Mary said.

The first church in Jerusalem was formed in the upper room. They were all very careful not to bring the attention of the rabbis upon themselves.

"John, when you go to the temple for class," Mary said. "Don't talk about Jesus. Tell them you don't know anything about Jesus. We don't want them to suspect that we believe that he is our messiah."

John agreed.

While he tutored John, Moses asked, "Did you hear about Jesus? He claimed he was the King of the Jews. Pilate had him killed."

"I knew something had happened," John said. "I saw the crowd. Then, mother and I took a walk. We didn't stay around the troops."

"I hope his followers return to their synagogues," Moses said. "In a few months, no one will remember Jesus."

John just looked at Moses. It was difficult for him not to say something, but he obeyed his mother.

"What are we going to study today?" John asked, changing the subject. "I want to learn more about writing the Greek language."

"That is a fine goal," Moses said. "We will spend extra time studying Greek. You could practice by writing a letter to your mother."

John smiled.

"She would like that," he said.

Aristopolus and Mary drifted away from the temple's activities. Aristopolus informed everyone that his business was growing so fast that he needed to attend to it. Mary worked in the fields every morning. The family met regularly with those who believed in Jesus. James, Jesus' brother, had moved to Jerusalem. Peter, John, son of Zebedee, and his brother, James, became the leaders of the Jerusalem church. They eventually found a building where they continued to meet in secret.

They continued to be very careful not to antagonize the rabbis. Jesus appeared too many people after his resurrection. The number of those who believed in him grew quickly.

CHAPTER 6

CHURCH IN JERUSALEM

Joshua worked very long days at his job in Caesarea. Ester, who had been accustomed to working with her mother in the fields and with the staff at her family home, was bored with her inactive life. "I need something to do," she said to Joshua one evening. "I want a job."

Joshua was surprised, but after putting himself in her situation, began to understand. He thought for a few moments.

"Why don't you talk to Simon who manages the wine outlet?" he suggested.

"You know more about wine than most people."

She looked at Joshua and her eyes got big. A large smile appeared on her face. She stood and when to Joshua and kissed him.

"I might just do that," she said. "I could work a few days a week."

Joshua was pleased that she liked his idea.

The next week, Ester talked with Simon. He was impressed with her knowledge about wine and offered her a part-time job.

"I can use help on days when I receive deliveries and maybe one day at the end of each week," he said. "As our business grows, I might need you more often."

She smiled at Simon and accepted the job.

"You won't be sorry," she said. "I will do a great job and your business will grow. When should I be here?"

They went to Simon's office. He looked at the delivery schedule.

Ester was scheduled to work on the next delivery day.

"When the wagon arrives this morning, I will be in the back unloading it," Simon said. "You can help customers in the front."

Soon, the wagon arrived and the driver went into the outlet. He thought he recognized Ester.

"Good day, Miss Ester," he said. "I haven't seen you in a while. Does Able know you work at his outlet?"

"No, I don't think so," she said. "I am just helping part-time. I was unhappy just sitting at home."

"You need an attendant and a child or three," he said. "May I mention to your father that you are working for us?"

"Certainly," she said. "I don't think they will be surprised that I had to do something."

Simon was surprised that the driver was familiar with Ester and her family. He quizzed her after the wagon departed.

"How do you know the driver?" he asked.

"My uncle owns the vineyards on Cyprus and all the wine outlets," Ester said. "Able lives next to our farm in Jerusalem and reports to my father."

Simon realized then that he had just employed the niece of the owner of the Cyprus vineyard. He cleared his throat.

"Then I am pleased that you came to see me," Simon said. "I will soon get deliveries directly from Cyprus. I am working out the shipping schedule with Able."

"That will help," she said. "Able's driver spends too much time on the road."

Ester and Simon worked well together and developed a prosperous business. Soon, they were receiving their wine directly from Cyprus and the driver began delivering wine to smaller towns in close proximity to the area.

When the driver returned to Jerusalem and told Aristopolus about Ester working at their outlet, Mary and John began planning a trip to Caesarea. John talked with his father.

"I don't want you and your mother traveling without an escort," Aristopolus said. "I will send someone with you."

"I know that the escort will protect us if I need any help," John said. "But, I am a young man now and getting stronger."

His father shook his finger at him.

"I want you studying, not fighting," he said.

John sensed that it wasn't a good time to question his father's judgment.

"What is the big fellow's name again?" John asked. "I like him. He has been our escort on several trips."

Aristopolus was still agitated by their conversation.

"I don't know," he said. "When you see him, you can ask him."

John understood about classes of people, but he wanted to call the driver by name.

A few days passed before the carriage was placed to be loaded. The carriage driver spoke with Mary.

"I have Aristopolus' permission to use our new horse for this trip," he said.

She glanced at the horse.

"I didn't know we had a new horse. I don't keep up with those things."

"I like the horse," John said. "I was with father when he picked him out. We saw a lot of horses that day."

"That is nice, John," she said. "Sit down; we need to get started."

They started their journey to Caesarea. John looked at the big fellow.

"What is your name?" he asked. "If you are going to be our escort, I should know your name."

He turned to John. He rubbed his hands together and puffed up his chest.

"They call me Maximus," he said.

"I can see why," John said. "It is nice to have you with us."

"Once a fellow called me Tiny," he said. "He has reconsidered and now calls me Maximus."

He looked at John and laughed loud and hard, pleased with himself.

On the second day of their trip, they arrived at Joshua and Ester's house. She greeted them and introduced Sipra, her attendant.

"What are you doing home?" John asked his sister. "I thought you were working."

"It is only part-time," she said. "I still spend many days at home. I am trying to grow a few plants."

She looked at the two potted plants in the window and sighed.

Mary and John spent the next few days visiting with Ester and exploring the area. Soon, it was time for them to return home.

"We will be leaving to return to Jerusalem," Mary said. "Where is John?"

"He and Maximus went to the harbor to feed the fish," Ester said.

"John should have asked me before he went to the harbor," Mary said. "Some days, he thinks he is a man."

When John returned home that afternoon, they packed the carriage and started for home.

Fifty days after Jesus was killed, the disciples and church members gathered at their church in the upper room of the barn. The Holy Spirit came upon them.

"I feel empowered," Peter said. "How do you feel, John?"

"I feel different," he said. "I feel like Jesus is with me."

The members discussed their latest blessing for several hours.

Two additional churches were started in different sections of the city over the next several months. Some members of the original church moved away to towns outside of the city and started their own churches. The church in Bethany grew quickly. Peter began visiting those churches outside of Jerusalem. On one occasion, he healed a woman who had been stricken ill. News of his power spread throughout the area. It was reported that other disciples were performing miracles as well.

Several months later after the incident in the upper room, John spoke to his mother.

"I will continue to go to the temple and learn from Moses, but I want to join the church," he announced.

"You are already a member," his mother said. "We are all members of the church."

"I want Peter to baptize me," John said. "I want to learn more from him. He knows all about Jesus."

"I will have to talk with your father," she said.

That evening, Mary talked with Aristopolus.

"John wants Peter to baptize him," she said. "No," Aristopolus said. "I don't want to draw attention to my family. The local Jews succeeded in having Jesus killed. I want to remain a friend of theirs."

"He will be disappointed," she said. "He is very impressed by Peter and his new powers."

"What new powers?" he asked. "I haven't noticed anything different."

"He healed a sick woman," Mary said. "When he attends church, people flock to him."

"I want John at the temple," he said. "It is important that he understands my position on this matter. We have a business to manage, and we must stay friendly with the rabbi."

Mary spoke to John.

"I am very disappointed," John said. "I thought father would understand. Yes, I will continue to study at the temple."

Mary took John aside and whispered into his ear. John smiled.

One day a few weeks later, Peter and John took a walk to the Jordan River. Peter baptized him that day. John never told anyone.

"I will continue to talk with Moses," John said. "He likes to tell me what the rabbis are doing about our churches."

Peter was very interested in what the rabbi were planning.

"Don't be too interested," he said. "If you hear anything about them wanting to harm us, please tell me at once. We must remain distant of them."

John agreed.

After baptizing John, Peter began feeling guilty. He knew about Aristopolus' concern for his son and family. He talked with Mary about the baptism.

"I know Aristopolus is opposed to the idea, but I went ahead and baptized John."

Mary's eyes grew worried as she put her hand to her mouth,

"You baptized John?" she exclaimed. "His father won't be pleased."

"I know," Peter said. "I protected John's identity and gave him the Roman name of Markus. We will call him Mark regarding all church matters."

"That may help," she said. "If I am asked, I will say that you baptized someone named Mark."

"Yes," he said. "Mary, I had to tell you. I was carrying a heaven burden. Please don't tell John that I talked you."

Still worried, she nodded.

One day as Peter and John walked to the temple to pray, they encountered a crippled man who was being carried to the temple. He looked at Peter.

"I have been crippled since birth," he said. "Rich man, give me money."

John moved closer to him.

"I can give you a few vegetables," he said. "I'm not a rich man, except in spirit."

He looked at John, and then at Peter.

"I don't want his vegetables," he said. "I want money."

Peter looked at him.

"What you need is mercy," he said. "I can give you God's mercy. Get up and walk."

Suddenly, the man felt a change in his body. He looked up at Peter. Then he stood and walked away. He never thanked Peter.

Several days later, Peter was stopped by the temple guards and taken to the high-priest who questioned him. He wanted to know how Peter cured the crippled man.

"By what authority do you perform miracles?" he asked.

"I didn't cure him," Peter said. "God did."

"Your God or our God?" he asked.

Peter looked directly at him.

"There is only one God," he said. "You know that. Our mothers taught us that."

The high-priest said nothing and walked away.

The small churches continued to grow. Members sold their belongings and funded those who taught full-time at the churches. It was an exciting time to be a Christian.

One day while John was studying with Moses, Rabbi Paul came into the room.

"Many of our members are giving money to rival synagogues," he said. "We of the Jewish faith should help each other and be united. It has been our strength for many years."

"What are we going to do?" Moses asked. "I know some of our most faithful members do not attend as often as before."

Not knowing the answer, Paul could only walk away.

The next time John saw Peter, he told him about Rabbi Paul's concerns.

"We have to be careful," Peter said. "We don't want them as enemies. They are powerful."

The church in Jerusalem remained underground.

Several months later, Joshua and Ester made a trip to Jerusalem. They arrived at her family home late in the afternoon.

"Joshua wants to see his parents," Ester said. "We will stay with you tonight and go to his parent's house tomorrow."

John walked into the room and sat down.

"We are very excited," she said. "I am with child."

Mary hugged her daughter.

"I am so happy for you," she said. "Your father will be pleased."

"Congratulations," John said. "I guess married life agrees with you."

Ester noticed that John seemed more mature.

When Aristopolus came home, he asked about dinner before he realized his daughter was in the room.

"Have a seat, dear," Mary said.

She looked sternly at him. He understood the situation.

"I'm going to have a baby," Ester announced.

Her father clapped his hands.

"This calls for a glass of wine," he said.

John went to the wine cellar and brought a special jug of wine to his father.

"Good choice, John," he said.

He poured everyone a glass, and they talked through dinner and into the night.

The next day, Peter visited with Mary and John.

"We are about to choose seven men to help with special church projects," he said. "Our people who speak Greek are upset with the Jews. I know you speak Greek, John, so I thought you might want to help us."

"I can't do that," John said. "I am still studying at the temple. Stephen can though. He speaks Greek."

"I will talk to Stephen, but I wanted to ask you first," Peter said. "I know Stephen has been very successful with his lectures and will help us."

"Someday, maybe, I will be able to help you," he said.

He tried to determine Peter's concern.

"We can change the day of my lessons," John said. "That way, you can go to the synagogue on the Sabbath and visit us the next day."

Peter thought for a moment, then nodded.

"That makes sense," he said. "I will see you this weekend."

Aristopolus arrived home from the market.

"When I passed through the north gate this evening, I noticed a man lecturing to a large crowd," he said. "I thought it was Peter. I don't think he saw me."

"What was he talking about?" Mary asked. "Did you stop and listen?"

"No," he said. "I never want to offend any of my customers, so I just pass by all those public meetings. I think Peter was defending his belief that Jesus was the messiah."

John wondered if his father had seen Stephen.

Moses was surprised how prepared John was with his Greek lesson.

"You know about as much Greek as I do," he said. "I don't think I can teach you anything more. Tell your father to see me."

John smiled as he walked home. When Aristopolus stopped by the temple, Moses recommended that he hire a private tutor to continue John's education.

When Aristopolus arrived home, he talked to Mary and John.

Have you seen Peter lately?" Aristopolus asked.

"I saw him last weekend," John said. "He is very busy. All of the churches want him to attend their services. He can only be at one church each week."

"Tell him I said hello," he said. "I think I am going to take a week away from work and go fishing with Jonas."

Mary turned to her husband.

"Will we be going with you?" she asked.

"Certainly," he said. "Tell the driver we will leave in a few days. I will tell Able to have Maximus work at the market."

The next days passed slowly for Mary. She was excited about seeing her friend, Ruth.

Aristopolus, Mary, and John ate breakfast at home. The driver loaded the carriage, and they headed to Sychar. When they arrived, Abraham greeted them. He had not seen Aristopolus for some time.

"Welcome. You must stay very busy," he said. "I enjoy the pleasure of your family's company several times a year."

"I don't take much time away from work," Aristopolus said. "I decided to relax and visit my brother. We are getting older."

"I am the same way," Abraham said. "It is difficult for me to go anywhere as well."

The next morning, they departed for Capernaum. They stopped along the Sea of Galilee to rest. As Aristopolus and John threw stones in the water, a wild animal watched.

"Did you hear that?" Aristopolus whispered. "I think a wild cat is hiding behind those bushes over there."

"Stay here father. I will get the others in the carriage," John said.

He didn't tell the driver or the others about the cat. He just insisted that they get into the carriage. Then he ran back to his father. The cat was crawling out from behind the bush at that moment. It stared at John and hissed. John looked into the sky.

"Go away!" John hollered, waving his arms.

Unaffected, the cat started towards him.

"Run son!'" Aristopolus yelled. "I will fight it!"

"No!" John said. "The cat will not hurt us. I can control him."

The animal moved closer to John. He stopped, bared its fangs, and hissed. It was about to spring.

"Stop," John said calmly. "I command you to leave this area."

The cat ignored him and continued to move closer.

Then John pointed at it.

"You should have listened to me. I had no interest in killing you."

All of a sudden, the cat fell dead. Aristopolus ran to John. They inspected the cat. Its body was limp.

"It was a large one," Aristopolus said. "How did you kill him?"

"I didn't kill him," John said. "The Holy Spirit stays with me and protects me. I have been greatly blessed. Please don't tell mother what you witnessed."

"When did the Holy Spirit join with you?" he asked.

"It was about fifty days after Jesus was killed," he said. "It is a great comfort to me."

Aristopolus was visibly shaken. He took John's hand, and they slowly walked back to the carriage.

"It took you both long enough," Mary said. "We have been patiently waiting."

Her arms were crossed and she stared at Aristopolus, waiting for an explanation.

"John had something he wanted to show me," he said. "We are ready now."

Aristopolus and John climbed aboard the carriage.

"You don't look well," Mary said to her husband.

She took Aristopolus' hand.

"You are trembling."

Aristopolus looked at her.

"I am fine now," he said. "John took care of everything."

He looked at John and then the driver.

"Onward to Capernaum," he said.

Aristopolus didn't say anything additional. He put his head on Mary's shoulder and eventually fell asleep. Mary turned to John.

"He will be fine by the time we arrive in Capernaum," she said.

John nodded.

They went to Jonas' house the following morning.

"Good morning, brother," Aristopolus said. "We have come to visit."

He wasn't talking to Jonas. Andrew had answered the door.

"Father has gone fishing," he said. "Come in."

They were led to the living room.

Andrew looked at John.

"Should I call you John or Mark now?" he asked. "Peter always refers to you as Mark."

Aristopolus listened carefully to their discussion. He was very disappointed that his son had gone against his wishes, but he decided not to make an issue of it at this time. He stared at John.

"At home I am John," he said. "I am Mark at the church. I should be safe here. You can call me John. I thought you were in Jerusalem with Peter."

"No," Andrew said. "I have returned home. I decided to help at our synagogue. I speak to members who ask about Jesus. If no one inquires, I help the rabbi with his duties."

"Are you going to start fishing again?" John asked.

"Probably," he answered. "Father and I have been talking about my future. I am still not sure."

Ruth changed the topic.

"Jonas has gone fishing," she said. "He will return this evening. Have a cup of tea."

They sat and talked the remainder of the morning. Late that afternoon, Jonas returned home.

"Welcome, brother," he said. "It is about time you took some time away from work. Would you and John like to fish with us tomorrow?"

"Yes, that would be good," he said. "John is not a fisherman. He will probably stay here with Andrew."

"That will be good for Andrew," Jonas said. "He hasn't been the same since Jesus was killed. Our rabbi is trying to help him."

They went to the inn for dinner. When dinner was served, Aristopolus noticed that the wine they were serving was theirs.

"I know that Barnabas grows grapes on Cyprus," Jonas said. "But, I didn't know that you sold his wine."

"I sell his wine throughout the area. We have several outlets. There is one in Capernaum."

"It sounds like you have a large business," Jonas said. "You must be doing very well.

"Business is good," he said. "Mary and I are starting to slow down. We have staff that has taken over and assumes more of the work each year."

"What about John?" Jonas asked.

"He has completed his studies at the temple," Aristopolus said, looking over at John. "He works a little with his mother, but he spends most of his time with Peter."

"Peter changed long before Jesus was killed," Ruth said. "He will spend the remainder of his life telling people about him. I worry. I hope they don't kill him."

"Peter is fine," Mary said. "We see him often, but no one knows. We have to be careful. We need to protect our business. He seems to be doing well. They have formed several churches in Jerusalem and more in the surrounding area."

"We are planning a church in Antioch," John added. "Several of our members have moved there."

For the next few days, the families were active. Aristopolus went fishing with Jonas. John went to the synagogue with Andrew, and Mary spent the days talking with Ruth.

At the end of the week, Aristopolus and his family returned to Jerusalem. Aristopolus explained his great disappointment in Mary and John concerning John's baptism. Aristopolus never regained complete confidence in his wife and son.

The following morning, Peter came to breakfast, visibly troubled.

"Is Mark available?" he asked. "We had a problem while you were in Capernaum."

"What happened?" Aristopolus asked.

John appeared and sat with Peter. They whispered to each other and then Peter excused himself and left.

"What did he tell you?" Mary asked. "I want to know what is happening."

John looked at his father.

"You told us that you saw Peter in a crowd at the north gate a few times," John said. "Well, he was listening to Stephen debate Jesus' message with the local Jews."

"I didn't know what he was doing," Aristopolus said.

"While we were away, the Sanhedrin had Stephen arrested," he said. "They put him in prison, held a trail, and had him stoned to death. Peter is very upset."

Mary looked at John.

"I am also very upset," she said. "Peter, you and the others may be in jeopardy."

"Peter doesn't know what will happen next," John said. "The members are not going to have church services for a while. They will continue to meet secretly."

"John, I want you to stay with us," Mary said.

"That is what Peter told me to do, he said. "He will visit and keep us informed of what is happening."

After a few months, Peter came to breakfast and sat with the family.

"John, do you know Paul, the Rabbi?" Peter asked. "He has left the area."

"Yes I know Paul," John said. "Why did he leave?"

"The head rabbi sent him to Damascus to check on the church we started there," Peter said. "While he was traveling, Jesus appeared to him and spoke to him. He has been converted."

Aristopolus stopped eating and looked at Peter.

"Jesus is dead," he said. "How could he talk with Paul?"

"I have seen Jesus after he was crucified," Peter said. "He has been resurrected. He spoke to Paul and told him many secrets. Their meeting was so dramatic that Paul was blinded for several days. Some Christians helped him escape Damascus alive. Jesus expects Paul to help us spread his message of good news."

Aristopolus didn't believe in Jesus' resurrection. He had heard many different stories and chose not to become involved. What he did know was that he loved his wife and family. He ignored Peter's explanation.

John looked at Peter.

"What are they going to do?" he asked. "What are we going to do?"

"They are holding a secret meeting at the temple," he said. "They don't know what to do. I think some of us who are known as trouble makers are going to travel for a while. John, would you like to go with me?"

Mary looked at John.

"That might be dangerous," she said.

"Staying in Jerusalem might be more dangerous," Aristopolus said. "I will fund a mission for you and Peter. I think that is what you call it when you travel and tell people about Jesus."

Aristopolus stared at Peter and John. Peter saw him in a different light. John went to his father.

"Thank you, father," he said. "We will be fine."

"I will protect your son," Peter said. "We will be gone for a while."

John went to his room, and he packed a few items. When he returned, he walked to his mother.

"Pray for us," John said. "We will be praying for you."

Mary held John's hand.

"We will pray for you every day," she said. "All of my children have left our home."

Aristopolus went to Mary and hugged her. She put her head on his shoulder and smiled.

"We have each other," he said.

Mary cried about John leaving home.

CHAPTER 7

MARK TRAVELS WITH PETER

Many changes took place within the Roman Empire and in the Christian church soon after Paul's conversion to Christianity. Caligula, who had been living with Tiberius for many years, became the next emperor. The year thirty-seven was a good year in terms of progress for the empire. Caligula gave out bonuses to the military, reduced taxes, and had two new aqueducts built in Rome. He especially enjoyed construction projects. Caligula had the temple to Augustus completed and built the largest ships in the world. He loved gladiatorial games and held many exhibitions for his people. During his first years as emperor, he worked very hard to be popular. Money was made available to improve the city of Caesarea, Judea, because it was the residence of the territorial Roman governor.

The most recognizable of Jesus' followers decided that it wasn't safe to remain in Jerusalem, and many moved away or went on mission. Some fled to Antioch, where the Christian churched flourished, and many were converted. The underground church in Jerusalem remained strong, but it remained fearful of the powerful Jewish rabbi.

"I am going on mission," Peter said. "Who would like to travel with me?"

John Mark looked at him, "I will travel anywhere you want to take Jesus' message."

Peter put his hand on John Mark's shoulder.

"Philip has gone on mission," he said. "He is doing quite well in Samaria."

"I can record your lessons in Greek, where are we going?" Mark asked.

Peter was pleased that Mark wanted to travel with him, but he was concerned for John's mother. As Peter and John departed, John spoke with his mother.

"You must do what you think is right for you," Mary said. "I am pleased that you came and talked with me. I will worry about you. It is a mother's duty to worry about her children."

"I will be careful," John Mark said. "I will have Peter to protect me."

"You will have the Holy Spirit to protect you," she said. "I am more worried about your soul than your being."

John Mark nodded.

"My soul is safely with the Lord," he said. "We will convert others by setting a good example."

"Work hard, pray regularly, and remember your mother," she said.

She gave John Mark a kiss.

He and Peter went outside and sat on the porch to talk about their mission.

"We will start toward Caesarea," Peter said. "Our first stop will be in Lydda. I know a family there."

John Mark put a few writing supplies in his bag. He planned to listen very carefully to Peter's lessons and then write a short summary of important points. When he was at a church or home in Jerusalem, he would expand his notes into a series of lessons. Peter went to the church and saw John, James' brother.

"John Mark is very young," he said. "Do you think he can be of any help to you?"

"Yes, I know that I can help him understand Jesus, and his record of what I say about Jesus' message might help others," Peter said.

"Your recollection of Jesus' stories is very inspiring to all who listen," James said. "If Mark records them, then we can all benefit from your lessons."

Two of Jesus' followers, who had remained in Jerusalem, decided to go with them.

The four men walked westward. It was a long walk to Lydda. They weren't accustomed to walking that far.

"I need to rest," a disciple said.

"We will wait for you," John Mark said. "It will take you a while to strengthen your legs."

They slept in an olive grove that night.

They arrived in Lydda on the second day. Peter found the home of the family he knew.

"You told me if I am ever in Lydda I should come and see you," Peter said. "My friends and I are headed to Caesarea."

"Come in, Peter," Amos said. "We have a man, Aeneas, who was paralyzed eight years ago, living with us. I will make room for you and your friends to stay in the barn."

"Thank you," he said. "This is my very good friend, John Mark. The other two are disciples of Jesus who are traveling with us."

"After you have rested return to the house, and we will eat," Amos said. "I will feed Aeneas first."

They went to the barn and rested. The disciple took off his sandals and rubbed his feet.

"It sure feels good to sit down," he said.

They smelled bread and became hungry. After an hour, they were invited into the house.

"I have some bread, cheese, and wine," Amos said. "Eat as much as you would like."

"Thank you for your hospitality," Peter said. "The bread smells really good."

"Everyone likes warm bread," he said. "There is plenty of grain."

They sat and ate.

"How is the church progressing in Lydda?" Peter asked.

Amos looked at him, "It isn't very active, but we have a few interested people. You could tell us a Jesus' story while you're here."

John Mark smiled at Peter and nodded.

The next day, several people came to Amos's house to listen to Peter.

"When you are finished with your lesson, why don't we pray for Aeneas?" John Mark asked. "It sounds like he could benefit from our prayers."

Peter told them about Jesus commissioning his disciples.

"Some have stayed in Jerusalem and some have relocated. We have gone on mission," Peter said. "I would like to pray with your friend."

They all went to see the paralyzed man in the next room. When Peter greeted him, Aeneas recognized him as a man of God.

"Will you pray for me?" he asked.

"That is why I came to see you," Peter said. "God can heal you."

Suddenly, Aeneas twitched as he lay in his bed. He looked around.

"I feel different," he said. "I somehow feel stronger."

He got out of bed and stood.

"I'm a little shaky," he said. "Hold my hand."

John Mark took his hand, and they walked outside. Amos stared at Aeneas in disbelief.

"Our friend is healed," Amos said. "Peter prayed for him and he was healed."

A neighbor approached the man.

"It is you, Aeneas," he said. "I didn't think you would ever walk again."

"I knew I would," Aeneas said. "I just didn't know how to communicate with God."

Word quickly spread that day that Peter had healed Aeneas. Later that evening when he was alone, John wrote a few lines about the miracle. He wrote just enough to engage his memory at a later date.

The next morning, when Peter went to the house, it was full of people.

"We want your blessings," a man said. "We want to know about Jesus."

"I wasn't the one who healed your friend," Peter said. "Your friend's faith in Jesus healed him."

The men continued to question the disciples.

"I am going on to Caesarea," Peter said. "Maybe, if you can feed and house one of the disciples with me, he would agree to stay and help you reenergize your church."

The disciple who had difficulty walking to Lydda came forward.

"I can't go any farther," he said to the men. "I am the one God has designated to stay with you."

"God works miracles in ways we don't understand," Peter said. "Our friend will stay with you and teach you lessons about Jesus."

The local men welcomed the disciple to be their teacher.

Amos heard a knock on the door.

"We have more visitors?" he asked.

When he answered the door, two men from Joppa appeared.

"Is Peter here?" they asked. "He must come to Joppa quickly. Our beloved Tabitha has died."

"How do you know of Peter?" Amos asked. "He is with us."

"We heard that he healed a man," he said. "We want him to heal our Tabitha."

"I will go with you," Peter said. "I feel God calling me."

He turned to John Mark.

"I am certain Amos will understand, we must leave," he said.

They bid farewell to the people of Lydda and departed.

Peter, John Mark, and their traveling companion left for Joppa. The two men from Joppa had provided a carriage for them. They stopped only once to rest the horses. They arrived that evening and found Tabitha's body washed and in an upstairs room.

"Tell me about Tabitha," Peter said.

"She was a great disciple of Jesus'. She always helped other people," a widow said. "She made clothing for us, the poor. She gave me what I am wearing."

Peter sent Tabitha's friends from the room. Then he, John Mark, and the disciple knelt and prayed. Tabitha's friends waited. Eventually, she stood up while Peter continued to pray. John Mark took her hand and led her out of the room to her friends. They were startled but overjoyed. Many wept and knelt to pray. A man named Simon went to Peter.

"I want you to stay with us," he said. "You should know I am a tanner."

"Do you believe in Jesus?" John asked.

"Yes, I do,' Simon said. "And I want to learn more about him."

They agreed to remain with Simon.

"I have plenty of room and enough food for everyone," he said.

"We do need to rest for a while," Peter said. "It's been an eventful day."

They drank wine and prayed with Simon. Later that evening Mark spoke with Peter and made a record of the events.

Two days later, Peter taught his lesson at the church in Joppa. The small building was so crowded that many had to stand outside. They came to see the man who had brought their friend back to life.

"Jesus is smiling," John Mark said. "You are doing a great service for him. You are a good shepherd."

As Peter spoke to the crowd, they mouthed his every word.

"We want you to remain indefinitely with us," Simon said

"I can't stay," Peter said. "I am going to Caesarea and then returning to Jerusalem."

Peter understood that Simon was desperate for Jesus' message. He kissed Peter's hand.

"We need to hear God's word from someone who knew Jesus," he said. "We believe what you say."

"Our companion here also traveled with Jesus," Peter said. "Maybe, he will stay with you."

Simon looked at Peter's companion.

"We need your guidance, will you remain with us?" he asked.

The disciple looked at Peter and then at John Mark. Peter nodded his head.

"I will stay with you," he said.

The church in Joppa gained a teacher who had traveled with Jesus.

After a month in Joppa, Peter awoke early one morning and turned to John Mark.

"I believe God told me in a dream last night to baptize gentiles as well as Jews," Peter said. "It took me a while to understand it."

John Mark went to Peter's side.

"Tell me about your dream," he said.

"I saw a street full of animals," Peter said. "God told me to kill my dinner and eat. But, many of the animals were the kind I am forbidden to eat."

"I guess he wants you to think about your restrictions," Mark said. "Your laws may be keeping you from doing what Jesus wants you to do."

"Yes,' he said. "That is it. All people are children of God. I must tell all of them about Jesus."

John Mark smiled.

"He did say to take his message to the world," John Mark said. "That would include gentiles."

Peter and Mark went for a walk later that morning. When they returned to the house, several men, who had been sent by Cornelius the Centurion to look for Peter, awaited him.

"We want you to come with us to Caesarea," one of the men said. "We have been sent by a great and devout man. He prays every day and fears God. He helps those who are less fortunate."

"We are going to Antipatrie next," Peter said. "John Mark and I planned our mission carefully."

"God spoke to Cornelius and told him about you," he said. "He is certain God talks to him."

Peter looked out at the men.

"God talks to me, sometimes," he said. "Many times, I don't understand what he is telling me."

"The people in Caesarea are waiting for you," he said. "You must come with us."

John Mark looked at Peter.

"I am looking forward to seeing my sister," he said. "I could use her husband's office to formalize my notes." "Maybe, we should go see her before we go see Cornelius," Peter said.

"You can see your sister later," the man said. "Our situation in Caesarea is critical."

"What is so important?" John Mark asked. "Is someone sick?"

"No," he said. "But, Cornelius and many other gentiles are waiting for you."

Peter stared at them.

"You want me to go into the house of a gentile?" he asked.

"Yes," he said. "We are all confused, but we are listening to God. We need you to explain God to us."

"Maybe that is what God tried to tell me in my dream," Peter said.
Mark stared at Peter.

"We can deviate from our schedule," he said.

Peter smiled at Mark.

Peter, John Mark, and several men from Joppa left with the men from Caesarea. Two days later, they arrive at Cornelius' home. He greeted them.

"Come in most honorable, Peter," he said.

He knelt before Peter.

"No," Peter said. "We only kneel to pray to our Lord God. I am a man like you. I understand we both serve our God."

Cornelius jumped to his feet. He didn't want to offend God or Peter.

"I didn't mean to dishonor God," he said. "I meant to honor you."

"You honor me and all Christians when you pray," Peter said.

Cornelius took Peter's hand. They went into a large room that was filled with people.

"We have heard of your miracles," Cornelius said. "We want you to tell us about Jesus."

Peter looked at John Mark and smiled.

"John and I have come to Caesarea to speak about Jesus," Peter said. "The first thing you must understand is that Jesus performs miracles. We are only his servants on earth."

As Peter spoke, the Holy Spirit came upon them. Cornelius looked at his attendant.

"Do you feel God is with us?" he asked.

"Yes, I do," he said. "I have never felt anything like this."

Cornelius called to Peter.

"God is with us," he said. "We can feel his presence."

"The Holy Spirit is upon you and your friends," Peter said. "God has greatly blessed all of you."

Cornelius looked at Peter.

"Baptize us, in the name of Jesus," Cornelius asked. "We have received the Holy Spirit and should now be baptized."

Peter spoke with John.

That evening, Peter and John Mark baptized all those who had come to Cornelius' house. They stayed with them for several days.

"Tell us another Jesus' story," Cornelius said. "How long did you travel with him?"

"I was with him before he started his ministry," Peter said. "Many of us were followers of John the Baptist. We attended a wedding where Jesus performed his first miracle. At the wedding feast, he turned water into wine."

Cornelius looked at Peter.

"When did he start healing people?" he asked.

"After the wedding, he went to Capernaum," he said. Many of us joined him there. That is where he healed a woman."

"I traveled with him for the next three years," Peter continued. "I am still traveling with him. You told me that you had just felt his presence."

"I hope he stays with me," Cornelius said. "Having God with you will keep you focused on doing good deeds."

One of the Jews from Joppa agreed to stay with them after the disciples left.

The next day, John Mark asked Cornelius if he knew where his sister, Ester, lived.

"I don't know many married women," he said. "I have a close circle of gentile friends. We don't associate much with the Jewish people."

"My sister knows about Jesus," John Mark said. "Her husband, Joshua, works for the government."

Cornelius thought for a moment.

"I do know a Joshua," he said. "He is a very important man. He works at the provincial court. He is a well-known lawyer."

"Take me to him," John Mark said.

They walked to a very large house. John Mark knocked on the door. An attendant answered the door and stared at John Mark.

"Are you Ester's little brother?" Sipra, the attendant, asked. "You have grown. Come in, I will get Ester for you."

She seated Peter and John Mark in a large living area. They were served wine and bread while they waited for Ester. Soon, Ester entered the room. She went to John Mark and hugged him. She looked at Peter.

"I remember you," she said. "You are Peter. You were a friend of Jesus."

"Yes, we were friends," he said. "Now, I am his humble servant."

She looked at her brother.

A second attendant entered the room. She had an infant and a young man with her.

"John Mark, this is your nephew, Jude, and your niece, Elizabeth," Ester said. "I am sorry I made you wait. I was feeding Elizabeth."

Peter and Mark looked at the children.

"I hope Elizabeth grows up to be as beautiful as you," John Mark said. "She looks like you and mother."

Ester blushed.

"And Jude looks like Joshua," she said. "Joshua will be home this evening."

"This is quite a house," John Mark said, looking around.

"Joshua has been promoted several times," she said. "He is doing very well."

"I can see that," he said. "Thank you for the wine and bread. Peter and I will enjoy a good home-cooked meal."

She looked at John Mark.

"Occasionally, I go to the market, but most of the time, Sipra does it for me," she said. "We have a large staff."

Sipra had their wine glasses filled.

"I attend many functions with Joshua," Ester said. "That requires a number of people to look after our family and our home."

They talked until Joshua arrived. He brought his aid with him. They entered the house. He saw John Mark, but wasn't immediately certain who he was. He looked at Peter, and then he recognized John Mark.

"Welcome," he said. "I haven't seen you for a quite a while."

"I missed by sister," John Mark said. "I still live in Jerusalem."

"My parents visited us from Jerusalem last year," Joshua said.

He pointed to the man with him.

"I have my aid with me," he said. "We must complete some work after dinner."

"This is my friend, Peter," John Mark said. "He and I are on a mission, sharing Jesus' story."

Joshua smiled at Mark.

"That's nice," he said. "How are your mother and father?"

"Mother is fine," he said. "Father has slowed down considerably."

"I hope he is enjoying life," he said. "He worked for many years; he deserves some time to relax."

"He isn't adjusting very well," he said. "He misses the market. Mother still picks vegetables a few days a week."

Dinner was served. The children ate with Sipra.

After dinner, Joshua and his aid went to the library; the others went into the living area and talked.

"I heard you say mother still picks vegetables," Ester said. "Good for her. As long as she can get her hands dirty, she will be content."

They were served another glass of wine. "Did you get this wine from Able?" John Mark asked.

"Yes, I did," she said. "We have a wine outlet in town, but I think this wine came directly from Cyprus."

"Did you know our nephew, Barnabas, is now living in Jerusalem?" he asked. "He is managing the market for father most of the time."

"Does he live with mother?" Ester asked. "She could use the company."

"He is living with Able's son," he said. "He is helping Able teach his son the business."

"I am pleased mother has help," she said.

"I think he planned to move in with her when I went on mission," John Mark said. "Mother invited him."

They talked for several more hours before Peter went to bed.

"Do you have a place where I could sit and write," Mark asked. "I am Peter's scribe. I make notes concerning our mission."

Mark and Joshua worked late into the night.

When Mark went to breakfast the next morning, Joshua greeted him.

"I am sorry I can't spend more time with you," he said. "I am due in Governor Cumanus' office in two hours. I have to advise him on a construction project."

"A meeting with the governor?" Mark asked. "I don't want to delay you. After I visit with Ester today, we will be returning to Jerusalem."

"She can show you the town," Joshua said. "We have a great harbor and a large military fortification."

"I will talk with her," he said. "I would like to see the harbor."

Just then, Ester came into the room, carrying Elizabeth. John Mark walked to Ester and kissed the baby.

"She is full of milk," she said. "What do you want to do today?"

"I thought I would like to visit the harbor before we start home," John Mark said. 'Your husband just departed."

"I usually don't see him in the morning," Ester said. "We do eat together almost every evening. I am very proud of him. We dined with the Providential Governor last month."

John Mark heard an apology about her extravert life style in her statement. He had noted that Ester enjoyed her new life style.

After she ate, Sipra took Elizabeth, and they went to the harbor. Several large Roman military ships were docked in the harbor along with many ships carrying cargo. The harbor was a beehive of activity.

"You certainly have a busy harbor," John Mark said. "I didn't associate Caesarea's being a provincial capital with all the military ships and men. I guess it makes sense."

"All the major Roman law cases are heard in our courts," she said. "They send people from all the cities to be judged here."

"I guess that is why Joshua is so busy," Peter said.

Ester nodded in agreement.

Later that afternoon, the three returned to the house and talked about their travel plans back to Jerusalem.

"I could have a driver take you to Jerusalem," Ester said.

Peter interrupted her.

"I am going to teach in Sychar," he said. "We will walk. We never know when we might meet someone searching for God."

"I understand," Ester said. I hope you find many people to enlighten."

Sipra handed John Mark a lunch that the staff had prepared for them. Peter and John Mark packed their things and started their walk to Sychar.

"When we arrive in Sychar, I want to see Jacob's well and talk with the townspeople," Peter said. "They already have a church."

The highway to Sychar wasn't a major highway. Most of the time, they didn't see any travelers. When it started to get dark, John Mark spotted a caravan that had stopped for the evening. Peter smelled food cooking. He approached the caravan leader.

"Your food certainly smells good," he said.

"Have a seat," he said. "We probably have a little extra."

He handed Peter and John Mark a piece of bread. The cook brought them a cup of broth.

"I am sorry we don't have any meat tonight," he said. "We do have some wine."

Mark and Peter washed the utensils, told a Jesus story, and slept near the caravan that night.

Two days passed before they arrived in Sychar.

"Do you know the location of the well?" John Mark asked.

"No," Peter said.

When they saw the inn, John Mark inquired about the well. Abraham gave them directions. After Peter located the well, he looked down into the water.

"This well provided water to the people of the area for many years," he said. "Jesus came here and waited for water carriers to come for their daily supply of water. I will do the same."

Soon, a few women arrived.

"Do you know about Jesus?" Peter asked. "I could tell you a few of his stories."

"I know of Jesus," one lady said. "I attend the church in town. You could tell your stories to all of its members."

She took Peter and John Mark into town and to the church. That evening, Peter taught a lesson to the Christians. Afterwards, he and John Mark slept at the church.

They next morning a local man, who was going to Jerusalem, offered them a ride.

"We thank you for the ride," John Mark said. "We have been doing a lot of walking."

When they arrived in the city, John Mark and Peter went to Mary's house. John Mark noticed that his mother was dressed in black. She greeted them.

"I have sad news," Mary said. "Your father died while you were on mission."

John hugged her and sobbed for a few moments.

"I am sorry I wasn't here for you," he said.

He wiped the tears from his face.

"I am fine," she said. "Able and Martha are very supportive. The members of the church have been visiting me in the evening."

John prayed with his mother. They rested and worked in the garden.

On the Sabbath day, after the service, a disciple approached Peter. "We would like to talk with you," he said. 'Come back to the church late this afternoon."

Peter agreed to meet with them. John Mark stayed with his mother. He told her about how Peter performed miracles.

"When we were in Joppa, he prayed for a woman who had died," he said. "She stood up and walked. The Holy Spirit travels with us wherever we go."

"What did the disciples want with him?" she asked. "They didn't look very happy."

"We converted a well know centurion, named Cornelius and his friends in Caesarea," Mark said. "Peter didn't have them become members of the Jewish faith first before he baptized them."

Mary looked at her son.

"Everything will be fine," she said. "You and Peter have a better understanding of Jesus' message than many of the members of the church."

John sat at a table and transcribed his notes in the words of Peter.

Peter returned before dinner.

"I think I finally convinced them," he said. "Many are still not completely satisfied. Someday, a formal decision will need to be made. For now, I am going to follow what I believe Jesus told me."

"Old customs are very difficult to change," Mary said. "Jesus will lead you."

That evening they drank wine together before they prayed.

CHAPTER 8

THE CHRISTIAN CHURCH IN ANTIOCH

After two years as emperor, conflicts between Caligula and the senate arose due to the excessive amount of money he spent on construction projects. The problem worsened, so the senate enacted a large tax to cover the expenses. The people immediately voiced their opinion against the tax and made it clear that they should not suffer for the emperor's spending habits. The senate quickly took action. They made an agreement with the Praetorian Guard, and the emperor was killed. Claudius became emperor. He was available because his family had kept him hidden due to his crippled limb, diminished hearing and poor sight. Although there was concern over his physical condition, Claudius took the appropriate actions as soon as he took office. The senate and the people relaxed as he undid many of the things that had caused the Empire's financial hardship.

Herod Agrippa, grandson of Herod the Great, had been granted a political office by the former emperor Caligula. When Claudius became emperor, he named Agrippa King of Judea. Agrippa proved to be a troublesome king. He persecuted the Christian Church in Jerusalem and killed James, the son of Zebedee. Then, Agrippa relocated to Caesarea and ruled Judea from that city. His problems with the church in Jerusalem continued, and he ordered that Peter be incarcerated.

When the Roman soldiers found the disciples, they had gathered to pray.

"We have come for Peter," a soldier announced. "King Agrippa has ordered that we take him to prison."

Peter was furious and chastised the ruler.

"He should be celebrating his religious holiday," he said. "Did he forget everything his mother taught him?"

The soldier became disgruntled by Peter's comment.

"I don't know anything about holidays," the soldier replied. "I am a good, well maybe not so good, pagan."

He laughed at Peter. Peter didn't respond, but he sensed the soldier's anger.

"What is the charge?" Mark asked. "We haven't harmed anyone. We aren't law breaking criminals."

The soldier didn't like Mark's attitude. He looked directly at him.

"Do you want to go with him?" he asked. "We have plenty of cells in the prison for all of you."

Mark sensed the soldiers frustration with them.

"No, we are peace-loving disciples of Jesus," he said.

"I don't know the charges," the soldier said. "I am only following orders. If he doesn't come with me, I will need to return with more soldiers to incarcerate all of you."

Peter looked at Mark.

"I will go with them," he said. "It isn't necessary for all of us to go to prison."

Peter left with the soldiers. Later, the disciples knelt and prayed for Peter's safety.

Peter was placed under the constant guard of sixteen soldiers. They didn't want to disobey Agrippa's orders, and they knew Peter had been credited with many miracles. When Agrippa heard what Peter had said, he was furious.

"He wants me to observe the holidays? Then, I will wait until after Passover to kill him. That should satisfy his concern for my mother."

Those present didn't respond. They were frightened by Agrippa's state of mind. They did as he ordered.

"The night before Herod was to bring him to trial, Peter was sleeping between two soldiers, bound with two chains, and sentries stood guard at the entrance. Suddenly, an angel of the Lord appeared and a light shone in the cell. He struck Peter on the side and woke him up. "Quick, get up!" he said, and the chains fell off Peter's wrist. Then the angel said to him, "Put on your clothes and sandals." And Peter did so. "Wrap your cloak around you and follow me," the angel told him. Petered him out of the prison, but he had no idea that what the angel was doing was really happening; he thought he was seeing a vision. They passed the first and second guards and came to the Iron Gate leading to the city. It opened for them by itself, and they went through it. When, they had walked the length of one street, suddenly the angel left him." (Acts, 12, 6-10, NIV)

He hurried to Mary's house and asked for Mark. When Mark saw him, he was very surprised.

"I thought you were in prison," he said.

Peter, still partially blinded, looked at Mark.

"I'm not certain what happened," he said. "I think God sent an angel to me. I followed the angel out of the prison. The guards didn't seem to see us. Whatever happened, here I am. I need your help."

Mark took Peter by the arm and led him to the upper room in Abel's barn.

The next morning, the soldiers arrived at Mary's house.

"We are searching for Peter," he said. "He escaped from prison last night. We want to search your house."

Mary hesitated for a moment.

"Only my son, John, is with me," she said.

The soldier thought she was stalling and moved towards her.

"Move to the side and don't interfere," he demanded.

Mary stepped aside, and the soldiers began their search. They looked in every room and then went to the stable. They were disappointed when they didn't find Peter. The soldier looked directly at Mary.

"If you see Peter, you must tell us," he said. "King Agrippa is very upset that he escaped. We had him chained in his cell and guarded. It would have been impossible for him to unchain himself and walk out of the prison without being seen. Agrippa thinks we weren't doing our job."

John pretended to be asleep. The soldiers tried to wake him, but when they figured out that he wasn't Peter, they let him be. They checked Abel's house and then his barn. They saw the barn was full of wine. Able gave them a few bottles, and they went on to the next house.

King Agrippa departed Jerusalem and returned to Caesarea. He honored Claudius with statues and ceremonies at the amphitheater. While he was speaking to the crowd, he suddenly fell ill. He motioned for his guards and they took him back to his palace. He was a very superstitious man and was convinced that he was being punished for his acts against the Christians. His pain grew worse and he never recovered. His comrades mourned his death. Fadus became the Roman ruler in Judea. Agrippa II was only a teenager and remained in Rome.

Peter was shaken by the miracle that had happened to him. He spoke to Mark.

"I'm not certain what God wants me to do," he said. "I do know that he has something special in mind for me."

Mark was worried and fearful.

"Maybe, you should leave Jerusalem," Mark said. "You know, many of your friends are in Antioch."

Peter thought for a moment.

"If I go, will you accompany me?" he asked. "You could record my lessons."

"Yes," he said. "I know that Barnabas will stay with mother and help her. I will tell her I am going with you to Antioch."

They planned their journey. They decided not to travel directly to Caesarea, and they didn't reveal their travel plans.

"We must be careful not to bring suspicion upon ourselves. I am fearful that I might be captured," Peter said.

"It is too long a walk from Caesarea and we shouldn't chance being recognized on a ship," Mark said. "I will pack all the dried food we can carry."

They rode to Caesarea.

One month later, they arrived in Antioch and located the largest church in town.

"Welcome travelers," Priest Evodius said. "Please stay with us."

"We sought this church, so we could become members," Peter said. "I am Peter, the one, who traveled with Jesus."

The priest tried to read Peter's face.

"We will get you food," he said. "We will discuss Jesus and his message tomorrow."

Mark turned to the priest.

"Thank you for the food and shelter. Peter did know Jesus very well. You will be convinced tomorrow. I would bring a few of your helpers with you. They will enjoy listening to Peter's stories about Jesus."

Mark and Peter slept in a room in the basement of the church.

"At least we don't have to stand watch for animals tonight," Peter said. "I never was a good watchman."

Mark knew the story about Peter falling asleep while he kept watch for Jesus, but didn't say anything. He just smiled.

They slept soundly until Evodius woke them the next morning. Peter spent the morning answering Evodius' questions. He never hesitated. When Evodius wasn't certain of Peter's answer, Mark would help Peter clarify his response.

"I have one more request," Evodius said. "Show me your knife."

Peter whipped his knife from his garment and displayed it before Evodius. He was startled by how rapidly Peter reacted.

"I am convinced that you are Peter," he said. "You honor us by joining with us. I have heard of your miracles."

Peter looked at Evodius.

"God performs the miracles," Peter said. "As you have noticed, I have become very good at asking for help."

Evodius placed his hands together and prayed.

"You will find God here with us," he said. "I want to introduce you to our church members on the Sabbath day as a new member of our priesthood. None of us ever traveled with Jesus, but a few members did hear Jesus speak."

"I thought I might try to find a few of my friends who left Jerusalem when Jesus was killed," Peter said. "I thought some of them traveled to Antioch. Do you have any members from Jerusalem?"

Evodius thought for a moment.

"Bartholomew was here," he said. "I have been told that he was a great help in starting our churches."

"What happened to him?" Peter asked.

"When he learned Thomas was going to India, he decided to join him," he said. "He has been gone for several years."

On the Sabbath, Evodius introduced Peter and Mark to the members of the church. The members were grateful to have a friend of Jesus as a member of their church. Peter spoke a few words and after the service met with several of the members. He started to teach lessons about Jesus during mid-week. His lessons became extremely popular. Mark faithfully recorded every lesson that Peter taught. The congregation asked that Peter be allowed to teach a lesson on the Sabbath. The priests of the church met with Peter. They had become a little concerned about his popularity.

"We are thankful that you have joined with us," Evodius said. "We have more people attending the church than we have room. We would like you to teach at a different church each Sabbath. We have three churches in Antioch."

Peter nodded.

"That is fine," he said. "If I am causing the priesthood any problems, I am sorry."

"They are good problems," he said. "We will learn from your experiences."

He gave Mark a parchment map showing the location of each church.

"You will start here next Sabbath," Evodius said, while he pointed to a mark on he parchment. "I still want you to teach mid-week at my church."

Peter agreed. At each location, the members would arrive early to find a seat. People who had never been in a church came to hear Peter.

"My name is Luke," he said. "I am a doctor here in town. I generally don't attend church, but my mother told me about you."

'So, you are a doctor," he said. "Do you have many patients?"

"I am a very busy man," he said. "Most weeks, I work six days."

"I am pleased that you are interested in learning about Jesus," Peter said. "I do the best I can to tell Jesus' stories as he told them."

"I will be coming back," Luke said. "My mother will be here every Sabbath."

After the service, Mark waited for Luke and his mother at the church door. He spoke to them and prayed for them.

After six months, the priests of Antioch met again. This time they named Peter the senior priest, Bishop of Antioch. He didn't have a church. He was the most popular teacher at all the churches.

Evodius visited Bishop Peter in his church office.

"I would like a copy of your lessons," he said. "Will you share what Mark is writing with the priesthood?"

"Certainly," Peter said. "That is why Mark is recording my lessons. Just speak with him."

Evodius thanked him and spoke with Mark. He provided him with a lesson he had recorded. After he had read it, he and Mark returned to Peter.

"If you would start from the beginning of Jesus' ministry and tell his story as you remember, Mark could fill in the social and travel details."

Peter smiled at Evodius.

"I could try to do that," he said.

Mark looked at Evodius.

"They may not be exactly in the order Jesus traveled," he said. "Peter's memory isn't perfect."

"Eventually, we would have a complete story about Jesus' life," he said. "You know that everyone who can read Greek will want a manuscript."

"Yes, I see," Mark said. "I hadn't thought of doing that. I already have many lessons written down. I will work with Peter and add detail as he remembers it."

Mark devoted more of his time to writing.

Over the next year, Mark wrote his gospel about Jesus, based on Peter's lessons.

Evodius looked at what Mark had produced.

"This is remarkable," he said. "I am going to send it to the university and have copies made for each church in town."

"This doesn't represent all of my stories of Jesus," Peter said. "I will remember more stories as time goes along."

Soon, Mark was teaching a mid-week lesson at a different church. Peter's story of Jesus' mission quickly gained popularity. The university sold copies of Mark's work to all who could afford to purchase it. Priests, from Jerusalem to Ephesus, used Peter's lessons as a teaching guide.

A year passed when Barnabas arrived at the church in Antioch. Mark greeted him.

"How is mother?" he asked. "Does she and Able still run the market?"

Barnabas put his hand on Mark's shoulder.

"Your mother died," he said. "Seth, Able's son, lives in the house and manages the market for his father. I couldn't remain in your mother's house, so I came to Antioch."

Mark was shocked. His eyes filled with tears, and he fell to his knees and grieved. Barnabas tried to console him.

After Mark had grieved and prayed for a few days, he was ready to talk with Barnabas again.

"How is my brother, Joseph?" Mark asked.

"He manages all of your uncle's businesses," he said. "All he does is work. He came to Jerusalem after your mother died. When I met with him, all he wanted to talk about was business."

Mark bowed his head and said a prayer for Joseph.

"He told Able to train me to manage the businesses in Judea," he said. "I told Able to train his son to manage the businesses."

"Why did you do that?" Mark asked. "A business opportunity like that doesn't come your way often."

"I don't want to be a businessman," Barnabas said. "I want to work for the church and learn from you and Peter."

Mark smiled at Barnabas.

"How is the church in Jerusalem?" Mark asked. "I miss my friends."

"After Paul's conversion, the rabbi in Jerusalem didn't trust anyone," he said. "They are a worried group. They are even having problems with the Roman government. Not everything is going in their favor."

"I have been told Paul is with his brother in Tarsus," Mark said. "Someday, he will come to Antioch."

"I am planning to go to Tarsus and bring him back here," Barnabas said. "I am going to rest for a few weeks before I go to see him."

Mark remained quiet.

The following morning, Mark ate breakfast with Barnabas and the other priests.

"I will walk with you around Antioch," he said. "We have a great river, the Orontes."

"I would like to see the island," he said. "Everyone in Jerusalem, who has ever been to Antioch, talks about the island."

They walked north and arrived at the market.

"When I go to the market, I always purchase a piece of fruit," Mark said. The market reminds me of home."

After they visited the market, they walked west to the river.

"This is a large river," Barnabas said. "How will we get to the island?"

"The Romans built several bridges across the river," he said. "They are always doing something on the island. The island gets crowded during the games."

"I'm not interested in the games," he said. "I do see a bridge."

They crossed the bridge onto the southern end of the island.

"The first thing we will see is the stadium," Mark said.

They walked around the island for two hours. After they visited the circus, they crossed another bridge and headed south.

"They didn't have any carriage races today," Mark said. "When the really good drivers are in town, you can't get onto the island it is so crowded."

Soon, they arrived at a complex of government buildings.

"This is our forum," he said. "You will see many government officials. I generally don't spend much time here as I don't want to draw attention to myself."

They returned to the church.

The following Sabbath, in response to their members' request, Evodius announced the construction of a large church building in town. Mark informed Peter that Barnabas had gone to Tarsus to talk with Paul.

"He hopes to bring Paul back to Antioch," he said.

"I think he could benefit by working with us," Peter said. 'When he was a rabbi, I didn't like him. He was at Stephen's stoning."

"He is a different man," Mark said. "We must receive him as a convert to the church."

They walked to the site of the new church.

"I can't believe how fast the church is growing," Peter said. "We are richer and have more members than the church in Jerusalem."

Peter looked at Mark.

"I think I would like to go to Rome," he said. "It is a great city, and it should have a great Christian Church."

"The Romans are pagans," Mark said. "It might be dangerous."

"Since converting Cornelius, I have baptized many gentiles who have converted," he said. "You know Luke, he has joined our church."

"He will be an asset to the church and to Jesus," Mark said. "I look forward to his contribution."

Peter spoke several more times about leaving Antioch and going to Rome.

Barnabas and Paul arrived from Tarsus. Evodius greeted him.

Paul looked at him.

"I want to study," he said. "I have been doing a great amount of praying. I will continue to visit with my brother and study with you."

Barnabas and Paul joined the priests in Antioch. They were quartered at the church.

After a few months, Paul approached Barnabas.

"I want to go to Adana and teach," he said. 'We can stay with my brother for a while. I want to perfect my lessons before I teach in Antioch."

"You could teach a midweek lesson," Barnabas said. "I could ask Mark."

"No," he said. "I want to go to Adana. I need to practice first."

Barnabas told Mark that he and Paul would be absent from Antioch for a while.

They headed west across the river. The river rushed mightily as it carried the spring rain water to the sea. Then, they headed northwest and followed the curvature of the Great Sea to Adana. They found the local synagogue.

"I would like to tell a story about Jesus," Paul said. "My friend, Barnabas and I are preparing to go on a mission."

They were welcomed by the membership. They remained with them a few days.

"We will return in about two weeks," Paul said. "I will tell another story at that time."

Barnabas was puzzled, but he didn't question Paul.

"Your stories are different than the other stories I've heard about Jesus," he said. "I guess you never traveled with him."

"No, I never traveled with him, but I knew him and I knew where he taught," he said. "My job didn't allow me to associate with him."

Barnabas didn't understand what Paul had said, but he didn't question it. They continued on to Tarsus.

When they arrived, Paul's brother, Aaron, answered the door.

"It is great to see you," he said. "How are you doing? Have you recovered?

"I am well," Paul said. "This is my friend and companion, Barnabas." They enjoyed a glass of wine.

"How is business?" Paul asked. "How are Hezekiah and Yona?"

"The tent business is good," he said. "Our brother and sister are doing fine. Hezekiah has a house full of children."

They talked into the night.

The next morning, Aaron went to the tent manufacturing facility. Paul and Barnabas stayed with Aaron's wife.

"I have never seen a tent making operation," Barnabas said.

"They make tents for the Roman army," she said. "You should talk to Aaron."

That evening, they talked to Aaron about making tents, and the following day they visited the facility.

"You have a lot of employees," Barnabas commented. "Making tents takes a lot of hard work."

"Yes, it does," Aaron said. "Paul was an accomplished tent maker. I hated to see him start teaching. He could have stayed with me. He is still welcome to stay with me at any time."

Barnabas looked at Paul.

"You have to remember, he is my older brother," he said. "I love him very much. He knows what I have planned for my life."

They stayed with Aaron about a week and then returned to Adana.

"Welcome," Joel said. "We enjoyed your stories about Jesus. Stay and tell us more."

They remained in Adana several days and then returned to Antioch.

The next morning, Barnabas found Mark.

"Paul is doing very well," he said. "He can write in Greek. He will make a great teacher for God."

"I knew Paul was educated," Mark said. "But, I didn't know about him writing Greek."

"He knows more about Jesus than you might think," Barnabas said. "He has heard Jesus speak. His family might have known Jesus' family."

"I only knew him as a devout rabbi, Mark said. "I tried to avoid him when I studied with Moses. On occasion, I would see him at the temple."

"Did you know that he was a tent maker?" Barnabas asked. "His brother is in the tent making business in Tarsus. He is quite wealthy."

"That explains a lot," Mark said. "I wondered how he could live like he did. He certainly wasn't a poor rabbi."

"Many rabbis are not poor," he said. "Some have business ventures."

"Not when they serve at the temple," Mark said. "There, they are dedicated to the work of God."

Paul entered the room.

"Good morning, Paul," Mark said. "So, you can make tents."

Paul nodded.

"Yes, I have made many tents in my life," he said. "Having a skill is a good thing, but I prefer to write."

"I, too, enjoy writing," Mark said. "I have been writing down Peter's lessons."

"That is very good," Paul said. "Peter might be able to remember what Jesus said. I don't think he would try to change it to suit his own life."

Mark didn't reply. He went outside into the church yard.

The next day, Evodius talked with Mark.

"Peter seems uneasy," he said. "I think he is distracted."

"He talked to me about visiting his wife in Capernaum," Mark said. "I think he is homesick."

"I will tell him to take some time away and visit his family," Evodius said. "It will do all of them good."

Later, Peter talked with Mark.

"I am going home," he said. "I haven't seen my family in a very long time. I will return in a few months."

"I will be here Mark said.

Peter packed a bag and departed.

A few weeks later, Evodius introduced Mark, Barnabas, and Paul to a disciple from Jerusalem named Agabus.

"He says the church in Jerusalem is starving," Evodius said. "He would like our help."

"We should help the people in Jerusalem," Paul said. "If we collect an offering, I will take it to them."

The offering was collected from the members of the Antioch church.

"I will travel to Jerusalem with you," Barnabas offered. "I would like to see my friends."

They traveled to Jerusalem. The church was desperate for money. They welcomed the offering from the members of the church in Antioch. Secretly, Paul's family and Able also contributed to the church. With their substantial help, the church recovered.

"When you return to Antioch, please express God's and our sincere gratitude for their help," a priest said. "We will be eternally thankful."

Barnabas and Paul returned to Antioch.

After visiting his family in Capernaum, Peter returned to Antioch. He found the senior priest and asked for Mark. Soon, Mark appeared. When he saw Peter, he ran to him. Peter hugged him.

"I have made my final arrangements," he said. "I am going to sail to Ephesus. I am having problems dealing with Paul."

Mark looked at Peter. He sensed his concern, but he didn't pursue Peter's thoughts about Paul.

"Why Ephesus?" he asked.

"It is a great Roman city," he said. "It has a great harbor and a great library. I might not write Greek, but my wife can read. She will read scrolls to me."

They discussed Ephesus for a while. Mark looked at Peter.

"Paul will be a good teacher for Jesus," he said. "He is with Barnabas and fine tuning his message."

Peter smiled.

"You don't need a finely tuned message," he said. "You need to convince people that you understand Jesus message and want them to understand it."

Mark agreed that Paul was insecure in his message.

"Setting a good example impresses people," Peter said. "That is one method Jesus used to get people's attention. I try to practice what Jesus taught."

Mark took Peter's arm.

"Yes, you do," Mark said. "It isn't always easy. I struggle with myself. I think Paul is struggling with his past."

Peter looked at Mark.

"Please pray for me, will you come with me?" he asked.

Mark knew he had to stay with Barnabas.

"No," he said. "I must stay with my nephew."

"I understand," Peter said. "He is a good, young man. He will be a great servant for Jesus."

"I know we can find someone to travel with you," Mark said.

"I already have someone," he said. "My wife has joined me. I will take her with me to Ephesus."

Mark secured a carriage from the church and drove Peter and his wife to the harbor. A week later, he returned to Antioch. He spent most of his time with Evodius and Barnabas. The priests of Antioch elected Evodius to a leadership position. He continued to serve the churches of Antioch. Mark was no longer recording Peter's lessons, so he spent his time turning Peter's lessons into a more detailed story about the life of Jesus.

CHAPTER 9

MARK TRAVELS WITH PAUL

After Paul became accustomed to living among the Christians, he became interested in going on a mission. Evodius worked diligently with the priests to plan several mission trips. Paul talked with Evodius.

"I know you are a friend of Barnabas," Evodius said. "Talk with him. He will help you find a few followers to help on your mission."

Paul met with Barnabas.

"Evodius encouraged me to go on a mission. It will be necessary to form a group. Barnabas, will you go with me?"

"Certainly," he said. "I am interested in taking Jesus' message to Cyprus. I know Mark, my uncle, would go with us."

"Mark, Peter's friend, is related to you?" Paul asked. "I don't think he considers me to be a faithful Christian. He remembers me as a rabbi at the temple in Jerusalem."

"Peter and Mark are both relatives of mine," Barnabas said. Mark would be a good scribe."

"I don't need a scribe," Paul said. "I already write very good Greek."

"If you want me to go with you, you will have to take Mark with us," Barnabas said. "He is familiar with Cyprus."

"I will take him, but he is yours to control," he said. "If I don't have to write, I will have more time to teach."

Two weeks later, they had organized a group that was eager to go on a Jesus mission. They walked to the harbor and found a ship scheduled to sail for Cyprus.

When they arrived in the town of Salamis, Barnabas directed them to the closest synagogue. The rabbi recognized him.

"Come in, Barnabas," he said. "Your father told me that you moved to Jerusalem."

"I did live there for a while," he said. "Now, I live in Antioch."

"What brings you back to our beautiful island?" he asked.

"Paul, Mark, and I are on a mission," he said. "We want to tell your members about Jesus."

The rabbi looked at Mark and thought he recognized him.

"Mark sure looks a lot like John, your uncle," the rabbi said. "I met John on several occasions."

"He is John," Barnabas said. "Now, he is John Mark. We call him Mark."

"My members ask me many questions about Jesus," he said. "They would be pleased to speak with you."

After Paul lectured at the synagogue several times, the people became very interested in Jesus' message. The rabbi grew concerned with Paul's popularity.

"I think it is time for you to continue on your mission," he said to Barnabas. "Paul is causing people to ask more questions than he is answering."

"We thank you for your hospitality," Barnabas said. "We will be visiting with my father for a few days."

They walked, south to the sea, rested, and traveled west along the sea. They walked for a few hours and then built a fire and watched the sun slip below the distant horizon on the sea.

Barnabas was awakened by Paul coughing. Paul tried to stand but fell to his knees.

He looked at Barnabas.

"I have had this problem a few times before when I am at the sea," he said. "I don't know what is wrong with me. I am going to lie down. I should be fine in the morning."

Paul curled up on the ground. Barnabas fell to sleep listening to Paul struggle to breathe. When Barnabas awoke, he didn't hear Paul. He went to his side.

"Wake up," he said.

He tried to arouse Paul, but Paul didn't move. He awoke Mark.

"Something is wrong with Paul," he said. "I think he stopped breathing."

Mark tried to awaken Paul. Barnabas looked at Mark.

"I am going to go to the vineyard and get a wagon," he said. "Stay with Paul. I will return as soon as possible."

Mark slept on the ground next to Paul.

After a several hours as the sun rose, Mark saw Barnabas approach with a helper and a wagon. They put Paul into the wagon and went to the vineyard.

"Welcome, we have been anxiously awaiting your return," the servant said. "I will send for your father. He is in one of the vineyards."

They carried Paul into the living area and put him on the floor. The others gathered around him. He started to take deep breaths. His open his eyes and looked at Barnabas.

"This is a wonderful home," he said. "Where am I?"

"You are safe," Barnabas said. "This is the largest and best vineyard on Cyprus. I grew up here."

Paul tried to stand. He was wobbly, but he stood.

"I am feeling better," he said. "There is something about the coast that doesn't agree with me. Tell me about the vineyard."

Paul looked at Mark.

"We distributed the wine in Jerusalem," Mark said. "Able, our neighbor, kept a barn full of wine."

Paul rubbed his eyes and pulled on his beard. He was beginning to get the picture. Joseph returned from the field and ran to his son.

"Barnabas, it is good to see you," he said. "Have you come home?"

"I've come to visit you for a few days."

"I know John," Joseph said, looking at Barnabas' companions. "Who is your other friend?"

"We are traveling with Paul. We are on a mission telling the story of Jesus, and Paul became sick."

Joseph looked at Barnabas.

"I was hoping you outgrew that," he said. "If you don't like Jerusalem, I could use you here at the vineyard."

"I will only be a few days. Then, we are traveling west," he said. "How are the grapes this year?"

"It is a good year," he said. "We are sending a ship loaded with wine to Caesarea each month. We sell everything I can grow."

"I will have your things put in a room for you," he said. "We will have a great dinner."

"The servants have taken care of us," he said. "We will rest until dinner. I think I will sit on the porch and look into the vineyards."

Paul went to his room. Barnabas and Mark sat on the porch and enjoyed the warm sun and gentle breeze.

After a while, a servant approached Barnabas.

"Dinner is served, sir," he said. "I have seated your friend Paul."

Dinner started with raw fish and white wine. The main dish was lamb and a dark wine. Desert was served with a sweet wine.

"I have never tasted such good wine," Paul said. "I especially like the wine you served with the lamb."

Barnabas was relieved that Paul had made such a fast recovery.

"Barnabas, my uncle who started the vineyard, developed that particular wine," Joseph said. "We produce over a thousand jugs a year."

They went into the living area and relaxed. Paul began to discuss Jesus.

"I have heard all about Jesus," Joseph said. "Every time I visited John Mark in Jerusalem, he would take us to church. Peter, their cousin, knew Jesus very well."

Paul sat back in his chair and enjoyed another glass of wine.

"The best story about Jesus is the one where he tells his followers to drink a lot of wine," Joseph said.

No one mentioned Jesus to Joseph again.

A few days later, Joseph had one of his drivers take the young men to Paphos.

"I will stay south of the mountain," the driver said. "It is much easier for the horses."

When they arrived in town, they thanked the driver and looked for a synagogue.

As they approached a synagogue, a Roman soldier saw them.

"Can I help you?" he asked.

"I am here to talk about Jesus," Paul said. "Do you know anyone who is interested?"

The soldier wasn't happy with Paul's attitude.

"I might," he said. "Follow me and we will go to the office of the proconsul, Sergius Paulus. He was appointed by Claudius and is probably the most powerful man on Cyprus."

"We don't mean any harm," Barnabas said. "We are just excited about being on such a beautiful island."

"The proconsul is interested in religion," he said. "He always has his advisor the sorcerer, Bar-Jesus, with him. I think he takes advantage of the proconsul."

The soldier took them to see Paulus.

"Come in," Paulus said. "You want to tell me about Jesus? Good, I can never get Elymas, Bar-Jesus, to tell me anything about him."

Paul recognized Elymas as a false prophet.

"He has been fooling you for a long time," Paul said, pointing to Elymas. "He is nothing but a sorcerer."

The proconsul was confused. Elymas stepped forward.

"He doesn't know what he is saying!" he cried out. "I am the true prophet; he is nothing but a teller of false stories!"

Just then, Paul pointed at Elymas, who suddenly became blind. At first, no one knew what had happened. Elymas reached for a chair.

"I can't see," he said. "Someone help me. I can't see."

Mark put his hand on the chair and helped him get seated.

Barnabas looked at the proconsul and then pointed at Elymas.

"He has been blind to the truth. Paulus, now you will hear the truth," he said.

They spoke with Paulus for several days. Paulus was astounded by the great miracles of Jesus. He listened to story after story. Finally, he looked at Barnabas.

"I want to be baptized" he said. "You are the true prophet. I will have Elymas sent away."

Bar-Jesus was disgraced and deported from the island. Others who witnessed Elymas being blinded now believed and were converted.

Paul was worshipped by the people.

"We must be careful," Mark said. "We must stress the fact that Jesus performed the miracles. We are just his servants."

Paul stayed very close to the proconsul.

Eventually, the proconsul asked Paul to stay with him as an advisor.

"I can stay for a short time, but I am sorry, sir, I am driven by the Holy Spirit. I must continue my mission," he said.

The proconsul was not happy and very disappointed.

"Can you change his mind?" he asked Barnabas.

"No, I can't," Barnabas said. "I am with him. We are all servants of God."

Paulus looked at them.

"I can give you a scroll that contains many of Jesus' stories," Mark said. "I traveled with Peter and recorded his lessons."

Barnabas further explained that Peter had traveled with Jesus."

"Thank you, son," he said.

He looked over the scroll.

"I can't read Greek, but I will have my advisor read the stories to me," he said. "This will be a great help."

Several days later, they sailed from Paphos.

Mark spoke to Paul, "The people there thought you were a God. You should have explained that Jesus performed the miracles."

Paul glared at Mark.

"Maybe,' he said. "God has filled me with the Holy Spirit. I am not Peter. I will do things my way. Make certain that you keep a good record."

Mark was disturbed with Paul's attitude. He knew that God should have been given the credit. He was also upset about the way Paul took all the credit and down played the fact that Barnabas was the reason that they went to Cyprus. He talked with Barnabas.

"I can't work with Paul," he said. "He is too consumed with himself. He needs to remember he is serving Jesus."

"Paul is filled with the Holy Spirit," Barnabas said. "God loves him. He is just different than Peter. Paul came from wealth. Peter came from poverty. He understood Jesus' message from a different perspective."

Mark shook his head.

"When we arrive in Pamphylia, I am going to find a way back to Jerusalem," he said. "I belong with the believers there."

"I will pray for you," he said. "Paul isn't going to be happy."

"He will get over it," Mark said. "The Holy Spirit has a lot of work to do with him."

"You do need to be away from him," Barnabas said. "I will tell him something."

When the ship docked in Pamphylia, Mark took his belongings and departed. Barnabas talked with Paul.

"Mark has gone to Jerusalem," he said. "I think he was home sick."

Paul shrugged.

"He wrote good Greek, but he was very immature," he said. "Maybe, he will grow in understanding by being with those in Jerusalem. We have work to do. Can you record my lessons?"

Barnabas wanted Paul to understand how valuable Mark was to them.

"No," he said. "I am not a scribe, and I don't think we will find anyone to help us along the highway."

"I wish we had a few others traveling with us," Paul said.

They remained in Pamphylia for a few weeks. Several converts joined them.

Meanwhile, Mark sailed to Caesarea and went to see Cornelius.

"I was here with Peter," Mark said.

"I remember you," Cornelius said. "Come in."

"How is the church?" Mark asked.

"It is good. We have several churches in town. Our procurator is very careful with those who believe in Jesus."

"That is good," he said. "Is he a Christian?"

"No," Cornelius said. "He is a pagan. He knows what happened to Agrippa and the history of Herod's family having problems with Jesus' followers."

"I wonder why Agrippa II isn't in Caesarea." Mark said. "He would be less tolerant."

"He is being educated in Claudius' court," he said. "He will be here someday. I'm not in a hurry for his arrival. I like Fadus just fine."

Mark visited with Cornelius the rest of the day and then decided to visit his sister, Ester.

He walked to her house and knocked on the door.

"Come in. When your sister returns, she will be overjoyed to see you," Sipra, Ester's attendant, said. "Joshua and she left much earlier to attend a function at the governor's palace. Fadus invites Joshua to everything."

"She must be a busy lady," Mark said. "I hope she enjoys all the popularity."

Sipra looked at Mark.

"She graciously attends the functions with Joshua," she said. "I think she would much rather be here with the children. I will have your things put in a room."

"Thank you, Sipra," he said.

"I will have dinner prepared," she said. "It will be quite late when they return."

Mark enjoyed a dinner of root vegetables.

The next morning, Mark slept late. When he went to breakfast, Ester was waiting for him.

"I am sorry I wasn't here when you arrived," she said. "I am so busy. If Joshua gets any more promotions, I don't know what I will do."

Mark hugged her and then looked down at her stomach.

"Yes, I am with child," she said. "Hopefully, this will be my last. I don't spend enough time with the two we have."

"Get another attendant," Mark said. "They can help you."

"I don't want help," she said. "I want to be with my children. I think they spend more time with their attendants than they do with me."

She wiped tears from her eyes.

That evening, the three sat in the living area and relaxed before the fireplace.

"I understand, you went to Cyprus," Joshua said. "Did you visit your uncle's vineyard?"

"Yes, we did," Mark said. "Joseph is managing the vineyards. He is busy and has very little time to spend with his family."

That is one of the costs of success," Joshua said. "But, it is better than poverty."

Mark was quiet.

"I remember when we visited the vineyards," Ester said. "It was a long time ago."

"A lot is still the same," he said. "The vineyards are much larger. Barnabas purchased all the land adjacent to his."

"Now, what does he do?" she asked.

"He rides around in a carriage and talks with the workers," Mark said. "In the evenings, he sits before the fire and drinks his wine. I think he is lonely."

After visiting with Ester for a few days, Mark walked on to Sychar. When he arrived at the inn, Abraham immediately recognized him.

"My guests love your family's wine, Abraham said. "I have people who come from town to eat dinner and drink wine with me."

He smiled at Mark.

"I will be staying only tonight," Mark said

Abraham nodded.

"Did you stable your horse?"

"I am walking," he said. "I'm traveling only with my pack."

Abraham thought for a moment.

"I will arrange a ride to Jerusalem for you," he said. "Many of my customers go to the city. Whenever your friend, Paul, and his family traveled to Jerusalem, they stayed with me. Now they live in Jerusalem. His sister, Yona, was married in Cana and now lives in Jerusalem."

Mark remembered the wedding and helping the servants pour the water that Jesus turned into wine. He was just a boy then. He paused for a moment.

"I guess you can call him my friend," Mark said. "I recently spent some time on Cyprus with him."

"I heard he had joined the church in Antioch," Abraham said. "I get the news from the travelers who stay with us. My son, Augustus, is managing the business now."

"You are lucky he wants to run the inn," he said. "Some sons don't follow in their father's footsteps."

"He loves the inn," he said. "He joined the new Jewish sect in town. He is very popular."

"He converted and joined a church?" Mark asked. "He shouldn't mix business and religion."

"He is a good manager," he said. "Travelers know that they will have a place to stay for many years. I am getting old, but I plan to remain here when I no longer can work."

He smiled at Mark.

The next morning, a couple gave Mark a ride to Jerusalem. They drove him to Able's house. Able saw him arrive and ran to him.

"I need a jug of wine for my friends," Mark said.

Able went into the house and returned. He handed Mark a bottle of wine. Mark gave it to the couple.

"You don't owe us anything," the man said. "We enjoyed your company. Is this the wine I purchase at the market?"

"I sell it there," Able said. "We also sell produce."

"We have been very good customers of yours," he said. "I see your fields on the way to the market."

"I love your produce," his wife said.

"I love your wine," the man said, as they drove away.

"I have returned to Jerusalem to live for a while," Mark said.

"You can stay in the room above the barn," Able said. "I will arrange for you to live in one of the new houses I had built for Joseph."

Mark didn't know Joseph was developing a housing complex in the area.

"I will need a job," Mark said.

"Go see Seth," he said. "He will give you a management job."

"I'd rather work in the fields," Mark said.

"Certainly," he said. "You can do whatever you desire. Business is very good. After you get settled, I will show you the houses."

Mark went to the room in the barn.

Two days later, Mark went with Able to the new housing complex.

"So far, he has built five houses," Able said. "I have already rented three of them. Two are still available."

They walked through the two vacant houses.

"Which one do you want?" Able asked.

"Which one will be easier for you to sell?" Mark asked. "I will take the other house."

Able pointed to the last house in the row.

"I will put a carriage and horse in the stable for you," he said. "Two servants come with the house. I am thrilled that you have returned."

"I don't know how long I will be here," he said. "I have no long range plans."

Mark moved into the new house that was only a five minute walk to his mother's house and fields.

The next Sabbath, Mark attended the church where Peter taught lessons and was surprised to see him. After church, he talked to Peter.

"I thought you were in Ephesus," Mark said. "I just returned to Jerusalem."

"I have been back a few months," he said. "My father died and I decided to visit with Andrew. He is doing well."

"Who is here with you?" Mark asked. "I know Barnabas and Paul are still on mission."

"James, Jesus' brother, is managing the church and John is helping him. I teach when I can." Peter said. "They keep me too busy at the church. I need a job. The church is very poor. Will you share lunch with me and my wife?"

"Certainly," Mark said. "I walked here."

"I drove a carriage," Peter said. "It belongs to a member of the church. He allows me to use it."

After Peter talked with James, and John, he went home with Mark. They headed north and entered Joseph's housing complex. They stopped several houses before Mark's house. He turned to Peter.

"We are neighbors," he said. "My brother, Joseph, owns all these houses."

"All I know is that I pay rent to a man named Able," he said. "He seems like a nice fellow."

Peter's servant served a cold, light meal. Mark began discussing his problems concerning Paul.

"He is different from me," Peter said. "I like the fact that he converts gentiles to Christianity."

Mark was a little surprised that Peter knew about and appreciated Paul's efforts.

One evening, a few days later, Peter came to visit Mark.

"I really have to find a job," he said. "The church doesn't have enough money to purchase food for the poor."

Mark thought for a moment.

"I might be able to help with both problems," he said. "I will talk to my friend, Able."

"The man, to whom, I pay my rent?" Peter asked. "I don't ever see him at church. How can he help?"

"Able owns several stalls at the market where he sells wine and produce. He might have food for the poor at the church, and a job for you."

The next day, Mark talked with Able.

"Peter needs a job," he said. "He is accustomed to hard work. He was once a fisherman."

Able smiled at Mark.

"Can he drive a wagon?" he asked.

"I know he can drive a carriage," Mark said. "I am certain he can drive a wagon."

"I might have a job for him," Able said. "I will talk with my driver who makes local deliveries. He has been asking for more pay and a job to deliver wine to my outlets."

"I will talk with Peter," he said. "He can help load the wagons each morning and make local deliveries."

"If he loads the wagons, I will pay him a little extra," he said. "That will allow you to have more time in the field."

Mark hugged Able and prayed with him.

Mark walked to Peter's house. Peter was at home.

"I talked with Mark," he said. "Are you willing to load a wagon and make local deliveries to the market six mornings a week?"

Peter looked at his wife.

"Certainly," he said. "What did he say about food for the poor?"

"I was so excited when he told me he needed a driver, I forgot to ask him," Mark said. "We will get food for the poor. I work in the fields and will see you each morning. I will tell Able the church needs food."

He stood and waved as he walked away.

Mark went back to see Able.

"I talked to Peter," Mark said. "He can drive and he wants the job."

"How much does he expect me to pay him?" Able asked. "I have a limit."

Mark looked at Able.

"He just wants to be treated justly," he said. "I want to give a bag of produce to the church each day."

"I will treat him fairly," he said. "I won't give produce directly to the church."

"I am going to pick a bag of produce each morning and take it to the church in the afternoon," Mark said.

"I didn't hear that," Able said, covering his ears. "Don't tell me anything about it; just take the produce."

He smiled.

"I understand," Mark said. "I will make it look like I am taking the produce home with me."

"That would be a good thing," he said. "You could give some to Peter."

He gave a little laugh and paused.

"Would you have a glass of wine with me?" he asked.

"Should field laborers drink with the big boss?" Mark asked.

"Only if the boss works for the field laborer's brother," he said.

He had his servant pour two glasses of wine. They walked into the field. Able handed the workers a jug of wine.

"It is hot," he said. "Have a drink and rest in the shade of the fruit tree for a few moments."

The workers smiled at Mark. They all knew his mother many years ago.

The following morning, Seth went to Peter, who was loading a wagon.

"My father told me you are our new local delivery driver," he said. "I manage the market for him. Welcome. He also told me you are part of Mark's family."

As Seth turned away, Peter waved to Mark and departed.

After church the following Sabbath, Peter visited with Mark.

"I can't make my comrades understand that we should be converting more pagans to Christianity," he said. "They insist that they become Jews before they become Christians. That requires circumcision."

"Have you converted any pagans here?" Mark asked.

"Two," Peter said. "Then they told me to cease direct conversions. I explained how many pagans are being converted by the church in Antioch, and those who go on missions from Antioch."

"What did they say?" Mark asked.

"They said they weren't aware of the practice, and they would send a messenger to Evodius," he said. "I know the bishop understands our great success."

"If he understands, he will support our position," he said. "He is a very reasonable bishop. He followed a great bishop."

"They called me bishop," Peter said. "I ran the church and was a rather popular teacher."

"Yes, I remember," he said. "I recorded your lesson and gave Evodius a copy of everything."

"Do you have a copy that you could give to this church?" he asked. "The young men who help me can all read and write. If they had a scroll of my lessons, they would learn faster."

Mark looked at Peter.

"Maybe, I could arrange for them to receive a scroll," he said. "I could teach them proper transcribing techniques while they copied my scroll."

"That sound like a good midweek lesson," Peter said. "I will introduce it to them this week."

Mark agreed to teach those who wanted to learn how to teach.

When Mark went to the midweek lesson, he took one very long scroll with him.

He showed it to his students.

"You are going to make a copy of this scroll," he said. "I will show you how to proceed and will monitor your progress. When you have finished, you will present the scroll to the church."

They had been given ink, writing instruments, and blank scrolls. One of the older students unrolled a blank scroll and started writing.

"Slow and steady," Mark said. "You must think ahead about what you are writing. I want two groups working at the same time."

The priest took their lesson very seriously. They worked on transcribing every week. After about three months, they had produced two scrolls that were acceptable to Mark.

The following Sabbath at the end of the service, a student presented the scrolls to the church.

"Thanks to Mark, we have learned how to transcribe the Greek language," he said. "I present one scroll written in Greek. Another scroll written in Latin was given to James, our senior priest."

"We are honored to receive these as part of our church library," James said, taking the scrolls. "Mark has written Peter's lessons in the form of a story of Jesus' life."

He took a scroll and read a short story to the members.

"Amen," they said.

As they left the church after the service, Peter talked with the members. He congratulated Mark.

"Nice job," he said. "I knew your work would be appreciated."

Mark knelt and said a short prayer.

As they walked to Peter's carriage, Peter pointed into the crowd.

"I see we have a few visitors from the synagogue," he said. "They stand outside to see who attends and to count their number. Some members consider it threatening."

"They might be looking for Paul," Mark said. "I know he is still looking over his shoulder."

They boarded the carriage and went to Peter's house. The servants served a light lunch. After lunch, Peter and Mark went for a walk.

"When they killed Jesus, I knew they acted in haste," Peter said. "I thought the rabbi would repent, and we would become friends again."

"Things are still getting worse," Mark said. "We won't live long enough to see our old friends again. I often think of Moses. He was a good teacher."

They walked to Able's house and drank a glass of wine and prayed with him.

Then they continued into the city. They went through the north gate and walked toward the temple.

"This is where they crucified Jesus," Peter said. "I wasn't here."

Mark didn't mention that he had been there with his mother. They continued to walk and talk. Finally, they started home. They arrived at Peter's house first. He waved at Mark.

"I will see you in the morning," he said. "Have a nice evening."

Mark went home and sat on the porch. He was able to watch the sun set from his porch. He closed his eyes and saw visions of heaven.

'God paints a beautiful picture' he thought.

When it became dark, he went inside. His servant served him cheese and wine before he went to sleep in his favorite chair.

The next evening after work, Peter visited with Mark.

"We haven't received a shipment of wine from Cyprus in two months," Peter said. "When I asked Able about it, he said the cold weather in Cyprus had killed one variety of grapes. We won't be getting any red wine for a year."

"That isn't good," Mark said. "But, Able can still sell the white and sweet wines."

"He fired the driver whose position I took over," he said. "I am very upset."

"It isn't your fault the weather was cold," he said. "He will find another job."

"If I hadn't taken his job, he would still one. I will talk with the driver," Peter said. "I am going to give him his job back."

"You should talk to Able," Mark said. "He worked for Able, not you."

Peter went to Able's house to discuss the problem and his guilty feelings.

"You could always share the job," Able said. "I could pay each of you one half of the wage. That way you would both be employed, and I could afford to keep both of you."

"That is fine," Peter said. "Will you talk with the other man?"

The following week, both men worked and received one half of a wage. This lasted for nine months until the shipment of grapes returned to normal.

One afternoon, Peter took Mark to the construction site for the new aqueduct. The hole for the pipe was about six feet deep and ran for more than a mile.

"The north side of town is growing so fast that the Roman government needed to provide a more efficient water system," Peter said. "They want more tax, so we get a new water system."

"That is great," Mark said. "When I was young, we had a drought. Our stream reduced to a trickle. Mother and I had to carry water for our crops. It doubled our workload, but we still had vegetables to sell."

"The new water system will make Joseph's land very valuable," he said. "He owns enough land to build about fifty more houses. He had been waiting for a new water supply."

Mark threw a stone into the hole.

CHAPTER 10

THE COUNCIL OF JERUSALEM

The business of selling wine and produce in Jerusalem flourished during the year forty-nine. It was warm on Cyprus and it rained occasionally in Jerusalem. The church in Jerusalem experienced some turmoil. Two priests were sent to Antioch to explain Jesus' message to the members of the Way. Those in Jerusalem became concerned when after three months their members hadn't returned.

Peter saw Mark at work in the field.

"I wonder what happened to the priests we sent to Antioch," he said. "I didn't think they would be gone nearly this long."

"You know Evodius," Mark said. "He will want to hear their position several times. He never agrees with anything until he is certain."

"He was certain about Luke's family," he said. "He helped them convert. That family is a good example. I don't know why he wouldn't think direct conversion is a good thing."

"Everything will work out in your favor," Mark said. 'Your results have proven your deed."

Mark and Peter anxiously awaited the return of their fellow Christians.

At the next Sabbath service, Mark saw one of the messengers who had gone to Antioch. After the service he talked with him.

"Evodius is talking with his priests," the messenger said. "He has been traveling to towns in the local vicinity. This is a controversial topic."

Mark became worried.

"He seems overly concerned," he said. "I hope he makes the proper decision."

"Evodius created a formal agenda for a council," he said. "He proposed the council be held in Jerusalem. He wants bishops and priests from all around the area to attend the meeting."

Peter joined the conversation.

"He can bring whomever he wants," he said. "I will invite the Lord. We should start praying. Is Paul going to attend?"

"Yes," he said. "He will be here."

'Good," Peter said. "He is a very good lecturer and will do a fine job of presenting our side."

Mark's brow furrowed. He had a problem visualizing Paul and Peter as compatriots with the same view on a controversial topic.

"I will be seated in the back of the room, taking notes," he said. "Peter, remember to tell the council about Cornelius."

Peter smiled at Mark.

"It should be a short meeting," he said. "If Paul needs help, I will be there."

Mark joined Peter's family and rode home.

When Peter arrived home from work the next day, he found a large pack of produce on his porch. He distributed the food to the poor, and then went to Mark's house.

"The poor thanks you for the food," he said. "Your arrangement with Able has been a great help to our members."

"We have a large crop this year," Mark said. "Tomorrow, we will probably pick two wagon loads of produce."

"It will be my pleasure to take them to market," Peter said. "I will see you in the morning."

Mark sat on the porch and watched the clouds in the sky. He visualized great white sailing ships and large white dragons. Finally, it became dark.

After Evodius talked with his priests, he decided that Paul should present the case for direct conversion of pagans to the council in Jerusalem.

"I want you and Barnabas to take several priests and go to Jerusalem," he said. "No one should be required to undergo procedures they don't understand before they become a Christian."

As they passed through Phoenicia and Samaria, they spoke at several churches.

"May I go with you to Jerusalem?" he asked. "I was converted from a pagan to a Christian."

Paul put his arm around him.

"Certainly," he said. "Join us. I will introduce you to our brothers in Jerusalem."

Several men joined the group from Antioch. When they arrived in Jerusalem, they were welcomed by the disciples.

"I have arranged for you to stay in a room above a wine storage area in a barn," James said. "You will be safe there. We will meet at the church. Please break bread with us."

The travelers ate and then went to their quarters.

A few days passed before the council began. They met in a large building that was used as a church. Believers, who were Pharisees, attended the meeting to enforce the laws of Moses.

"The Gentiles must be circumcised," a member said. "God gave laws to Moses that must be followed."

A feeling of excitement filled the room.

"God didn't intend his laws to deter men from coming to God," Paul said. "We need God, and he needs us."

The man whose faces had become red spoke again.

"God's laws must stand for all time," he said. "Moses didn't say follow these laws for a thousand years, or five thousand."

"God's laws, and therefore God, are timeless," John said. "It is an interesting concept. Man created keeping time to make life simpler."

The man interrupted John's discussion.

"We don't know how God kept time," he said. "Our laws keep us safe and clean."

Peter stood and joined the discussion.

"When I was in Caesarea, I baptized a pagan," Peter said.

A hush fell over the crowd. No one really wanted to confront Peter.

"He was a Roman centurion named Cornelius," Peter said. "He is now a devout believer in Jesus and leads a church in Caesarea."

He looked at the membership. They all looked at the ceiling.

"He has brought many Roman soldiers to God," Mark said. "That is a good thing. They would still be pagans if they had to become a Jew before they could talk with God."

The crowd answered, "Amen."

Peter continued.

"God, who knows the heart, showed that he accepted them by giving the Holy Spirit to them, just as he did to us. He made no distinction between us and them, for he purified their hearts by faith." (Acts, 15, 8 – 9, NIV)

Paul stood next to Peter.

"I have baptized many pagans," he said. "They are now serving God. The Jews in Antioch don't understand. They have named us Christians to separate themselves from us. They are losing member to us. Christians know God."

They debated the situation for several days. At times the discussion became heated. The crowd became silent as Barnabas and Paul told about the many miracles that they were able to perform. Finally, James stood and spoke.

"Peter has told us how God took a Gentile for himself," he said. "You should know this would happen. If you don't know, read your scripture."

James read scripture from the prophet Amos. The crowd listened. When James finished, the crowd began to whisper to each other. James paused for a few moments.

"We must not make it difficult for Gentiles who have found God," James said. "We should do as the prophet has written."

"What about the other laws?" a member asked. "Many of our laws help us to be healthy and safe."

The disciples agreed to eliminate the requirement for circumcision, but to keep the law concerning consumption of polluted food. The disciples created a letter that clearly stated the position of the Christian Church.

The members chose two men, Judah and Simon, to accompany Barnabas and Paul as they took the letter to churches in Antioch, Syria, and Cilicia. The men traveled to Antioch last. Evodius convened the priests from that area and read the letter to them. Judah and Simon spoke with authority about the great decision the central church in Jerusalem had made. The priests understood and were pleased with the outcome of the council. Paul and Barnabas remained in Antioch. The other disciples returned to Jerusalem.

Evodius spoke to Barnabas and Paul.

"You have represented the church in Antioch well," he said. "Representing God is very rewarding. Some days, it can be challenging. Jesus' message will always be challenged."

Barnabas taught a mid-week lesson concerning the council in Jerusalem.

CHAPTER 11

MARK AND BARNABAS ON CYPRUS

Barnabas became the leader of the priests in Antioch.

"Your lecture, where you compare Jesus to the path in light and the path without Jesus to the dark path, is very popular," Evodius said. "I would like you to teach our priests."

Soon, Barnabas became a mentor to the young priests. They looked up to him and sought his guidance on many topics.

Paul was noted for his success on mission and spoke with future missionaries.

"We were able to convert many Gentiles to Jesus' message," Paul said. "If you study hard and practice telling Jesus' story, someday, you will be ready to go on a mission."

The priests continued serving the faithful in Antioch.

After many months, Paul spoke to Barnabas.

"I want to return to the churches that we helped create during our first mission," he said. "Would you be willing to travel with me?"

Barnabas hesitated. He felt close to God in his current position training priests.

"Evodius has given me an assignment to work with the young priests," he said. "When are you planning to leave?"

"I am a little nervous staying here in Antioch with all these Jews," Paul said. "They might send someone from Jerusalem to find me."

"I will be finished with my current classes in two weeks," Barnabas said. "We will need a scribe. Mark would probably travel with us."

Paul thought for a moment. Barnabas noted a wrinkle in Paul's forehead.

"Mark, your uncle, who deserted us?" he asked. "I don't think so."

Barnabas was surprised that Paul remained so agitated.

"He is much more mature," Barnabas said. "When we were in Jerusalem, I talked with him. He has traveled with Peter."

Paul realized that taking Mark on mission with them was important to Barnabas. He didn't want to continue the conversation and decided to speak with Barnabas at a different time.

"I will think about it," he said.

After a few days, Paul approached Barnabas.

"I think I would like to depart in about one month," he said. "Can you possibly be ready by then?"

"I can be prepared. Have you thought about Mark?" he asked. "I would like to spend some time with him."

Paul decided to face his problem.

"Yes, I have prayed about it," he said. "Unfortunately, we can't take him with us. I need someone who is trustworthy and dedicated to our mission."

Barnabas was stunned and became defensive.

"Then, you will have to find another priest to go with you," he said. "If you can't forgive Mark and help him understand God, I, myself, will go on mission with him."

Paul understood Barnabas' position, but he wasn't about to take Mark with him.

"I am certain you can help him more than I can," he said. "You are his relative. I am just a servant of God."

"Yes, I am his relative," he said. "I love him very much. I'll do want I can to help him understand God's message."

Paul accepted the fact that he wasn't going to change Barnabas' opinion.

"I will miss you," he said. "You have been a great help to me."

"I have wanted to return to Cyprus," he said. "I will take Mark with me."

"I will pray for you and find a team to go with me," he said. "Many people come to Antioch to go on mission. We have no shortage of priests."

Paul took Silas on his second missionary journey.

Barnabas met with Evodius at the church.

"I would like to take Mark on a mission to Cyprus," he said. "My father manages a large vineyard, on Cyprus, and will provide for us."

"I hate to lose you," Evodius said. "We need more priests. Paul and Silas have just departed and will be absent for at least two years. Will you perform Silas' duties until I find a replacement for him?"

"Yes, I'll teach his lessons," he said. "Please begin your search."

"I will talk with members of my bishopric," he said. "They might recommend someone."

Evodius held Barnabas's hand. He hoped Barnabas would forget Cyprus.

"Thank you," he said. "I am certain Mark will benefit from the fine example you will provide."

They went and prayed. Soon, Evodius found a replacement to teach Silas' lessons.

Several weeks later, Barnabas traveled to Jerusalem. He found Mark working in a field. When Mark saw Barnabas he stopped working and greeted him.

"Come with me to Cyprus," Barnabas said. "We can visit my father and teach the story of Jesus in the churches."

Mark hugged him. He looked forward to returning to Cyprus.

"I will have to tell Able," he said. "I will go with you, but it will take me a while to make the necessary arrangements."

Mark motioned to a man working in the field.

"Can I help you, sir?" he asked.

"I am going home for the day," he said. "Barnabas is my nephew and is here to visit. If you see Able, tell him I will talk with him tomorrow."

Barnabas turned to the worker.

"I know Able very well," he said. "He works for my father."

The worker didn't have any idea about Able having a boss, but he knew if Able had a boss, he had to be important.

Mark and Barnabas walked to his house. A few houses before he was home, Mark pointed to a house across the road.

"That is where Peter and his wife live," he said. "We have been neighbors for a while."

"You mean one of Jesus' disciples?" he asked. 'I didn't know he was living in Jerusalem."

"Yes," he said. "His wife is a very good cook."

When they arrived at Mark's house, he introduced Barnabas to his servants, and then they sat in the living area and talked. Barnabas told Mark about his disagreement with Paul.

"He can certainly hold a grudge," Barnabas said.

"I am pleased that I'm not working for him," Mark said. "We have made some progress with the churches in Jerusalem."

The following morning, they went to see Able.

"Good day, sir," he said. "Are you having a good morning?"

Able looked at him. He wondered why he wasn't working in the field.

"Yes, I am fine," he said. "How are you?"

"Able, I've decided to go to Cyprus with Barnabas," Mark said. 'I will give you time to find someone to take my job in the fields. I won't need the house."

Able was surprised. He looked at Barnabas and recognized him.

"I can keep the house until you return," he said. "Those houses are in great demand."

"I don't plan on returning," Mark said. "I will remain on Cyprus with Barnabas and Joseph."

Able thought about Mark's statement and his relationship to his boss.

"I will find someone to take your job," he said. "Plenty of people are looking for full-time work. I could sell the house tomorrow."

They walked to Able's house and sat on the porch and talked. Mark worked with Able for one additional week.

When Mark and Barnabas departed, Able allowed them to ride in a wagon that was scheduled to deliver wine to Caesarea. When they arrived, they walked to Ester's house.

"Come in," she said, excited to see her brother.

"Do you remember our nephew, Barnabas?" Mark asked. "We are going to Cyprus and need a place to stay until our ship sails."

Ester scrutinized Barnabas.

"Yes, you both can stay with me," she said. "Joshua is in Rome on business. He won't return for several weeks."

They all went to the living area.

"Do you attend church?" Mark asked. "I know Cornelius. He helps with a church in town."

Just then, two children, an infant and two attendants entered the room.

"Occasionally," she said. "Joshua isn't allowed to attend church. He tries to remain out of the religious quarrels. I don't know Cornelius."

The attendant introduced Ester's children. Mark had already met two of them.

"I will check the schedule of the ships in the morning," he said. "I am looking forward to seeing our brother."

The next day, they purchased passage to Cyprus. The ship was scheduled to depart the following day. Early in the morning, Ester rode with Mark and Barnabas to the harbor. Mark gave Ester a kiss and walked up the ramp onto the ship.

As they boarded, a mate approached them.

"May I show you to your quarters?" he asked.

"We have passage to Cyprus," Mark said.

"Follow me," the mate said.

He showed them to their cabin.

"Dinner will be served at four bells on the second dog watch," he said.

Mark started to explain that he didn't understand the ship's bell.

"That is six o'clock for land lovers," the mate said. "Welcome aboard. We have a good wind."

After the ship was loaded, the crew rowed it into position and raised a small sail. Wind filled the sail and the ship headed to the open sea. Mark carefully watched the sailors' every move. When the ship finally cleared the harbor, they raised the main sail and the ship rapidly gained speed.

The ship docked at Amathos. Barnabas knew the town well. He hired a driver to take them to his father's vineyard. His father was working when they arrived, but a servant recognized him.

"Welcome home, Barnabas," he said. "I will prepare your room for you and put your guest in a spare bedroom."

"This is Mark," he said. "He is my uncle."

"Very good sir," he said. "I will make the proper arrangements."

They sat on the porch of the house and looked out at the vineyards. Just before dinner, Joseph returned from the vineyards. He saw Barnabas and ran to him and hugged him. He had tears in his eyes.

"Welcome home, son," he said. "I have been praying for your return. My prayers have been more than answered. You brought my brother with you."

He sat and a servant served them cool wine. They talked until dinner.

"I am through with traveling," Barnabas said. "I plan to teach Jesus' message throughout Cyprus."

"The people here love you,' Joseph said. "Governor Paulus talks about your healing powers. You are very popular."

"I have heard that emperor worship is popular," Mark said. "I remember the cults, to pagan Gods, in the cities."

"The cities all have pagan temples," he said. "Paphos has a large temple dedicated to Aphrodite. I would stay away from the cities. The churches are in the smaller towns."

Barnabas wondered how his father knew about the temple to Aphrodite.

"The first thing I plan to do is write down my thoughts," Barnabas said. "Mark is going to help me turn it into a theological statement."

They spent the next year at the vineyard, praying and writing. Barnabas decided it was time to visit a few churches. They headed west toward Paphos and stopped at the first small town.

"They still call the churches synagogues," Mark said. "I guess they still think of themselves as Jews."

"As long as they have Jesus in their heart, I don't care what they call their gathering place," Barnabas said. "They seem like a wonderful group of people."

He smiled at Mark.

Before they arrived in Paphos, they stopped in two additional towns. They walked to the center of the city.

"I don't remember the temple being this large," Mark said.

His head was tilted upward at a strange angle as he talked.

"It was this large the last time we were here," Barnabas said. "Many people in town worship Aphrodite."

They stopped on a street corner and started to tell the story of Jesus. Several people stopped to figure out what they were doing.

"Is Jesus related to Aphrodite?" he asked.

Another local man overheard the question and approached them.

"Move on," he said. "We aren't interested in your cult. In this town, we worship Aphrodite."

Barnabas wasn't pleased with the man's attitude.

"You should learn about Jesus," Barnabas said.

"I heard Jesus' story," he said. "I wasn't impressed."

"Then, I am sorry for you," Barnabas said.

"You are sorry for me?" the man asked, becoming visibly agitated. "This is my town."

Mark moved between the man and Barnabas and the people standing close by scattered. Soon, the man returned with a Roman soldier mounted on horseback. The soldier pointed at Barnabas.

"What are you doing?" he asked.

"I am telling a Jesus story," he said. "Everyone should have an opportunity to learn about Jesus."

"This island is Roman," he said. "We worship the emperor. Move on, or I will take you to prison."

"You don't scare me," Barnabas said. "I'll move on, but I will continue to tell my stories about Jesus."

The soldier moved his horse closer to Barnabas. He pulled a mallet from behind his shield and raised it above his head. Then, he hit Barnabas across his brow. He fell to the ground. The soldier and the man quickly left the scene. Mark knelt and held Barnabas in his arms and prayed for him. He remained unconscious for some time. Eventually, his eyes opened.

"What happened?" he asked.

He placed his hands on his head. He felt a bloody lump and was relieved he was alive.

"You had an argument with a soldier," he said. "He took exception to what you said. Then he hit you on the head and rode away."

"I remember the horse," he said. "That is all I remember."

Mark pulled Barnabas up to help him stand.

"My father warned me to stay away from cities," he said. "Take me back to the vineyard."

The next day, they started to walk east toward the vineyard. They stopped and taught a lesson in each small town they visited. When they arrived at the vineyard, Barnabas head was still swollen and discolored. Joseph looked at him.

"I guess you visited Paphos," he said. "They worship Aphrodite there, and pledge allegiance to the emperor. You didn't listen to me."

Frustrated with his son, he shook his head and walked away. Mark was quiet. Barnabas wasn't able to walk very far without feeling weak and sick to his stomach. For the next few days, they sat on the porch. Mark read Peter's lessons to Barnabas and prayed with him.

Barnabas slowly recovered, physically and spiritually.

"I have to be smarter," he said. "We can work on my epistle this week."

A few days later, Barnabas spoke to Mark.

"I'm ready to do a little more traveling," he said. "But, I'm not going west. You don't have to worry about that."

"Good," Mark said. "Where do you want to go? No more cities. The smaller towns are much safer."

"I thought we might visit towns north of the vineyard," he said. "You know, toward the great sea."

"When do you want to depart?"

"Tomorrow," he said.

Mark was surprised and concerned.

"Are you certain you will be able to walk?" he asked.

"I feel fine," Barnabas said. "I need to become more active. I can't sit on the porch indefinitely."

"I will be packed and waiting," he said. "I'm looking forward to a good walk."

The next day they only traveled a short distance, before they stopped for dinner. While at the restaurant, they heard a priest talking.

"Good evening, sir," Barnabas said. "I noticed that you are a priest."

The man nodded.

"I am," he said. "I try not to look too conspicuous. I don't want to draw attention to myself."

"We are priests as well," he said.

"I thought I recognized you," he said. "You were here with another fellow several years ago."

"Correct," Mark said. "He is on a mission west of Tarsus."

"I guess he didn't like our island as well as you," the priest said. "I love the island."

"It is my home," Barnabas said. "My father manages the large vineyard."

"Barnabas' vineyard?" he queried. "I knew Barnabas."

"Yes," he said. "I was named to honor my grandfather."

The priest thought for a few moments.

"Are you staying at the vineyard?" he asked. "I like their wine."

"Yes, we are," he said. "I have returned home and plan to remain on Cyprus."

"Would you like to come and tell my members about Jesus?" he asked. "Some of them will remember you. I am certain they know your father. They might have even worked for him."

Barnabas and Mark agreed to meet with the members.

They stayed with the priest at the church for a few days. They met with the members and told Jesus stories.

"Did you know Jesus?" a member asked.

"Yes," Mark said. "I talked with him on several occasions. My cousin, Peter, traveled with him."

The member was impressed and invited them to dinner. The local priest attended dinner with them. It was a joyous evening.

They continued north. They stopped and taught in several towns. Barnabas looked at Mark.

"I want to go to the city before us," he said. "I won't cause any problems."

"You didn't plan to cause any problems the last time," Mark said. "You seem to have a very short memory."

"I can't ignore the people in the cities forever," Barnabas said. "I only want to look around. I promise you won't have to carry me."

He rubbed the spot on his head where he once had a bump and smiled at Mark.

They walked into the city and were amazed by the size of the pagan temple. Mark looked at Barnabas.

"Yes, it is a very large temple," he said. "Don't even think of speaking about Jesus here. The people haven't been friendly. No one has spoken to us."

"I agree, it is a city," Barnabas dejectedly said. "But, city people need to hear about Jesus."

Mark shook his head, ignoring Barnabas' comment.

"We will take a different highway going south," he said.

"I guess I promised," he said. "This time, I will follow you."

When they arrived in the next town, a man greeted them.

"My wife is sick," he said. "My neighbor told me that you could heal people who are sick."

"Are you Christians?" Barnabas asked.

"My wife believes in Jesus," he said. "Will you heal her? The children and I need her desperately."

Barnabas looked at the man and held his hand.

"I can't," he said.

The man looked at Mark. He squeezed Barnabas' hand and pleaded for help.

"He can't heal her, but Jesus can heal her," Mark said. "She will be healed because of her great faith."

They walked to the man's house and prayed with his wife. The husband watched them pray for her recovery. He knelt with them.

"I don't know how to pray," he said.

"That is fine," Barnabas said. "We will do the praying."

She awoke and looked at Barnabas. Her husband was amazed.

"Thank you," she said. "I don't know you, but I can tell you are a man sent by God."

The husband offered to pay Barnabas a great sum of money.

"We don't take money," he said. "We would be pleased to dine with you and your wife."

The husband had the servants prepare a special meal. After dinner they went into the living area of the house. Barnabas looked at the man.

"Give your extra money to the local church," he said. "I am sure the priest will use it wisely. The poor are always with us."

"I will talk to the priest," she said. "We will use the money to feed the hungry. We have a few poor families in town."

Barnabas hugged her and they continued south on their journey.

After two weeks, they arrived at the vineyard. Joseph spoke with them.

"The grapes are ready to pick," he said. "We could use your help."

"We were very successful in the small towns up north," Barnabas said. "I would like to continue telling Jesus' story."

Joseph stared at him.

"Do you like your nice, large room?" he asked a bit impatient. "Do you like dinner every evening?"

Barnabas just looked at his father. Before he could say anything, Mark spoke.

"I am good at picking produce," he said. "I can pick grapes for you."

Barnabas smiled.

"You are correct," he said. "I should be more appreciative of your hospitality. Sometimes, I get so excited about helping other people; I neglect those who are helping me. I need to pray."

"Thank you for everything," Mark said.

"We will be ready to join the workers in the morning," Barnabas said. "I haven't picked grapes for a few years."

They retired early. They knew the work would be physically challenging the next day.

The following morning, they arose early and joined Joseph for breakfast.

"It is good to see you," Joseph said. "I shall keep you busy for a while."

Barnabas grimaced at Mark.

"Eat a large breakfast," he said. "We won't return to the house until dinner time."

They rode in a wagon to the grapes. Soon, Barnabas looked at Mark.

"I am tired," he said. "I am a teacher not a field worker."

"You will get used to it," he said. "I worked many days in my mother's vegetable fields."

"My feet hurt," he said. "My head is throbbing."

He sat down on the ground and took off a sandal.

"I think something bit me," he said. "My foot is red."

"Catch the culprit and bite it back," Mark said, chuckling. "We don't have time to sit on the ground. The grapes won't pick themselves."

"I'm thirsty," he said.

A worker heard Barabbas complaining and brought him a drink of water while Mark kept on picking grapes. Eventually, Barnabas went back to work.

"You haven't been doing enough physical work," Mark said. "Getting up and down is work."

"It is quitting time," a worker announced. "Get into the back of the wagon."

Mark helped Barnabas into the wagon.

When they arrived at the house, Barnabas took off his sandals and stretched out on the floor of the porch.

"Call me for dinner," he said. "I will be sleeping on the porch."

"I will help the workers put the grapes in the building with the press," Mark said.

About the time Barnabas was able to work all day, the crop was picked. The field hands now worked in the building pressing juice from the grapes.

Barnabas and Mark had worked in the vineyards for two weeks.

After dinner, Joseph spoke with them.

"The grapes have been pressed," he said. "The juice is stored in large barrels and will ferment for a while."

"What do you do with the grape skins?" Mark asked.

"The red and black wines have the skins in the barrels," Joseph said. "The wine will be strained before it is put in jugs. The skins from the white grapes have already been buried in the field where we will grow grain next season."

"I didn't know you grew grain," Mark said.

"We grow almost everything we eat," he said. "We make bread every day. We use a great amount of grain."

After breakfast one morning, Barnabas talked with Mark.

"I had a dream last night," he said. "I dreamt that I was being drawn to Salamis. It was like someone spoke to me."

"Salamis is a city," Mark said. "They worship Zeus. The largest building in the city is their temple to Zeus."

"When we were there with Paul, we were successful," he said. "I think we can be successful again."

"I don't want to go to any more cities," Mark said. "Your father has warned us, and we have had more than one close call with the pagans."

"I must go to Salamis," he said. "It is time I take a stand for Jesus in the cities. I have decided to start in Salamis."

Mark shook his head.

"You might be killed," he said. "That is too great of a sacrifice."

"If that is what is required to convert the pagans and Jews in Salamis, I will be glad to join my God."

Mark realized they were going to Salamis and was worried about Barnabas' safety.

"When do you plan to depart?" he asked. "You should tell your father."

"I'm not going to tell him," he said. "He will just give me another lecture about being safe and staying in the small towns. I want to go as soon as you can be ready."

Barnabas packed a copy of his epistle in his pack. They headed east along the Great Sea. Mark walked slowly and talked with Barnabas.

"I see a sailing ship," he said. "The ship is so far away, it seems to be standing still on the horizon. I wonder where it is taking its cargo."

"Many ships travel just south of Cyprus," Barnabas said. "We are between Caesarea and the other part of the world."

Mark visualized a drawing of the Roman Empire and nodded in agreement.

That evening, they stopped by a grove of carob bushes. They ate berries and pods for their dinner. Mark built a fire and skipped stones on the water. They looked at the moon's reflection in the water. It appeared as a gold glimmering spot. Mark looked into the sky.

"God paints a beautiful picture," he said. "It is very peaceful at the sea."

Barnabas moved closer to the fire.

"It is getting cool," he said.

They slept under the stars and the light of the moon.

The next day, they avoided Kition and walked north. Soon, they could see the sea again.

"I want to spend one more peaceful night on the sea before we go into the city," Mark said.

"I will make the fire tonight," Barnabas said.

They looked for ships and gazed at the sky.

The next morning, they walked into Salamis. They went to a church that they had first formed when Paul was with them. The priest provided them a place to sleep.

"I have something for you," Barnabas said to the priest.

He handed him a copy of the epistle that Mark had written for him. Mark was surprised.

"I didn't know you brought your epistle with you," he said. "I hope the Jews don't read it."

The priest accepted it.

"I will read your scroll this afternoon," he said. "What are you going to do today?"

"I thought I would find people who want to hear about Jesus," Barnabas said.

"You could help me teach the mid-week lesson tomorrow," the priest said.

"That is a great idea," Mark said. "In the meantime, we will visit the theater."

They walked north to the large, outdoor complex. "This is impressive," Barnabas said. "I wonder how many people attend the performances."

"I don't know," Mark said. "I know I want a hot bath."

"I guess we have time," Barnabas said.

They walked to the hot baths.

"The town is lucky that the Romans built such a great aqueduct system for them," Mark said.

"I like the hypocaust heating system," Barnabas said. "I like my baths really hot. These are the best on the island."

The next day, Barnabas met with the priest to prepare the mid-week lesson.

"I read you epistle," he said. "Will you tell our members about your ideas concerning the lighted path?"

Barnabas spoke to the members about how Jesus was the light that would keep them from stumbling in the dark. They appreciated his lesson.

The following day, the priest questioned Barnabas about the remainder of his epistle.

"Do you really believe the Jewish religion to be a false religion?" he asked. "God provided us with guidance a long time ago."

"The Christian religion is the only true religion," Barnabas said. "Anyone who isn't a Christian belongs to a false religion. They have been misled."

The priest stared at Barnabas.

"That is strong language," he said. "Many people wouldn't agree with you."

"I will defend Christianity," he said. "People must see the light."

That evening, Barnabas talked with Mark about his conversation with the priest.

"I thought he would be a great supporter of my ideas," he said. "He liked my ideas about light and darkness, but he seems upset by my calling religions other than Christianity false religions."

Mark looked at him.

"He is probably a Jew," he said. "Most of Jesus' disciples were once devout Jews."

"They saw the light and became converts," Barnabas said. "I plan to convert many more Jews and pagans."

The next day, a priest spoke to Barnabas.

"A rabbi came to see us today," he said. "He has invited you to defend your epistle at his synagogue."

"Who gave him Barnabas' epistle?" Mark asked. "We didn't want it to cause any problems."

"Tell him I will come to his synagogue tomorrow," Barnabas said. "I will pray today."

Mark turned to Barnabas.

"This is not good," he said. "You know that he wants to do more than discuss the epistle with you."

"It is time," he said. "You don't have to go with me."

"I will be with you," Mark said.

They prayed for the remainder of the day.

The next day, Barnabas and Mark went to the synagogue. They were met by an irate group of Jews.

"You think your religion is the only true religion?" a rabbi said. "We have great news for you."

"I am listening," Barnabas said. "I will try to answer your questions."

A small group of men rushed Barnabas and put a rope around his neck. They yelled at Mark.

"Unless you want a rope yourself, go outside!" a man yelled.

Mark ran outside, knelt on the ground, and prayed. He heard a struggle and knew Barnabas was in trouble. Barnabas was dragged by the rope out into the street. He was bleeding profusely. Mark couldn't stand to watch as Barnabas was stoned to death.

After what seemed like a long time, a man spoke to Mark.

"You can have your friend's body," he said. "We don't want to burn it."

Mark carried Barnabas' body to the church. A priest loaded the body into a wagon, and he and Mark drove to the vineyard.

The following day, Joseph and Mark buried Barnabas at the edge of the vegetable field.

CHAPTER 12

MARK IN COLOSSAE

Emperor Claudius' reign was so effective that those around him became envious of his success and plotted to kill him. In the year fifty-four he was assassinated. His adopted son Nero became emperor. Early in his reign, Nero was guided by his mother and the senate. He appointed Herod Agrippa II the ruler in Judea.

Mark was grief stricken over the martyrdom of Barnabas and stayed for a period of time at the vineyard on Cyprus. He prayed about what he should do next to serve his God, Jesus. He spoke to his brother, Joseph.

"Paul has made it very difficult for me," Mark said. "I am known as the disciple who deserted him. When he saw me at the council in Jerusalem, he said that he would put in a good word for me with the people of Colossae."

"Where is Colossae?" Joseph asked.

"It is about a three day's walk east of Ephesus," Mark said. "It is in the beautiful Lycus River Valley."

"I am familiar with the Meander River and the town of Laodicea," Joseph said.

"Yes, that is the area," he said. "The Lycus River flows into the Meander River. Colossae is on the great Roman highway that runs east."

"If they are expecting you, it might be a good place to help the bishop," Joseph said. "I would remain on Cyprus until you are certain what you are called to do. You don't have to rush into anything."

Mark thanked his brother for his understanding and hospitality.

"I might visit a few churches north of the vineyard," he said. "When Barnabas and I visited them, they enjoyed listening to our stories."

Mark spent the next two months taking short trips and teaching at the small churches north of Amathos.

When he felt ready to leave Cyprus, Mark spoke to Joseph.

"I am happy that I stayed with you," he said. "You have been very kind to me."

"You are always welcome here," Joseph said. "We will miss you. Are you certain you don't want to work for me in Jerusalem?"

"I am certain," he said. "Able is doing a fine job."

He gave his brother a hug.

"I will pack my things, and travel to Ephesus," he said. "I am ready to get on with my life."

"I will have my driver take you across the island," he said. "Many more ships depart from the north side of the island going to Ephesus than the south side of Cyprus."

Mark went to the port of Kyrenia. He was impressed with the large number of ships in the harbor. With their sails all stowed, the top half of the ships appeared as skeletons. Soon, he purchased passage and boarded a ship bound for Ephesus. He stood at the ship's rail and looked out at the dark blue sea. He remembered many good times with Barnabas. He thought about the nights they spent together looking at the moon's reflection on the water. Now, he was aboard that ship that sailed on the horizon. Tears formed in his eyes. He looked to the sky and prayed.

As the sun rose the next morning, he smelled breakfast. He started toward the odor. It was a beautiful, sunny, warm day. His nose guided him to the galley. He found a seat and ate a large breakfast and then went and stood by the ships rail and watched the ship cut through the sea.

When he arrived in Ephesus, he walked along a street paved with tiles. He asked a stranger for directions. The man directed him to the largest church in town. Mark proceeded to the prayer rail at the front of the church and began to pray. When he stood, he heard a greeting. He turned and saw a man in a robe.

"Good day," the priest said. "Welcome to Ephesus. What brings you to our town?"

"I am on a mission, and I plan to go on to Colossae," he said.

The priest looked at Mark and pondered for a moment.

"Epaphras, one of Paul's disciples, started a church in Colossae," he said. "I am certain he will appreciate your help. Do you know Paul?"

It was the question Mark didn't want to hear.

"Yes," he said. "I traveled with him for a short time,"

"Good," he said. "Before you depart, remain with us for a few days. You can dine with Paul this evening."

Mark was very surprised and didn't want to appear unappreciative.

"He will be here this evening?" he asked. "I haven't seen him since we spoke in Jerusalem."

The priest nodded.

"He lectures in the park or at a church, on occasion," he said. "He spends most of his time writing at the library."

"I guess he writes to the churches that ask for his help," Mark said. "He started so many churches, he can't return to all of them."

He paused for a moment.

"I will be leaving for Colossae in a few days."

The priest looked at Mark.

"Paul has never been to Colossae, but he writes to Epaphras," he said. "You will like Colossae."

"I don't plan to stay there," he said. "I just want to help the priest for a while."

He thanked the priest for the conversation and help. He was taken to his room where he stretched out on his bed and fell asleep.

"It is six o'clock," the priest said, knocking on the door.

Mark jumped to his feet, and then followed the priest to dinner.

When they arrived, Mark saw Paul. Paul stood and he hugged him.

"It is good to see you, Mark," he said. "I understand that you are going to Colossae. They will be expecting you. I spoke to Epaphras about you."

Mark was relieved. He had prayed for a gracious greeting. He smiled at Paul.

"Thank you, Paul." he said. "Did you know Barnabas was martyred?"

"We have all heard the bad news," he said. "Tell us what happened."

Mark addressed the priests for a few moments and then blessed the food. After dinner, Paul told Mark about the library.

"They need a larger library to hold all of their scrolls," Paul said. "They have scrolls they don't even know what they contain. They are lucky to have a librarian that knows where everything is located and that is willing to help us who like to read."

"How do they store them?" he asked. "Have you looked at them?"

"Yes, you must visit the library while you are in Ephesus. It is a great experience," he said. "It is my favorite place in the world to relax and write. When I need a particular scroll, I explain what I am doing to the librarian, and he locates useful material and brings it me."

Mark agreed to visit the library.

After a few days, it was time for Mark to depart, and he started east. He decided to follow the great highway that followed the river. He faced east and the bright sun's reflection in the river made it difficult for him to see. He stopped in a small town to purchase a head cover.

"I need something to keep the sun from blinding me while I walk," he said. "I have been shading my eyes with my hand."

"I have a head cover that goes down over your forehead," the shopkeeper said. "If you tip your head slightly forward, you will be fine,"

Mark pushed his long hair from his forehead and tried on the head cover.

"I'll take it," he said. "It is definitely better than just wrapping my head."

He continued along the highway. He slept near a caravan for safety. When he reached the Lycus River, he turned and headed south. The river appeared chalky in color due to the many mineral deposits in the water. He saw field after field of green grass full of sheep. Occasionally, he saw a shepherd leaning on his crook. He was impressed by the majestic mountain that he saw in the east. When he arrived at Colossae, the highway circled north around the town, and he walked toward a gate in the city's wall. He was detained while several wagons loaded with merchandise entered the town. He noticed that one wagon was loaded with wool, and he remembered all the sheep he had seen. Finally, he was inside the gate.

"Can you direct me to the church?" Mark asked.

"I don't know what church you are talking about" the stranger said. "But, the synagogue is two blocks ahead of you."

Mark went to the synagogue and was directed to the church. It was a house that was converted to a meeting place. He knocked on the door and a man answered.

"I am looking for Epaphras," Mark said. "Paul told me about this church and the priest."

"You have found me," he said. "I, too, am a disciple of Paul."

Mark wanted to make a good first impression.

"I knew Paul before he became a Christian," Mark said. "I also knew Jesus. He visited our home in Jerusalem when I was young. Peter baptized me."

Epaphras wasn't certain what he had said that made Mark so defensive.

"Come in," he said. "I have known Paul for several years. I hope you came to help me."

"I did come to help you, but you will also have to help me," Mark said. "Do you have lodging for an assistant?"

Epaphras smiled at Mark.

"You can stay with me," he said. "The house is provided to me by a member of the church."

Mark finally seemed to relax.

"We will make a good team" Epaphras said. "Now, tell me about Peter."

"I will do better than that," he said. "I have recorded his lessons about Jesus."

He looked in his pack, found a scroll, and handed it to Epaphras.

"If you will give me materials to write, I will make you a copy of the scroll. Do you read Greek?"

"Yes," he said. "I have an epistle Paul wrote to me from Corinth, but he has never given me any of his lessons about Jesus."

Mark went with Epaphras to his house.

During the next few weeks, he proceeded to make a copy of his scroll.

On the Sabbath, they attended church, and Epaphras introduced Mark to the members.

"Paul sent Mark to us," he said. "He has met Jesus and talked with him."

Then, Epaphras taught a lesson about ethics. After the service, they returned to the house.

"We have many problems in our church," he said. "That is why I taught about ethics."

Mark thought for a moment.

"I would like to read the epistle that Paul sent to you," he said.

Epaphras looked over several parchments.

"Here it is," he said.

He handed the letter to Mark.

"I will study it and discuss it with you tomorrow," he said.

He took the scroll to his room. After he had read it several times, he talked with Epaphras.

"First it seems that Paul feels that your members are slipping back into their old habits," he said. "They aren't studying the message of Jesus."

"Many of my members were pagans and Jews," Epaphras said. "They have laws and creeds of their own that they follow."

"Paul wants them to understand what is proper," Mark said. "He wants them to gain this knowledge by studying Jesus' message."

Epaphras looked down at the parchment as Mark pointed to a passage.

"He wants them to know the mystery of God," he said. "By studying and knowing Jesus' message, they will gain the treasures of wisdom and knowledge."

Epaphras took the parchment from Mark and reread the message aloud.

"I think you are correct," he said. "He doesn't want them to memorize laws. He is interesting in them knowing and understanding the laws well enough to make informed decisions."

He looked at Mark.

"Yes, that is part of it," Mark said. "He also talks about their ideas concerning demonic spirits."

"They are afraid of many natural things," Epaphras said. "Thunder and lightning for instance frightens them more than it should."

"We need to teach them about the Holy Spirit," he said. "When they understand Jesus message and allow the Holy Spirit to help them, they will know nature is part of God's world."

"I should have studied what Paul wrote to me," he said. "They will continue to consider their existence a nightmare until we help them see the light."

Mark nodded in agreement.

The following Sabbath, Epaphras taught a lesson concerning the message of Jesus.

"Jesus' message is the good news," he said. "It is the truth. Other writings and messages are conjecture about God. Jesus gave us the truth."

A few members answered, "Amen."

Epaphras taught loud and long. He waved his arms and stared into the sky.

After the service, many members stayed and talked with Epaphras. He talked with Mark as they walked home.

"Never have I received so many comments and congratulations," he said. "I think you have pointed me in the direction that Paul suggested."

"I didn't always understand Paul's words or actions," Mark said. "It takes a while to know someone well enough to discern their writings."

Epaphras smiled at Mark.

After a Sabbath service, a few months later, a member talked to Epaphras.

"I would like you and Mark to join my family for dinner tomorrow evening," he said. "It won't be fancy, but my wife grows a garden and is a good cook."

When they visited with the family, Mark commented about the garden.

"My mother had a garden," he said. "I often worked in the garden with her. We always had fresh vegetables."

He had visions of vegetables dancing in his head.

After a wonderful dinner, they went home.

"He is an important man in the church," Epaphras said. "It is good to know he is happy with my lessons."

"All men are important to God," Mark said. "I am pleased that he has expressed his agreement in such a positive manner."

During the following year, Mark remained with Epaphras and helped him create and practice his lessons.

Mark talked with Epaphras, "You no longer need me. I think Paul would be pleased with our efforts and our results. I am now going to Ephesus."

Epaphras was surprised. He knew Mark wouldn't stay indefinitely, but he wasn't prepared for him to leave.

"But, I count on you to help me to keep teaching the proper message," he said.

"It is time," Mark replied. "Your members are again in tune with Paul's desires. They are comfortable with your message."

Epaphras dejectedly looked at Mark.

"I will miss you," he said. "What are you going to do in Ephesus?"

"I am going to the library," he said. "I want to read their scrolls concerning our religion, and I want to write."

After a few days, Mark followed the river to the highway and went west. He smiled as he thought about the progress they had made helping the people of Colossae correctly understand Jesus' message. The Holy Spirit was in his heart and the sun warmed his back as he walked. He wasn't a tall man, but he cast a long shadow.

When he arrived in Ephesus, he went to the church hoping to find Paul.

"I have been working for Epaphras at Colossae," he said. "Now, I want to stay in Ephesus and study. If I teach a lesson, will you give me quarters and food?"

"Yes," the priest said. "You are welcome to stay with us. You will have to do what is necessary at the church."

"Where is Paul staying?" he asked. "Does he still live with friends?"

"No," he said. "He has continued his mission. He told me he was going to Macedonia."

"I missed him," he said. "Well, I know I will see him again, someday."

The following morning, he visited the library.

"I would like to read all the scrolls in your collection concerning Jesus," he said.

The librarian looked at him.

"We have a few scrolls that mention Jesus," he said. "One scroll, written by Thomas, is a listing of Jesus' sayings. We have an untitled scroll that people seem to like. It mentions Jesus."

"I would like to look at that scroll first," he said. "I have visited churches that consider the Gospel of Thomas part of their scriptures."

"If you like that sort of thing," he said. "You might want to visit the Temple of Artemis. It is a very interesting structure. I think it has been rebuilt three times."

"I would like to see the scroll," Mark said. "I have seen too many pagan temples. It seems every city has a temple built to honor a different God."

The librarian brought him the scroll.

"When you are finished, please return it to me," he said. "I haven't classified it."

He started reading the scroll and then motioned to the librarian.

"This is only a partial scroll," he said. "I don't think you have the entire scroll. It is very interesting so far."

"I have read it," he said. "I thought you might like it. Most Christians like the part about Jesus being sent down by God to remove ignorance from our earth."

"It is correct," Mark said. "Many teachers are foolish because they try to understand the world by analyzing the law."

The librarian was quiet and walked away. Mark continued to read. The untitled work clearly stated that fear was a result of ignorance. Mark made several notes.

Later, he returned to the church.

"Did you find anything interesting?" the senior priest asked. "We also have a few scrolls here."

"Yes," Mark said. "Your library has a good collection. I have already found one that I wasn't familiar with."

When Mark returned to the library the following day, he began to study the scroll written by Thomas.

Mark thought, 'Paul certainly had a copy of this text. He quoted freely from Thomas' recollection of Jesus' sayings.'

The librarian came up and spoke with Mark.

"What do you think of this scroll?" he asked.

"I like it very much,' he said. "I will read a section to you. Thomas wrote that Jesus said: 'When he who seeks, finds what he looks for, he will become troubled. Then he will be astonished and be able to control himself.'"

The librarian looked at Mark.

"That is good," he said. "It makes sense. That is probably why so many people follow Jesus' saying."

Mark smiled at the librarian.

Mark realized that Luke and Matthew probably had read a listing of Jesus' sayings as well. Many believed that Jesus would soon return, but Thomas believed that the kingdom of God was already upon them. That afternoon, Mark visited the large park in the center of town. He listened to a man teach.

"I have with me a letter written by Peter, the great disciple of Jesus," the man said. "He denounces Moses."

Mark was astounded and couldn't restrain himself.

"I doubt that," he said, bluntly.

The man glared at Mark.

"I suppose you know Peter," he said. "Look at this letter. You will see Peter's name."

Mark took the parchment and quickly analyzed it.

"This isn't Peter's writing," Mark said, about to explain further.

The man interrupted.

"I suppose you are an expert in detecting his writings," he said. "Who are you?"

Mark slowly spoke to the man and those around who listened.

"I am Mark. I traveled with Peter for years and recorded all of his lessons. Your parchment is written in Greek. I know that Peter didn't write much at all, and he didn't know Greek."

"I guess you probably knew Jesus, too," he said. "Then, tell us your story."

"I met Jesus on several occasions," Mark said. "I was too young to travel with him, but he visited our family home."

The man quickly realized that he was on sinking ground with this subject. He grabbed the parchment out of Mark's hands and walked away. Everyone close by who had been listening, jeered the man.

The next day, a priest spoke to Mark.

"I heard about the incident in the park yesterday," he said. "That man is a false prophet, and he will return tomorrow. I'm sure he will look for you before he reads anything out loud or tries to solicit money."

Mark hesitated before he spoke.

"It is unfortunate that many people are usurping the good names of the original disciples," he said. "They will answer for their actions at judgment."

"Amen," the priest responded.

After a year in Ephesus, Mark decided to visit his sister. He spoke with the priests who had shown him great hospitality.

"It is time for me to leave to visit my sister," he said. "I haven't seen her for many years."

"Where does she live?" he asked.

"In Caesarea," Mark said. "Her husband is an important lawyer with the providential government."

"We will miss your faith," he said. "We pray every day, but we lack the confidence that your experiences have given you."

Mark smiled at the priest.

"Have a safe journey," the priest said. "I will pray for you and your sister."

After a few days, Mark boarded a ship. The ship's first stop was Cyprus to load wine. Mark watched two wagon loads of wine carried aboard. He remembered the vineyards and harvesting grapes. It was a pleasant journey to Caesarea. When he arrived at Ester's house, Sipra answered the door.

"Come in," she said. "Your sister will be pleased to see you. Joshua is at work."

Ester entered the room and beamed a big smile.

"It is great to see you, Mark," she said. "Where have you been living?"

"I have been in Colossae and Ephesus," he said. "At first, I was with Paul. After a short time, I went to work with Epaphras in Colossae. I stayed with him for over a year and returned to Ephesus."

Ester looked at her brother.

"Paul is now here in Caesarea," she said. "Joshua knows him quite well."

"What is he doing here?" Mark asked. "I didn't know your husband converted to Christianity."

"He didn't," Ester said. "Paul is in prison. He has talked with Governor Felix and with Joshua."

"Why was he arrested?" he asked. "I thought he was on a mission."

"After his mission, he went to Jerusalem," she said. "He visited with your friends."

"He should have been safe with them," Mark said. "They have become accustomed to dealing with the Romans and the Jews."

"Paul went to the temple and a few Jews recognized him," she said. "They aroused the crowd and then began to beat Paul. The Roman soldiers rescued him."

"The soldiers probably saved his life," Mark said. "The crowd might have killed him. He isn't very popular with the Jews who once trusted him."

"The soldiers sent over a hundred men with Paul to Caesarea," she said. "He was brought here so he would be safe."

"That is a lot of soldiers to transport one prisoner," he said. "Someone was looking out for him."

"When he arrived, it looked like a parade. Many people lined the street."

"He is a Roman citizen and has the right to a Roman trial," he said. "I hope Joshua will ensure he is treated fairly."

Ester looked at Mark.

"Joshua treats everyone fairly," she said. "Felix doesn't want to get involved with Paul and doesn't know what to do. Maybe, you should go see him."

"No," Mark said. "I don't want to bring any problems into your house. I will have a priest visit him and then talk with me."

"The priests at our church visit with all the prisoners," Ester said. "So, it would look normal for them to visit Paul."

The following day, Mark visited the local church and found the senior priest.

"My friend, Paul, is in prison," he said. "I want someone to go and talk and pray with him."

"Why don't you go to him?" the priest asked. "I would go with you."

"My sister is married to Joshua, the Roman lawyer," he said. "I don't want her to be associated with this situation."

The priest nodded.

"I understand," he said. "You are doing the proper thing. I will pray for all of us. After I visit with Paul, I will come and see you."

"Ester said that I could depend on you," Mark said. "We will be waiting."

Mark returned to Ester's home.

The priest went to the prison.

"Good day, father," the guard said. "Who do you want to visit?"

"I am going to pray for Paul today," he said. "He is a follower of Jesus."

The guard took him to Paul.

"You have a visitor," the guard said, gruffly.

The priest looked at Paul and spoke to him softly.

"Your friend, Mark, sent me," he said. "He is worried about you. He can't visit because his sister lives here, and he wants no harm to come to her family."

Paul took the priest by the hand.

"I understand," he said. "Tell him, eventually, they will send me to Rome. I don't know how long I will be here. I will probably be here longer than Felix is governor."

The priest smiled.

"We will pray, every day, for your safety," he said. "I will inform Mark that you anticipate a trial in Rome."

The next day, Joshua came home from work and he, Ester, and Mark sat in the living room and enjoyed red wine.

"We are getting a new governor," he said. "I am to meet him next week. His name is Festus."

"Is Felix being transferred?" Ester asked. "He isn't a very good governor and hasn't been popular."

"He is being recalled to Rome," Joshua said. "The citizens of Caesarea have complained about him. He might be in trouble."

"Will Festus deal with Paul?" Mark asked.

"From what I know about him, Festus is a man of action," he said. "If he doesn't know what to do, I have been told to contact Agrippa II."

Two week later, Mark, Ester, and Joshua were in the living room.

"The governor asked me about Paul today," Joshua said. "He wanted to know why Felix hadn't dealt with the problem. I think he already knew the answer."

"What has he decided to do?" Mark asked

"When Agrippa II visits next week, we will consult with him," he said.

Joshua came home the following week, very excited.

"I met Agrippa II today," he said. "I told him about Paul. He wanted confirmation that Paul requested a Roman trial, and I said that was correct."

Then he smiled at me and said, "I don't understand what Felix's problem was. We will give Paul a Roman trial. Send him to Rome."

"When I told Festus what Agrippa II said, he was very pleased," Joshua said. "Festus said that after we send Paul to Rome, he won't be our problem any longer."

"Can you give him any help in Rome?" Mark asked.

"He won't need my help," Joshua said. "He has served enough time in prison. I expect they will put him under house arrest. Governor Festus is sending his recommendation."

They gave a toast to Paul.

Mark stayed with his sister for another month before he departed for Rome.

CHAPTER 13

MARK IN ROME

Young Nero married Claudius' daughter, his step-sister, and spent most his time with her. Nero's mother, Agrippina, with the help of the senate, ruled the empire. Financial conditions were so severe, Nero insisted that many public services and construction projects be started to help people find work. With all of the new projects, a new wife, and his mother, Nero was too busy to be concerned about religion.

Felix, the displaced governor of Judea, was recalled to Rome, accused of inciting minor disputes. He used the disputes as a cover to seize the property of those involved with the disputes. He was never punished for his alleged wrong doings.

During Mark's trip to Rome, a storm raged in the great sea. His ship groaned and was tossed about by the heaving waves so badly that the vessel snapped and cracked. The passengers were frightened. Mark went to the galley and prayed that God would be with them. Suddenly, the storm subsided, but the ship was damaged and docked in a harbor on Crete.

"We will be staying in Crete for a few days," the captain said. "Our safety is more important than our schedule."

The first mate arranged for the passengers to stay at an inn for two evenings. On the third day, the passengers were told the ship would sail in two hours.

"A ship docked this morning to load grain," he said. "The captain told me that the storm has subsided. It is time for us to proceed on to Rome."

Several days later, they docked in Ostia. Mark took his pack and proceeded to walk to Rome, following the Via Ostia. As he approached the city, he went through the Porta Capena and turned left at the wall around the Palatine Hill. Then, he followed the Tiber River north until he saw a complex of houses. He knew he was close.

"Can you direct me to the church?" he asked. "I am new in town."

He was directed to a house two blocks away. He entered the building and saw a man kneeling at the altar. The man rose and turned to Mark.

"I am so glad to see you," Peter said. "As you can see, we use this house as our church. I live next door."

They talked for a few more moments and then went to Peter's house. Peter located his wife and made the introductions. Mark remembered her. She hugged him.

"Welcome to Rome," she said. "You are an answer to our prayers. We have a fairly active church and Peter needs help."

Mark quietly thanked God.

"What brings you to Rome?" "Peter asked. "Did you know I was here?"

Mark wasn't exactly certain how to answer his question.

"When I was in Caesarea visiting my sister, Ester, a local priest told me about Paul being in prison. Paul told the priest that he would eventually be tried in Rome."

Peter looked at Mark.

"I haven't gotten news that Paul is here," he said. "We are careful and haven't encountered any problems."

"Maybe, he hasn't arrived yet," he said. "Why don't I record your lessons for you?"

"Do you have a copy of my old lessons?" Peter asked. "I could give them to those who have been helping me."

"I have my own copy," Mark said. "That is all I carry."

"Will you make a copy for my helpers?" Peter asked. "They can read Greek." Peter found a place for Mark near his home and assigned Mark duties at the church. Mark worked diligently making a copy of Peter's lessons.

A few days later, Mark was working at the church when Peter walked in.

"A group of Roman prisoners arrived yesterday," he said. "Let's go and determine if Paul is among them."

The two men walked to the prison and talked to the warden. He checked the manifest.

"Yes," he said. "I have a prisoner named Paul."

He motioned to a guard. When the guard returned, he had Paul with him.

"If you will be responsible for him, I will release him under house arrest," the warden said. "I will assign Thaddeus to be with him."

The warden introduced Mark and Peter to Thaddeus. He was an older, burly, prison guard. He nodded to both men.

Paul was allowed to live and teach in Rome. On many occasions, Mark went and listened to Paul lecture in the park.

"If you will believe in the message of Jesus, you will be given grace," Paul said. "Jesus' grace is your salvation. This grace will allow you to perform great works and be in control of your actions."

Mark took notes so that he could talk later with Peter about Paul's lessons. Several times a week, people would gather in the park to listen to Paul.

One afternoon, Mark stopped by Paul's house and talked with Thaddeus.

"Peter and I would like to invite you both to dinner," he said. "Peter's wife is a very good cook."

"That is fine," Thaddeus said. "My wife is so busy with our children; she doesn't have the opportunity to make dinner for all of us. When I get home from work, I eat whatever I can find."

Paul and Thaddeus visited Mark the following week.

"Paul may be under house arrest, but it is better than being in prison," Mark said. "How long will they control his movements?"

Thaddeus looked at Paul before speaking.

"I have been told that he will eventually be set free," he said. "The emperor isn't interested in these minor matters. When we have satisfied the request of Agrippa II, he will have his freedom."

After dinner, they went outside and sat on the porch.

"If you are interested, I can get you access to the Pompey Theatre," Thaddeus said. "It is named for one of Rome's past great military leaders."

"We might like to attend," Peter said. 'Where is it located?"

"It is just a few blocks from here," he said. "I will make the arrangements for you."

"Do you know someone?" Mark asked.

"One of my best friends is a guard at the theatre," he said. "He allows several people to come in each night."

On occasion, Peter and his wife attended the theatre.

The following week, Paul spoke again in the park.

A local man asked him. "How did you get to Rome?"

Paul smiled.

"I came via Malta," he said. "I am a guest of the emperor. I was in prison in Caesarea, and Governor Fetus sent me to Rome to be tried."

"How did you get to Malta?" he asked.

"While we were sailing, a violent storm struck," Paul said. "The ship was destroyed, but we made it ashore on Malta."

The man was puzzled.

"If your ship was wrecked on the sea, why didn't you escape?" he asked.

Paul looked at him.

"It was my duty to help rescue those who were drowning," he said. "God kept me safe and gave me strength."

The man scratched his head.

"If your ship sank, how did you get here?" he asked.

"Publius, the local city administrator, sent for me," Paul said. "His father had been very sick in bed. I prayed for him and God healed him."

"You prayed and God healed," the man repeated.

"The administrator was so pleased that our captain had taken me to see his father, he sent out a ship for us," he said. "If the captain hadn't gotten us to Rome, he would have been in trouble. The captain put a good word in for me at the prison. Then, my friends, Mark and Peter arrived."

"That is a great story," he said. "I enjoyed that story more than the Jesus story you told yesterday."

"The story I just told you was a Jesus story," Paul said. "I prayed to Jesus, and he healed the man."

Still puzzled, the man shook his head and walked away.

A month later, Mark was at the church when he noticed a man praying at the altar. He walked over and the man faced him.

"I am Luke," he said. "I have come to Rome to find Paul."

"I am Mark," he said. 'I am a friend of Paul's.'

Luke smiled at him.

"He has told me about you," he said. "Will you take me to him?"

Mark wondered what Paul might have told him.

"Yes, follow me," he said.

They walked to the park and found Paul and Thaddeus. Paul saw Luke, stopped speaking mid-sentence, and went to him. Then he turned to the crowd.

"This is my friend and great physician, Luke," he said. "He has traveled with me and has helped me tell the story of Jesus."

The people in the park greeted Luke in unison. Thaddeus explained all about Paul's house arrest to Luke. Later, Thaddeus talked with his superior, and Luke was given permission to live with Paul.

They returned to Paul's house later in the day.

Mark came to visit.

"How did you know Paul was in Rome?" he asked.

"I was in Antioch helping the church," he said. "I met a man from Caesarea who told me about Paul. I decided to join him."

"He is lucky to have such good friends," Mark said. "I was in Caesarea when Paul was jailed there. Did you come straight to Rome?"

"No," Luke said. "I visited my parents first in Troas."

Paul looked at Luke.

"I remember a day when we had a small problem in Troas," he said. "You were a great help that day."

They told Thaddeus about the man who fell from a window.

The following week, a box was delivered to Paul. Thaddeus opened it.

"You received a parchment and some money," he said. "I will have to make a record of it."

Paul read the letter and counted the money.

"Who sent you money?" Thaddeus asked.

Paul smiled.

"My sister, Yona," he said. "She worries about me. She owns a retail outlet in Jerusalem. Am I allowed to write to her?"

Paul was given permission to send an occasional letter to his sister.

Mark was in his office at the church, when Peter came to see him.

"I heard that Nero had his mother put to death," Mark said. "I guess he tired of her telling him how to run the empire."

Peter was shocked. He couldn't imagine anyone killing his own mother.

"How did he have her killed?" he asked. "Was she poisoned?"

"No, he had her taken on a boat that was supposed to sink," he said. "The boat sank, but she swam to shore. A guard posted on the shore stabbed her to death."

"I hate to hear that," Peter said. "She might not have been emperor, but she was a good advisor to the senate. I hope Nero is as steady as his mother, Agrippina."

"We should say a prayer for her soul," Mark said. "She was one of God's children, even if she was a pagan."

While Thaddeus and Paul walked in the park, a soldier approached them. He waved at Thaddeus.

"You don't have to guard him any longer," he said. "He has been set free by the court. The requests of Agrippa II have been satisfied, and we have no charges against him."

Thaddeus turned to Paul and announced that he was a free man. Paul dropped to the ground and prayed.

That evening, he and Luke visited with Peter and Mark.

"I am free," Paul said.

"What are you going to do?" Mark asked.

Paul pointed west.

"I have always wanted to go to Spain. I am getting old. If I don't go now, I probably never will."

He thought a moment and then looked at Luke.

"Luke, I could use a companion. Will you travel with me?" Paul asked.

Luke had already established a good rapport with many people in Rome. He thought about them.

"No," he said. "I have a lot of work to complete with the church. I will be here when you return."

Paul dejectedly walked away.

Peter, Luke, and Mark continued to serve the Christians in Rome.

A few weeks later, Mark and Peter were at the church when a man came to them.

"I am Simon Magus," he said. "I have heard you do great things. You heal the sick."

"God heals the sick," Peter said. "We just ask him to help us. Many of his followers have received the Holy Spirit and can, with God's help, perform miracles."

Simon looked at Peter and said, "Give me also this ability so that everyone on whom I lay my hands may receive the Holy Spirit."

"Peter answered: "May your money perish with you, because you thought you could buy the gift of God with money!" (Acts, 8, 19 -20, NIV)

Mark and Peter were stunned and glared at Simon.

"The Holy Spirit can't be sold," Peter said. "God gives the Holy Spirit to those he trusts to use it properly."

Simon spoke with Peter and Mark the rest of the afternoon.

A few days passed before Mark and Peter went to the park and listened to Simon teach.

"I gave my wife, Helen, a body and sent her down to earth," he said. "Earth was again a prison for her."

Mark looked at Simon.

"Do you claim to be God?" he asked. "You say you have the power to put a soul in a body and send it to earth?"

"I'm not God," he said. "I'm a supreme being sent by God to do his work among the people of the earth."

"You aren't supreme," Peter said. "You have mastered the power of a magician. You aren't a God, and you weren't sent by God."

Peter was furious.

"I told you I wasn't God," Simon said. "My God has given me great powers. I know your God has given you the power to heal people. Why shouldn't my God give me special powers?"

Mark tugged on Peter's robe.

"Easy Peter,' he whispered. "Simon is trying to get you riled."

Peter's face had already turned red. His hand was on the handle of his knife.

"Then, he is doing a good job," Peter said. "Hold me back."

"The powers of my God are greater than the powers of your God," Simon said.

"What can your God do for his people that my God can't?" Peter asked.

"He allows me to fly," Simon said. "I can fly above the hills of Rome. I can fly like a bird."

"I would be interested to see you fly," Mark said. 'Give us a demonstration of what God does for you."

Simon grinned. He had tricked Mark into saying just what he hoped he would say.

"I challenge you, Peter, and your God to a demonstration in the Forum," he said. "If your God has real power, bring him with you to the Forum tomorrow. I will bring all my followers. It will be packed with spectators."

"We will be there," Peter said. "My God is always with me."

Mark tugged on Peter's arm.

"Now you have done it," he said. "We know you shouldn't challenge God."

Peter smiled at Mark.

"Sometimes I can't see past my red hair," he said.

The following day, they went to the Forum. When Simon appeared, he was wearing a great robe adorned with gold. He waved to the crowd.

"I have come here today to demonstrate the power of the real God," he said. "After I fly over the hills of Rome, Peter will entertain you with a demonstration of the power of his God."

Mark and Peter knelt on the ground and prayed. Then they stood and went to Simon.

"Your followers will be my followers in a few moments," Simon said.

He waved to the crowd again and then flew up into the air.

Peter gasped.

"I can't believe it," he said. "He can fly."

"We had better pray," Mark said.

They knelt on the ground, as Simon flew away. After several moments, he reappeared over the Forum. Peter looked into the sky and continued to pray.

A moment later, Simon came crashing to the ground. Both of his legs were broken. The crowd jeered him.

"He is a phony!" a pagan cried out. "Their God is more powerful than his!"

The crowd rushed to where Simon laid. They seized his badly broken body, dragged him from the Forum, and stoned him to death. Mark and Peter made a hasty departure for the church to pray.

"I will have to record this for you," Mark said.

"Put it on a different scroll," Peter said. "I don't want it recorded with Jesus' message."

"I will title it the Acts of Peter," Mark said.

Soon, the church heard of Peter's encounter with Simon. The following Sabbath, many pagans came to hear Peter speak about Jesus. After the service, they stayed and talked to Peter about Simon.

Several months passed before Mark told Peter he was ready to leave for Africa.

Peter looked at Mark in disbelief.

"What will you do in Africa?" he asked.

"I want to take Jesus' message to those in the Pentapolis west of Alexandria," Mark said.

"Luke and I will remain in Rome," Peter said. "I wish you great success."

Although Mark remained in the city for a short while longer, Luke quickly assumed all of Mark's duties concerning the church and Peter's lessons.

It was a solemn day for the men when Mark left for the port. Before he departed, the three drank wine, ate bread, and prayed together.

CHAPTER 14

MARK IN AFRICA

Aulus Vilellius ruled as the governor of the western province of northern Africa. He considered his job good training in preparation to be emperor of the Roman Empire. The political climate in Rome was for the most part peaceful and in Africa life was prosperous. Paraetonium was a great port city, and the harbor was generally filled with ships that transported grain to Rome.

Paul had gone to Spain on a mission, while Luke remained in Rome with Peter.

Peter had assumed firm control of the church in Rome. He was well-liked and spoke with great authority. Luke worked closely with him, attending all of his lessons. Mark planned to return to Africa, the land of his birth.

"Luke, take this scroll," Mark said. "I have recorded Peter's lessons, and I find them very useful as a teaching aid."

He handed Luke a large scroll.

"Thank you, I will continue what you have started," he said.

"I will be leaving tomorrow," Mark said. "I will miss Peter very much. Please take good care of him."

"I will," Luke said. "I'll walk with you to the port tomorrow."

The next day, they made their way to the port. Mark boarded a ship destined for Paraetonium. The sea was choppy, and Mark remained in his quarters most of the trip. When they arrived in Africa, he said a prayer.

He walked down the ramp and planted his feet on familiar soil. He journeyed to the city of Cyrene. As Mark walked through the lush valley, he remembered his family's garden. He smiled and looked up at the bright, blue sky. He spent the afternoon walking and communing with God.

The next day, he looked for the house of his friend, Simon. He spoke with a stranger on the street.

"I am looking for my friend, Simon," he said. "Do you know where he lives?"

"What does he look like?" he asked.

Mark thought for a moment.

"I don't know," he said. "I haven't seen him in thirty years. I guess he would have a long, gray beard. The last time I saw him was when he visited Jerusalem for Pentecost."

"You must be talking about the old Jew who lives down the street," he said. "He lives in a very large house on the right-hand side of the street. He likes to sit on his porch and look at the clouds in the sky."

The man pointed to the house.

Mark walked to the house and knocked on the door.

When Simon came to the door, he didn't recognize Mark. Mark was surprised by how old he appeared. Simon scratched his head.

"You stayed with my father, Aristopolus, in Jerusalem during Pentecost about thirty years ago." Mark said.

He looked at Mark, blankly.

"I'm sorry. I am old," he said. "My memory hasn't been very good."

"You carried the cross for Jesus," Mark said.

Simon's eyes glowed, and he slowly smiled.

"Oh, yes, I remember. Jesus had fallen, and his cross was on top of him. The Roman soldier began screaming at him. I did carry his cross. I don't remember why I helped him. It was as if I was told to carry his cross. I never understood what made me do it."

He smiled and motioned to Mark to come in.

"This is a very large house, and I have an extra room," he said. "You can stay with me."

Mark picked up his pack and entered Simon's house.

"What brings you home, Mark?" he asked.

Mark realized that Simon did remember him and his family.

"I want to teach the people of Cyrene about Jesus," he said.

"Make certain you teach them the truth," Simon said. "Some have mistakenly taught that I was crucified in Jesus' place. Some teachers will say anything to gather a large crowd. The larger the crowd, the wilder their stories and the more money they can collect."

"I did read that you were crucified in Jesus' place,'" Mark said. "Many incorrect stories have been written about Jesus."

"I am glad we have writers like you and Matthew," he said. "I read a scroll written by Matthew that someone had altered."

Mark thought back for a moment.

"Once I revisited a church where I had given a copy of Peter's lessons," he said. "Someone had translated the scroll to Latin and added several incidents that never happened."

Simon held out his hand.

"It is said that Thomas felt Jesus' side," he said. "Hold my hand."

"I will tell everyone I meet you and that you are alive," Mark said. "I saw Jesus before and after he was crucified. You don't look much like him."

"By the time the resurrected Jesus appeared to the crowds, I was on my way to Africa," he said. "I didn't want to be associated him or with the Christians. I was frightened by the manner of the crowd and just wanted to get home."

"It was a good thing that you left," Mark said. "Soldiers were on every street for many months. The rabbis never did admit that Jesus was resurrected."

"I wish you good luck," Simon said. "After you have started a few churches, I might tell my Jesus story if it will be of any assistance to you."

Mark looked at Simon and smiled.

"What can I tell you about Jesus that will help you?" Mark asked. "You must be curious."

Simon thought for a few moments.

"What did Jesus tell you about Hell?" he asked. "Is Jesus' judgment going to be like the Jewish eye-for-an-eye?"

"I never talked to Jesus about that" Mark said. "Jesus told Peter about Hell. Later, Peter told me."

"Now, you can tell me," Simon said.

"It is a little like what you learned as a youngster," Mark said. "Your punishment in Hell is related to your sins on earth. If you are a blasphemer, you will be hung by your tongue."

"Stop, that is enough," Simon said.

He rubbed his hands together. He was visually shaken.

"What did Jesus tell Peter about heaven?"

"Jesus told Peter things that Peter was instructed not to tell anyone," Mark said. "Jesus often told people not to reveal what he did and what he said."

"Does heaven have streets paved of gold?" Simon asked. "Will I have a perfected body and be able to fly?"

"Gold will have no special value," he said. 'You will be able to go where God wants you to go."

Simon pondered the idea of gold not having any value.

"People who have hoarded gold are going to be surprised," he said.

Mark looked at him.

"The people in heaven will be beautiful, have cream colored skin, and curly hair," he said. "Heaven will be full of flowers that bloom forever."

"That sounds much better to me," he said. "I don't have much time to improve my position,"

"Your position was greatly improved when you started believing in Jesus," Mark said. "I have been helping people see beyond the cross. You helped Jesus get beyond the cross."

Mark and Simon said a prayer.

Mark waited until Simon opened his eyes and asked. "Do you know many Jews or Christians?"

"I see a few Jews at the synagogue," Simon said. "I don't attend as often these days. I don't think I know any Christians."

"If people aren't Jews what religion are they?" Mark asked. "What God do they worship?"

"The oracle that Alexander the Great visited lived in the desert not far from here," Simon said. "Many people still believe in the special powers of Alexander's oracle, Amun."

Mark thought for a moment and then stroked his beard that had started to turn gray.

The following week, Mark talked to several people in Cyrene before he found a man named Adam at the synagogue. Adam was familiar with the Christian religion.

"I would like to start a church and teach lessons about Jesus' message," Mark said. "Do you know anyone who would be interested in learning about Jesus?"

Adam nodded.

"I am interested," he said. "And I have many friends who would be as well. Our rabbi has warned us about how Jesus divided the members of the synagogues in Judea."

"Talk to your friends," he said. "I am currently living with my friend, Simon. I have plenty of time. We will need a place to meet."

"I will get back to you," Adam said.

Mark thanked him.

After dinner, Mark and Simon sat in the living area.

"When you departed this morning, I thought about Diogenes and how he walked the streets, day after day, looking for an honest man," Simon asked. "I visualized you walking the streets telling your story of light and dark. Did you find any Christians?"

"No, I didn't" he said. "But, I did find an interested Jew named Adam."

"You must have been to the synagogue," he said. "Adam is one of the wealthiest men at the synagogue. He grows grain. He and his neighbors grow grain under contract for the Roman government."

A large smile appeared on Mark's face as he considered how many good men Adam might know.

"He said he would talk to his friends and tell me if they are interested in learning about Jesus," Mark said. 'I told him we would need a place to meet."

"I am certain Adam has plenty of buildings," Simon said. "He owns many barns and houses. He must own fifty slaves."

"I hope I get to see his farm and meet his friends," he said. "I would love to tell them about Jesus."

After it turned dark, Simon went to sleep. Mark went outside and sat on the porch. He enjoyed watching the stars twinkle. The moon was out, but it was cloudy, so he couldn't read. He went to his room lit a few candles and read one of the scrolls he had written. He enjoyed rereading Peter's lessons. He knelt next to his bed and prayed for Luke and Peter.

During the next two weeks, Adam talked with his neighbors.

"I am interested in starting a church here in our town, close to the farms," Adam said. "I will need support from you and your families."

Adam's closest neighbor seemed very interested.

"My wife is always reading the scroll I purchased for her," he said. "I think she said it was written by a woman named Mary."

"I will acquire a building in town. You hire Mark," a neighbor said. "We will bring our families to church."

"I suppose I am going to have to provide him with a horse and carriage," Adam said. "He is living with an old man named Simon."

They reached an agreement, and Adam planned to visit Mark.

Two weeks later, Adam met with two friends who had shown an interest in establishing a church, and they traveled to see Mark in Cyrene. Adam knocked on the door. The servant answered and seated the visitors in the living area.

"You have visitors," the servant said.

"I will be with them in a few moments,' Mark said.

He put away his writing tools and went to the living room. When Adam saw Mark, he stood.

"We have come to speak with you about a church," Adam said. "We can provide a building to meet."

"That is good," Mark said. "Someone will have to provide transportation for me."

Adam looked at him.

"I will provide you with a horse, driver, and carriage," he said. "It is part of our offer. We can also pay you a small stipend."

Mark smiled and looked at Adam.

"We will start immediately," Adam said and then paused for a moment. "I would like my son to be your helper,"

"Your son can manage the church," Mark said. "Simon will occasionally tell a Jesus story. He met Jesus and helped him."

"I didn't know that you knew Jesus," Adam said to Simon. "I have known you for years, and you never mentioned that."

"I didn't want to draw attention to myself," Simon said. "Yes, it is true. I did talk with Jesus."

"The church will require attention," Mark said. "I will teach your son how to maintain the church, and I will teach him about Jesus. Can he write Greek?"

"He can only read Greek," Adam said. "His tutor isn't very proficient at writing."

Mark smiled and said. "I will teach him."

"My son needs to know how to write Greek," another neighbor said. "You could teach a mid-week class concerning Greek."

Mark was pleased by all the interest. Everyone seemed satisfied.

A few days passed when a man arrived at Simon's house.

"I am Mark's new servant and driver," he said. "I guess I will be working for you as well."

Simon's servant greeted him and took him to the kitchen. Then he located Mark.

"Your new servant is here," he said.

"That was quick," Mark said. "He will be our driver, maintain the stable, and help you."

"It will be nice to have a carriage," the servant said. "I enjoyed our old driver and horse."

The servant showed the new driver to the stable. He bedded the horse and cleaned the carriage.

The following Sabbath day, Mark and Simon traveled to the country. Adam's son, Matthew, had arranged for a building to be used as the church. It was full of people. Mark was pleasantly surprised. After everyone was seated, Adam introduced Mark and Simon. Mark stood, walked to the front of the church, and spoke to the people.

"You are probably wondering by what authority I come to you to tell Jesus' message," he said. "I didn't travel with Jesus, but I met him several times. He was a guest at our family home. I also spoke with him after his resurrection."

The crowd was pleased that Mark knew Jesus.

"I traveled extensively with Peter, one of Jesus' disciples," he said. "I recorded many lessons that Peter taught. I also traveled, for a brief period, with Paul."

The crowd buzzed about Mark being Peter's scribe.

"I will teach a lesson each week and on mid-week I will teach about the Greek language."

After the service, the members formed a line and spoke to Mark. Simon waited at the back of the church. Adam approached Mark.

"Today, we will eat bird and roots with my family," he said. "You will visit a different family each Sabbath. Everyone wants to meet you and Simon."

"We will be pleased to break bread with you," Mark said.

After dinner, the driver returned them home to Cyrene. During the first year, the church membership grew substantially. After a Sabbath service, Adam talked with Mark.

"We are going to build a church," he said. "We want you to work for us on a full-time basis."

Mark looked at Simon.

"We will also rent a building on the edge of Cyrene," Adam said. "Matthew and Simon can manage that church. You have several young men who are learning Greek and can help you after the new church is built."

Mark went to talk with Simon.

"Don't worry," Mark said. "If you have any questions, I will help you."

"Do you think I can actually help people?" Simon asked. "I really didn't know Jesus."

"You have already helped many," Mark said. "You helped our savior in a very tangible way."

"Then, I will assist you as much as I can," he said.

Mark returned to Adam, and they spoke.

"Simon has agreed," Mark said. "I will have my students make a copy of Peter's lessons for Matthew."

"The new church will include two offices for priests, two classrooms, a library, and a large meeting room," Adam said. "I'll ensure it is large enough."

Mark smiled at Adam. He visualized a large church full of members listening to him teaching one of Peter's lessons. He prayed that the Holy Spirit would always be present.

For the next three months after Sabbath services, Mark and Simon would eat dinner with a family and visit the construction site of the new church. The church was about half built.

"It is going to be a grand building," Simon said. "It will be your responsibility to make it a grand church."

Mark and Simon walled around the construction site. Simon grew tired.

"Not so fast, I can't keep the pace you are setting," Simon said.

Mark helped Simon into the carriage and returned home.

A few days later, Simon talked with Mark.

"I am old and haven't been feeling well," he said. "I don't think I will be able to help with the church in Cyrene."

Mark knew Simon was old, but he was surprised he felt so poorly. He wanted to encourage him, but didn't want him to feel guilty if he was too weak to help.

"You won't have to help Matthew," Mark said. "I will help him. There are also several men who I have been training to become priests."

"Thank you," Simon said. "I am tired."

The driver took Mark to see Adam.

"Simon isn't well," Mark said. "I would like to send one of my students to work with Matthew in Cyrene when the church opens."

"I am very sorry to hear that," Adam said. "Please don't send either of Matthew's brothers."

Mark didn't know what Adam meant.

"Your sons are all good students, and someday, they will be fine priests," he said. "You might have to build more churches."

Adam grinned.

"I hope that is the situation. You get them prepared to teach, and I will build each of them a church," he said.

The new church near the farms opened to standing room only. After the service, many members talked with Mark.

"I am very pleased that you are with us," Adam said.

"This is a much better arrangement for all of us," Mark said. "It is a beautiful church."

The church in Cyrene opened the following week. Christianity gained a foothold in the Pentapolis.

Soon, Simon became very ill.

"I need a doctor," he said. "If he can't heal me, I will need you to talk to God on my behalf."

Mark sent for a doctor.

"The doctor will be here, soon," he said. "He will give you a powder that will help."

Simon tried to smile. When the doctor arrived, he went to check Simon.

"Unfortunately, I can't do anything for him," the doctor said. "He is old and very weak. He won't live long."

Mark knelt and prayed for Simon.

A week passed before Simon died. He had made legal arrangements for his home to become a church. He was buried near the new church at the farms. His house became the third church in Cyrene.

Adam approached Mark.

"Now that Simon's house is being converted to a church," he said. "I will build you a house on a small piece of land next to the new church. You and your staff should live with us."

Mark realized that he didn't have a place to live, so he agreed. Adam built a suitable home for them, and they moved into it three months later.

Adam and his two neighbors visited with Mark at his new home.

"Mark, we need to talk to you about two things," Adam said. "First,

I want you to send my son, Benjamus, to Cyrene to be the priest for the third church."

"He was my first choice," Mark said. "I think he will do a fine job. I will send an assistant with him."

"Second, we are going to promote you," he said. "You are now our bishop. Your bishopric will include all the churches we've started.

Mark was pleased that they had confidence in his ability.

"The central church will probably want to know what we are doing," Mark said. "I think James, Jesus' brother, is still in Jerusalem."

Mark realized that Adam was taken back by his comment.

"This is our business," Adam said. "They can manage their churches, and we will manage ours."

"It would be a nice gesture if you informed them of our success." Mark said. "They try to help all of the followers of Jesus."

"I will tell him the next time I visit the temple," Adam said. "I haven't been to Jerusalem in several years. I don't feel like it is a requirement for me to visit the temple any longer."

Mark smiled at Adam. He wondered if he would ever visit the temple.

"On occasion, we would like you to travel to the other churches," Adam said. "You can check on them and teach a lesson. I need you to ensure that all of the priests are correctly teaching Jesus' message."

"I trained them and gave each a copy of Peter's lessons," Mark said. "They should understand the importance of telling Jesus message as we remembered it."

Mark agreed that he and his assistant would visit at least two churches each month.

He would teach a lesson, speak with the church staff, and review Jesus' message. He was to ensure that all his students continued to follow their copy of his scroll containing Peter's and his lessons.

One Sabbath after the formal service was completed; Mark asked if anyone had a question. A man stood.

"My name is Rheginos," he said. "I would like you to teach a lesson concerning our resurrection. What will happen to me when I go to heaven?"

Mark was surprised by the question.

"I will teach a lesson for you at the next Sabbath service. Bring all your friends," he said.

"We will be here," Rheginos said. "We will have dinner for you next week."

The following week, Mark started his lesson.

"I was at his crucifixion," Mark said. "My mother became sick and took me home. Peter wasn't present at the actual crucifixion, but spoke of the event."

"Where was he?" Rheginos asked.

"It wasn't safe for anyone associated directly with Jesus to be at the crucifixion," Mark said. "The disciples knew that the body on the cross didn't contain Jesus' soul. Jesus was actually was looking down on the soldiers and the crowd."

"You mean he wasn't suffering," Rheginos said.

"Those who don't have a complete understanding of Jesus' message think that he suffered," Mark said. "Those of us who understand know he was with his father."

The members mumbled among themselves.

"I will now tell you about a vision Peter had of Jesus," Mark said. "I recorded it for him."

"What about me?" Rheginos asked. "I am certain my body will rot. I have found rotted animal bodies on my farm."

"That is correct," Mark said. "Your body isn't eternal. It will break down, but your soul will experience a spiritual resurrection."

"I think I am beginning to understand," Rheginos said. "Resurrection is a complicated thing."

Mark nodded his head.

"When I first saw the resurrected Jesus in the upper room of my neighbor's barn, he did appear a little pale to me," Mark said. "So, I guess he was suffering concerning the actions of his closest friends."

Mark closed his lesson and greeted the members as they filed from the church. He met Rheginos after the service and went to his house for dinner.

Mark enjoyed a great dinner with Rheginos' family.

"My oldest son wants to learn about Jesus and how to write Greek," Rheginos said. "Will you work with him?"

"I would be honored," Mark said. "What is his name?"

"His name is Garus. He always attends the Sabbath service. I will have him start attending the mid-week lessons as well."

"What does he want to do when he grows up?" he asked. "Does he want to be a farmer?"

"He isn't a child, he is a young man," Rheginos said. "He is a good son. He will do whatever I ask of him. I think I would like him to be a priest. I might even send him to the school in Alexandria."

"I will look forward to working with him," Mark said.

The children didn't eat at the same table with Mark and Rheginos.

After dinner, Rheginos introduced Garus to Mark. They sat on the porch and talked. A mild breeze blew across the farm. The crops swayed in the wind. Mark saw God at work on the farm.

A few months passed before Adam spoke to Mark about another church.

"I have talked to my friends. We have decided to build another church for the servants and slaves," he said. "We want you to assign a priest to manage it."

"That is an excellent idea," Mark said. "I would like a good servant to help the priest who I assign to the church. That will make them feel like the church is really theirs. I don't want them to feel that they are being forced to worship God."

Adam pondered Mark's request.

"I will have my wife's attendant, Sara, talk to you," he said. "I think she can read."

Several days later, Sara visited Mark. He was impressed with her and explained Adam's idea to her.

"Can you read Greek?" Mark asked.

"No," she said. "But, I can read Latin fairly well,"

"I will have my students transcribe a scroll into Latin for you," he said.

A church for the farmers' staff and slaves was built at the edge of the farm. Mark trained a priest and a member of the church to teach and manage the new church. Sara often taught the lessons. Her scroll was her most prized possession.

Aulus Vilellius, the governor from the west, was told by the emperor to visit the port city. He was to inspect the grain that was being shipped to Rome. He and his troops spent several days in Paraetonium. They watched as the dock workers carried the grain aboard a ship.

"Stop," a soldier ordered. "I want to inspect the contents of that sack."

The worker dropped the bag on the ground. The soldier cut it open and inspected its content.

"This looks good," Aulus said. "Feed the grain to our horses. I will pay the harbor manager."

Aulus ordered his troops to open several more sacks of grain.

"These are the cleanest sacks of grain I have inspected so far," Aulus said. "I want to ensure that this farmer is given a long term contract."

Aulus talked to the harbor manager and traced the paper work for the grain order. He found out that it came from Adam's farm.

"Find out where this farm is located," he said. "I want to make a personal visit and speak with the owner."

The sergeant obtained directions to Adam's farm.

They journeyed to an area just south of Cyrene. Beautiful fields of grain, waving in the wind, were visible to the horizon.

"That is the farm," the sergeant said. "The large house must be where Adam lives."

The troops rode on to the farm house. A servant saw them approach.

"Mr. Adam, we have visitors," he announced.

Aulus and two soldiers entered.

"We would like to speak to the owner of the farm," Aulus said. "I have good news for him."

The servant returned with Adam. He looked at his company.

"Welcome," he said.

"I inspected the grain you ship to Rome," Aulus said. "I liked what I saw. I want to sign a long term contract with you to continue to provide grain to Rome."

Adam blinked.

"And who are you?" he asked.

"I am the governor," he said. "We would like to increase the amount of grain that the government purchases from you."

"I could grow about twenty-five percent more grain," Adam said. "I have a piece of land that is not being used. I would have to clear it."

The governor went to his carriage and returned with a contract. He handed it to Adam.

"The contract is for the increased amount of grain," he said. "I gave you an increase in price."

"Did you include any money for me to clear the land?" he asked.

"No," Aulus said. "I can't pay you to improve your farm."

"The expansion would be an expensive operation for me," Adam said. "I can't sign a contract for only three years."

Aulus looked at Adam.

He walked back to the carriage, modified the contract and returned to the house. Adam looked it over again.

"That is good," he said. "A ten year contract is better. I hope you can help my neighbors as well."

While Adam signed the contract, Aulus looked out of the window.

"I would like you to show me the fields," Aulus said. "This is a beautiful farm."

Adam boarded Aulus' carriage and they rode on a path between the fields. Then they came to the church.

"What is that building?" Aulus asked.

"It is where we come to worship God," Adam said.

Suddenly, Adam felt uneasy. He knew Aulus was once a pagan priest.

"That is good," Aulus said. "I am certain you worship a God that provides rain and kills insects. Farmers are important to God."

Aulus seemed very proud of his knowledge about farming.

"Yes we do," Adam said. "Our God is very good to us. You can see our beautiful crops in the fields."

"Your farm makes me think of God," Aulus said.

Adam smiled at him.

"Me too," he said.

The next day, Adam visited with Mark.

"The governor and I rode through the fields yesterday," he said. "He was impressed that our God provided rain and protection for our farms."

Mark didn't comment about the governor's visit.

"I visited the new church," Mark said. "Sara is doing a fine job. She encourages everyone to attend the Sabbath and the mid-week lessons. The church is doing well."

The following Sabbath, Mark visited the third church. Benjamus stopped to talk with him.

"I have a family that wants to be baptized," Benjamus said. "What is the best way for me accomplish this?"

"It is desirable to immerse the person in cold running water," Mark said. "On the farm, I use a small stream close to the church."

Benjamus looked at Mark.

"I would like you to suggest two topics that I can use to create lessons," he said. "I am using the scroll you provided me."

"I like to stress to my members that they should love one another," Mark said. "When people love one another, they help each other. Second, explain to them to avoid evil desires. We must keep our minds clean. They should focus on Jesus."

Benjamus took Mark to a nearby stream. The sun glistened on the water. Mark put his hand into the stream.

"This will be fine," he said. "Not everyone can be baptized in the Jordan River."

Benjamus thanked him for the help.

CHAPTER 15

MARK RELOCATES TO ALEXANDRIA

Mark was alone in his large house. While he relaxed in his favorite chair, he fell into a deep sleep. Suddenly, a bright light appeared. His vision seemed so real that he thought that he was awake. The bright light stood before him. Mark felt like it was telling him that it was time for you to move to the city. He knew he had served God well in Cyrene, but the city offered him a new great challenge.

Mark was startled. He woke up when he tried to determine what had happened. The sound of his voice surprised him. The vision was so real that he became perplexed. He didn't tell anyone. He planned to wait until he had another vision.

He visited with Sara at the church located on the other side of the farm. When he arrived, Sara saw him.

"Come in," she said. "I am preparing the church for the Sabbath lesson."

They both sat to review her lesson. She read Latin from her scroll.

Mark cautioned, "Be certain that you speak loudly and slowly. Your members need time to think about what you are saying."

She nodded that she understood and tried again.

"That is much better," he said. "Slow and steady is the best way to keep people interested."

The following night, Mark drank wine and prayed for a long time before he went to bed. Soon, he felt the urging to go to the city. He was less startled than before. He was certain that many people in the city were ready and wanted to learn about God. He had a very restless night, but the next morning Mark wasn't frightened as he understood that God gave him instructions. He thought about what he should do next and decided to visit Adam.

The next Sabbath, after the service, he spoke with Adam.

"I need to meet with you in private," he said. "I think God communicated with me."

Adam arranged to visit Mark at his house later that afternoon. Mark considered very carefully what he was going to tell Adam. He spent most of the morning praying. When he arrived, Mark was kneeling and praying in the living room. Adam approached him.

"What has God been saying to you?" he asked. "I talk with God, and he answers me, but not through conversation. It is more that I am enlightened."

Mark looked at him. He was pleased with Adams concern.

"I have had two visions," he said. "During each visit, the messenger from God told me to go to the city. He explained that many opportunities await me there."

He watched Adam's facial expression. A look of serious concern appeared on Adam's face.

"Has he told you which city?" Adam asked.

Mark paused.

"No, not exactly," he said. "I have only considered Alexandria."

"Maybe you should determine what God is thinking," Adam said. "He will provide the details to you."

Mark appreciated Adam's advice.

"I will pray longer this evening," he said. "I don't want to make a mistake."

"I will visit with my neighbors and get back to you," he said. "Stay in contact with God."

Adam was a little surprised by Mark's experience, so he talked with several of his neighbors.

"Mark is being told to go to Alexandria. You travel to Alexandria, don't you?" Adam asked.

"Yes, my brother lives in that area," Rheginos said. "I think we owe it to Mark to help him follow God's direction. I will talk with him."

"He will be very difficult to replace," Adam said. "I know he has trained many of our sons to be priests, but he has met Jesus and now Jesus has given him a new opportunity."

They continued their discussion for a long time, but finally Adam agreed that Rheginos should talk with Mark.

Several days passed before Rheginos went to see Mark. He found him praying in the church.

"Adam and I have talked," Rheginos said. "He told me that you are being called to Alexandria."

Mark was pleased that Rheginos was concerned enough to come and visit with him.

"Yes, I am certain I have received direction from God," Mark said. "I don't know what to do. We have great churches in this area, and I have learned to love all our members."

"We want to help you answer God's calling," Rheginos said. "We know God sent you to us. The churches in this area would miss you, but they can be maintained by the men you have trained."

Mark thought for a few moments.

"You are probably correct," he said. "The churches are doing very well, and I have faith in our priests."

Rheginos looked at Mark.

"If you will mentor and give my son, Garus, direction in Alexandria, I will arrange for both of you to have a place to stay in the city," he said. "I know a few people in Alexandria."

Mark looked at Rheginos in wonderment.

"I have been teaching your son for several years; does he want to go to the city?" Mark asked.

"I would like to send him to the university," he said. "My brother lives in that area and has several rental houses in the city. I am certain that I can rent one for the both of you. Are you interested?"

Mark thought, 'now, I am getting the direction for which I prayed'.

"I am very interested," he said. "I will make arrangements with my priests and Adam for the churches we have started."

"I will tell my son that he and you will be traveling to and living in Alexandria," he said.

Rheginos left to give his son the news that he was going to the university.

The following Sabbath, Mark told the members of the church, at the farm, that he was leaving for Alexandria. After the service, a line of members formed outside the church. They asked many questions.

"Why are you considering leaving us?" a member asked. "We love you and we need you."

"I have been called by God to go to Alexandria," Mark said. "I am perfectly happy here with you. I never planned to leave."

The members crowded around him.

"Who will you appoint as our new bishop?" a member asked. "Will you return and visit us?"

Mark hesitated for a moment.

"It is up to the leaders of the church to elect a new bishop," he said. "Adam will announce the new bishop at the next Sabbath service. I will miss all of you and the farm. I will come back and visit you."

Adam waved to Mark as he boarded his carriage.

Finally, Mark had spoken to almost all the members and went to Adams house for dinner.

"We will give you a horse and carriage to keep as a going away present," Adam said. "You will need transportation to get around Alexandria."

"Thank you," Mark said. "Garus and I will enjoy the carriage very much. I will have him take our belongings to our new house. I must walk to Alexandria. I need time to think, and I think very well while I am walking. I have walked across many countries in my life."

They agreed, without much discussion, that Matthew would be the new bishop. He prepared to move into the house. He and his father would promote and move other priests as needed.

After the carriage and wagon were loaded, Garus and a slave headed to Alexandria. A week later, Mark started walking to the city. He saw the slave with the empty wagon returning to the farm. The Great Sea was on his left as he walked east. He wore the head covering that he purchased for his trip to Colossae. He carried a fishing net that Peter had taught him how to use and occasionally would stop at the shore to fish. It was as if Peter was standing there with him.

"Throw it high and far, allow it to sink slowly," Peter once told him.

Mark smiled to himself as he remembered the days along the Sea of Galilee, fishing with Peter.

A month passed before Mark arrived in Alexandria. He approached the city from the west, and the first thing he saw was the stadium on his right, close to the lake. He remembered that Rheginos told him to walk beyond the Royal Palace on his left. He entered the Jewish section of the city. He looked at the parchment he had been given as a map. He went south two blocks and found a house that looked like what Rheginos had described. He knocked on the door. Garus answered and hugged him.

"I have been worried about you," he said. "Come in and meet our attendant and servant."

Mark didn't know Rheginos had given Garus money to acquire an attendant and slave. He walked through the house.

"Your uncle provided us with a very nice home," Mark said. "I didn't expect anything nearly this grand."

"I have been working on getting it fixed up," Garus said. "It is only about a ten minute walk to the university. I start my classes in two weeks. I am really glad you are here to tutor me."

Mark smiled at Garus.

The attendant took Mark's pack to his room. Then they relaxed in the living room and drank wine. When Mark tasted the wine, he was certain it was from his brother's vineyard on Cyprus. He had visions of grape vines and workers picking the grapes. He looked through the wine glass.

"This is a fine wine," he said.

Garus looked at him through his glass of wine. The glass wasn't very clear and Mark looked blurred.

"All I see are wine legs," he said.

"I shall teach you all about wine and bread," Mark said. "Breaking bread together is a fine thing."

The next day, Mark showed his damaged sandal to Garus.

"I need to fine a cobbler," he said. "I damaged my sandals walking from Cyrene. I want to have them repaired.

"I can purchase you a new pair of sandals," Garus said. "Father told me to take good care of you."

The attendant looked at Mark.

"I know a cobbler," he said. "His name is Anianus. He has a small business in the barn behind his house. It is only a block away. He made Garus a new pair of sandals."

"I don't need a new pair," he said. "I prefer to have my old sandals repaired."

Garus shook his head. He thought, 'so this is the way it's going to be.'

They agreed to visit the cobbler after lunch.

A few hours later, they walked to the cobbler's house.

"He has a nice business in his barn," Garus said. "He has made my uncle several pairs of sandals."

They walked to the barn and found the cobbler working on a new pair of boots for a Roman soldier.

"Good day, gentlemen," Anianus said.

He noticed Mark's sandals.

"Take off your sandals," he said. "I need to see that left one."

He inspected the sandal very carefully and tossed it down.

"I will have to make a few new holes, but I can repair it," he said. "I am busy with an order of new boots for the army."

Mark was pleased that he would fix his old sandal.

"I don't have an extra pair of sandals," he said. "Can you repair them while I wait?"

"You can see I am busy making a pair of boots," he said. "I am very busy working for my largest customer."

Garus wasn't happy about Mark having to wait.

"Do you know another cobbler who isn't so busy?" Garus asked. "My friend is also a busy man."

Anianus didn't want to lose the business, so he stared at Garus and picked up the sandal. He grabbed his awl, placed it on the sandal, and swung his hammer at it very swiftly. When the hammer struck the awl, the awl broke into two pieces. One piece went partially through Anianus' hand. When Garus looked at Anianus' injury, he passed out. Mark quickly grabbed Anianus' hand, and pulled the piece of awl all the way through. Then he picked up a handful of dirt, spat on it, and placed it on both sides of Anianus' hand. Anianus mumbled a few words as he looked at the sky. Mark could tell he was very upset. He held his hand and talked to him. He could see tears in Anianus' eyes.

"I will say a prayer," he said. "Please don't move your hand. Please pray with me."

Soon, the cobbler's hand stopped throbbing. Mark continued to press his hand firmly.

"Did you pray to your Jewish God?" he asked.

"I used to be Jewish," Mark said. "Now, I follow and teach the message of Jesus, our savior."

Anianus looked confused.

"You will be fine," Mark said. "Do you make many boots for Roman soldiers?

Anianus had picked up the broken awl with his good hand and was inspecting it.

"I make a pair every week," he said. "They send me a different soldier each day after the Sabbath. I look very carefully at his feet and his worn boots. He returns the day before the next Sabbath and claims his new boots."

"How does your hand feel?" Mark asked.

"It is fine," he said. 'It doesn't even feel like I injured it. Your friend has decided to join us."

He pointed towards Garus. Garus' eyes opened, and he looked around the shop. Mark helped him stand.

"Anianus is healed," Mark said. "And you will be fine."

Mark removed the clay from Anianus' hand. The wound was completely healed. Anianus inspected it and wiggled his fingers. He was astounded by the miracle.

"You healed my hand," he said. "I have never heard of such a thing."

"Jesus healed your hand," Mark said. "Remember, you prayed with me? I asked him to help you."

Anianus picked up an awl and very carefully made a few holes in Mark's sandal. He sewed it together and handed it to him.

"What do we owe you?" Garus asked. "I pay my friend's bills."

Anianus didn't look at Garus. He spoke to Mark instead.

"You don't owe me anything," he said. "I will visit and talk with your friend in a few days. I needed to think about what just happened."

Garus' legs wobbled and he motioned to Mark. He grabbed Mark's arm and walked from the barn.

"I think I will hold onto your arm for a while," he said.

Mark stopped and steadied Garus.

"I don't feel very strong," he said. "Tell me what happened back there?"

"You saw Anianus hit his hand with the awl and you collapsed," Mark said. "His hand is fine, and my sandal has been repaired."

Mark slipped off his left sandal and held it for Garus to inspect.

"I thought I saw him really injure himself," Garus said. "He said something about a miracle."

"When you feel stronger, we shall talk about it," Mark said. "I think we should slowly walk home."

Garus held very tightly to Mark's arm and they slowly proceeded.

When they arrived home, they sat on the porch. Mark crossed his legs and examined his newly repaired sandal. 'He does nice work,' he thought. When the attendant approached them, Mark asked for two glasses of wine.

"Give Garus a big glass," he said. "He isn't feeling very well."

They sat on the porch and watched the sun disappear. The moonlight was bright, and the moon seemed to smile at Mark. As Garus finished his second glass of wine, the stars began to twinkle. Mark gave him a large piece of bread.

The next week, they went to the university. Mark went to the university library, and Garus met with his professor. The professor spoke to him in Greek, and Garus answered him in perfect Greek.

"You speak Greek very well," the professor said. "Can you translate from Latin to Greek as well?"

"Yes, I can write Greek," he said. "Mark, my mentor, has taught me well. He is in the library reading."

The professor handed Garus a scroll written in Latin.

"Translate the first sentence into Greek," he said.

Garus immediately read the first sentence out loud in perfect Greek.

"No, I meant for you to write it in Greek," he said, handing Garus writing materials. Garus quickly wrote the sentence in perfect Greek.

The professor looked up from the parchment.

"Well, you don't need to take any Greek classes," he said. "What do you want to study?"

"I plan to become a priest," Garus said. "I want to study Greek and Roman history. Maybe even Persian history."

"I would like to meet your mentor. What is his name?" the professor asked.

"His name is Mark," Garus said.

The professor and Garus walked to the library. Garus introduced Mark to his professor.

"Where do you work?" the professor asked.

"I don't have a job," Mark said. "I just arrived from Cyrene."

The professor didn't hesitate.

"Would you like to try and teach a class concerning speaking Greek?" he asked.

"Certainly," he said. "I have taught many men how to read, speak, and write the Greek language."

"Could you teach any other topics?" he asked.

"I plan to teach about Jesus," he said.

The professor looked at Mark with wide eyes.

"He is the one who created the great sect of the Jewish religion they call Christianity," he said. "How do you know about him?"

"I met him several times, and I traveled with his greatest disciple, Peter," Mark said. "I recorded all of Peter's lessons."

"I don't know if the president of the college would be interested in offering a course about Jesus," he said. "I will talk with him. Your Greek class will start next week."

The next day, the professor came to see Mark.

"I have talked to the president of the college," he said. "Your Greek class will be full."

Mark looked at the professor, waiting to hear more.

"What did he think about me teaching about Jesus?" he asked.

"He isn't ready to offer a course based on the life and teaching of Jesus," he said. "He is going to have a few of his friends, who are rabbis, visit you."

A wrinkle of disappointment appeared on Mark's face.

"I can find someone interested in learning about Jesus," Mark said. "A group of farmers helped me create many churches in the area in and around Cyrene. I will speak with his friends."

"They will visit you in a few days," the professor said. "I would like to ask you a few questions about Peter."

Mark was curious why the professor wanted to know about Peter.

"Was Peter proficient in Greek?" he asked, "What kind of work did he perform before he started following Jesus?"

"He couldn't write in any language," Mark said. "He didn't have the opportunity to go to school. His family fished to make a living. I did his writing for him."

"How did you know Peter?" he asked.

"I am related to him," Mark said. "My father and Peter's father were brothers. My family visited them in Capernaum many times. I was also related to Barnabas."

"I don't know Barnabas," he said. "What did he do?"

"He traveled with Paul and taught at the church in Antioch."

"I have heard of Paul," he said. "We have heard many stories about him. I must return to the university now. I will be seeing you."

The professor said a few words to Garus before he departed.

The next day, three rabbis came to see Mark.

"We are friends of the president of the university," a rabbi said. "We are very interested in learning about Jesus. Each of us manages a synagogue. We have many members who are interested in learning about Jesus."

"I am interested in teaching about Jesus," Mark said.

"We want you to work with us," he said. "How do people worship Jesus?"

Mark explained the role of Christian churches, bishops, deacons, and baptism. The rabbis were surprised that one didn't have to be a Jew to become a Christian. Mark agreed to speak with them again in a few days.

"I start teaching at the university next week," he said. "I want to teach a mid-week evening class about Jesus. I will wait a week for your decision."

"We have already made a final decision," a rabbi said. "We also know Garus' uncle very well. He is going to provide us with a building. We will see you next week."

The following week was very busy for Mark. Anianus, the cobbler, came to visit one day.

"I have had time to think about the miracle you performed," he said. "I want to know more about your Jesus."

Mark didn't know where to start.

"I told you, I didn't restore your hand," he said. "Jesus healed you. I am only a servant of Jesus' message."

"I want to learn more about him," Anianus said. "I have told many of my friends about you and your Jesus. They also are interested in learning about him. We don't all worship the same God. Some of us don't worship any God, but we all work hard and care for our families. We are good, honest men."

"Right now, I am working with a group of men to start a mid-week school," he said. "I will invite you to the opening."

Anianus was pleased with idea of a new school.

"I will bring my son," he said.

Mark had the attendant serve them wine and bread. They talked for another hour, and then Anianus went home.

Mark enjoyed teaching Greek at the university. One evening, as he sat reading, a rabbi visited him.

"We have rented a building for your mid-week class," he said. "You can start teaching lessons next week."

The next day, Mark went to see Anianus and invited his children to attend the classes as his guest.

"I will also attend," Anianus said. "I don't work late in the evenings."

He looked at Mark.

"I might miss my awl and hurt myself," he said. "I like to work in sunlight."

Mark smiled at him.

"That makes a great amount of sense," he said. "The sun can light you awl, and Jesus will provide a well-lighted path for you to follow."

"I want you to teach me everything you know about Jesus," he said. "It is important that my family understand Jesus."

The building was almost completely full for the first day of lessons. The rabbis were overwhelmed by the school's success and decided to build a larger building. They contacted Garus' uncle, and construction work quickly started. By the next study period, Mark was teaching Greek at the college and lessons concerning Jesus and his disciples at the school. The school charged a fee to cover all costs, and it operated five days a week. One of the rabbis stopped teaching at his synagogue to teach the Jewish religion at the new school.

After two years, Mark was the dean of the large school and teaching every Sabbath at a church that had been constructed for him.

"My family and I are pleased that you built this church," Anianus said. "We want to join with you and the other members."

Anianus' family was the first family to be baptized at the new church.

"After the service today, we will join at the stream," Mark said. "We are going to baptize several new members."

The pagans in the neighborhood were concerned by what they witnessed.

The new school offered a course that was created to train priests. Garus came to visit with Mark.

"I have finished my studies at the university," he said. "I would like to help you at the school and at the church."

"Your father is very proud of you," Mark said. "Years ago, he told me he hoped you would attend the university and become a priest."

"You have made it possible for us to reach our goals," Garus said. "When are you going to build another church?"

"I'm not the one to make that decision," he said. "The members decide when they want to support another church."

"The church where you teach is too small," he said. "I think they are planning to build more churches."

During the next year, two new churches opened in Alexandria. Mark provided trained priests to them. Garus began his new job.

"I am pleased you have taken the responsibility of managing our newest church," Mark said. "I will be sending priests-in-training to help you. I will expect you to teach them exactly as I taught you."

"Everyone who graduates as a priest has made a copy of your scroll and knows all of Peter's lessons," he said. "We will continue the tradition as Peter saw it."

"I want you to work especially hard with my friend, Anianus," Mark said. "He is a great convert. He is well respected."

The churches in Alexandria grew at an astounding rate.

Garus' uncle visited with him and Mark. "I received a message from my friend in Rome," he said. "He explains how more than half of Rome has been destroyed by fire."

"Where did the fire start?" Garus asked.

"In the circus area, just south of the Imperial Palace," he said. "It started on a very windy night. It spread quickly, destroying the circus and all the buildings around it. The fire swept through the area so fast that many people didn't have a chance to escape. Almost everyone in that area died. The fire also spread north, damaging the palace."

"Did the soldiers put the fire out?" he asked.

"No, it burned for five more days," he said. "After the fire at the palace was extinguished, the soldiers evacuated families from the city into the fields and provided blankets, food, and water. The fire continued north, destroying everything in its path."

Mark tried to visualize what he heard.

"Did many temples burn?" he asked.

"After the main blaze was almost put out, another fire started and destroyed several of the temples northeast of the palace."

"What started the fire?" Mark asked.

"It depends on who you ask," the uncle said. "The Christians say Nero started it to clear land for a new building project, and it got out of control. He just wanted to expand the palace and the fire almost totally destroyed the palace. He lost many personal items."

"I am certain Nero will blame it on the Christians," Mark said. "I hope my friends will be safe."

They continued to talk for a few hours and then Garus' uncle went home.

A few months passed, Anianus visited with Mark.

"I have received reliable word that Nero started persecuting Christians in Rome," he said. "The pagans in Alexandria have become very disturbed by our success. They might use Nero's persecution to cover their desires. If I were you, I would go west for a while."

Mark considered what Anianus had told him. He met with the priests, who he had trained, and the lay leader of the Christians.

"I have ordained Anianus, Bishop of Alexandria," he said. "He has many friends and will keep you safe while I visit western Africa."

"I know the Romans have killed your friends, Peter and Paul," Garus said. "It is not safe for you to remain in Alexandria. We will be God's representative; you should go to your friends in the west."

"Many more than two friends have been killed. I think Jerusalem will be the next target of Emperor Nero. Will you travel with me?"

"No," he said. "My place is here in Alexandria. We will wait for your return."

Mark and one attendant left Alexandria and traveled west. As the sky turned dark, they stopped by the sea and slept under a tree. A storm blew, and it rained hard for a short while. When the sun finally broke through the clouds, the attendant turned to Mark.

"I can't go on," he said. "I couldn't sleep all night. I miss my family. I must return to Alexandria."

Mark was disappointed with the man, but he realized he should have been more involved in choosing his attendant. They returned to Alexandria. When he saw Garus, he approached him.

"My attendant only lasted one day," he said. "I need a more mature attendant."

"Why don't you take a priest-in-training with you?" Garus asked.

"Can you make a recommendation? I don't want to make that choice."

"I would take Bakus," he said. "I think he will be a fine priest."

Garus talked to Bakus, who agreed to travel with Mark.

The two started west along the sea. By noon, they passed the spot where Mark had slept a few evenings before.

"We are making good time," Mark said. 'You are a walker."

"I worked with my father," he said. "He grows grapes. He has a very small winery outside of Alexandria."

"My brother has a winery on Cyprus," he said.

They walked until the sun started to set. Without saying a word, Bakus put down his pack, opened it, and took out a net he had brought with him. He walked to the shore.

"You start the fire and I will catch dinner," he said, calling back.

Mark gathered some wood. By the time the fire was hot, the fish was cleaned, and Mark started cooking.

"We make a good team," he said. "Many of Jesus' disciples were fishermen."

Finally, they saw a sailing ship and realized that they were approaching Paraetonium. They headed toward Cyrene. Mark was happy when he saw Adam's farm. A servant saw him approach the house and met him at the door.

"Good day, Mr. Mark," he said. "I am sorry to inform you that Mr. Adam has died. But, you are welcome to stay with us."

Mark was grief stricken. He knelt and prayed. Bakus talked with the servant. They were escorted to the living room and served wine.

"I will send word to Bishop Matthew that you are home," the servant said. "He will want to talk with you. Are you planning to stay with us awhile?"

Mark looked over at Bakus.

"We might stay a year," he said. "The situation in Alexandria has become unsettled. The pagans are reacting to Nero's persecution of the Christians in Rome."

"We have plenty of room for you and your attendant," he said.

"Bakus is a priest-in-training," he said. "He will help me teach."

The next day, Matthew came to see Mark and brought Sara with him.

"It is good to see you," Matthew said. "The churches are doing well. Sara's church is doing very well. All of our staff members and servants are attending her church."

"Does she teach the Sabbath lesson?" Mark asked.

"No," he said. 'She teaches the mid-week lesson and only assists with the Sabbath lesson."

They talked most of the day. Matthew asked Mark and Bakus to attend a different church each week as a guest lecturer.

"I will be pleased to tell your members about our success in Alexandria." Mark said.

"Mark healed an injured cobbler," Bakus said. "It was a miracle."

"My members would like to hear about that," Matthew said. "What happened to him?"

Mark didn't answer.

"I will teach your members about Jesus' power to heal," Mark said. "I, myself, have no power outside of my faith in Jesus."

Matthew understood.

Later, he took Mark to Adam's grave. It was located in a very grassy spot that received a great amount of sun. It was beside the church at the farm. As Mark stood at the grave, he could see the church and the fields of grain. It was a peaceful location. They knelt and prayed for Adam's soul. The breeze gently blew, bending the stalks of grain towards Adam's grave.

"I think the grain is honoring Adam," Mark said. "I am certain he is with God, looking down on his farm."

Bakus proved to be a quick learner. After six months, he was teaching the Sabbath lessons. Matthew gave Bakus the position of priest in Sara's church. The priest at that church began working with and helping Mark. After one and a half years, Mark decided it was time to return to Alexandria. He decided to visit Jerusalem before returning to Alexandria.

CHAPTER 16

MARK'S DEATH

Soon after the great fire in Rome, Emperor Nero encouraged the persecution of the Christians. By the time two years had passed, Nero had rebuilt much of the city. He instituted many programs to help the people of the city who lost their homes or were affected by the fire. Although his popularity increased, Nero remained an unstable ruler. He suffered from paranoia and eventually expanded his persecution to include all people who worshipped one God. He specifically targeted those living in Rome and Jerusalem. In the year sixty-six, he sent Vespasian and his son, Titus, to Judea to confront the Jewish revolt. Vespasian had been the governor of North Africa and was known for his trickery and greediness. Mark, who was aware of Vespasian's behavior, became exceedingly worried. He felt compelled to visit Jerusalem.

Mark and his assistant prepared to sail to Jerusalem and talk with the followers of Jesus.

"I feel strongly that we should visit Jerusalem," he said. "The members of the church there are facing a great threat. I will write to remind them of Jesus' divinity and our purpose as his servants."

"I have never been to Jerusalem," he said. "I am looking forward to the visit."

They walked to the port in Paraetonium, and found a ship bound for Caesarea. Mark was pleased to learn it would only make one stop in Amathos, Cyprus.

When the ship arrived in Cyprus, Mark started towards the ramp. He planned to make a quick visit to his brother.

"Sir," a mate said. "You aren't allowed to leave the ship. We will only be here for two hours."

"My brother lives here," Mark said.

He thought for a few moments.

"Two hours probably isn't long enough for me to get to his place and back," he said.

Mark was very disappointed and frowned.

"You might like to stand at the ship's rail in the sun and watch the dock workers load the wine we will deliver to Caesarea," the mate said.

Mark and his assistant walked to the ship's rail. As they watched the workers, Mark noted a man on the dock watching the operation. He turned to the mate.

"I see my brother," he hollered. "May I go onto the dock and visit him?"

The ship's captain heard Mark's request as he headed toward the ramp.

"Which one is your brother?" he asked.

"The man standing on the dock with the sack in his hand," Mark said. "He manages the largest winery on the island."

"Follow me," the captain said. "I am going to see him. When we transport his wine, he gives me a few bottles, and in return I post a guard with his cargo."

They walked over to Joseph.

"Mark, is that you?" he asked. "I haven't seen you in years. Are you going to Jerusalem?"

"Yes, I am going to visit the church there," he said. 'I am living in Africa. I will return to Alexandria after I talk with the faithful."

They hugged each other and talked until the mate demanded that Mark return to the ship.

When the ship arrived in Caesarea, they found a wagon loaded with wine destined to an outlet. Mark and his assistant talked to the driver.

"Do you know a woman named Ester?" Mark asked. "She used to work at the wine outlet."

"I think I have met her," he said. "She is related to the owner of the outlet. My wagon is loaded. Get on board, and I will take you there."

When Mark and his assistant arrived, the manager of the outlet took them to Ester's house. She was surprised to see Mark.

"Come in," she said, "I will have a servant put your things in a room. You must stay with me for a few days."

Mark introduced Ester to his assistant.

"I can only stay until tomorrow," he said. "We are on our way to Jerusalem."

"Do you have a driver for tomorrow?" she asked. "We can provide transportation for you. I think Joshua was able to get Paul released. How is he doing?"

Mark smiled at Ester.

"He is fine," he said. "He is on a mission in Spain and plans to return to Rome. I am living in Africa now. I will spend the remainder of my life in Alexandria."

Mark decided not to tell Ester about the disciples in Rome being killed. He didn't want her to worry about him. Ester tried to remember her time in Africa. She visualized a large garden and working with her mother. As she looked into the sky, she smiled. Mark stayed with his sister for two days before departing for Jerusalem.

Mark directed the driver to the church. Matthias greeted and spoke with Mark.

"I have come to see James, Jesus' brother," he said.

"James was killed two years ago," he said. "I am trying to manage the church myself. Many of our members have fled Jerusalem."

"I have a scroll I wrote to help your members understand persecution," he said.

He handed the scroll to Matthias.

"The only person still here who you might remember is Mary," Matthias said. "She has been with me for several years."

Matthias introduced Mary Magdalene to Mark.

He had heard of Mary, but never met her.

"I am worried for your safety," Mark said. "The emperor has declared that he would eliminate all people who worshipped one God. He has already killed those in Rome, including Jesus' closest disciples."

"We are also afraid of the persecution," Matthias said.

"I'm returning to Alexandria," he said. "Any of you who are able to leave are welcome to travel with me."

Mary became excited.

"I will go with you," she said. "I have been a marked woman since I talked with Tiberius. He still tells people about the white egg that turned red while I held it before him."

"Talk with your friends and the other members," he said. "I am planning to leave as soon as possible."

Mark walked around Jerusalem that day. He didn't talk with anyone, but he visited his old house and Able's barn.

After two days, Mary approached Mark.

"I was able to gather five people who will go with us to Alexandria," she said. "As usual, I am the only woman."

Mark didn't have sufficient money to purchase passage on a ship for all of them, so they had to walk to Alexandria.

After a few days, they reached the Great Sea. One evening, as they sat around a fire, Mark asked Mary about her background.

"I was born in Magdala," she said. "Many people call me Magdalene, because Mary is such a popular name."

"How did you come to meet Jesus?" Mark asked.

"When I was a child, my parents purchased a boat from John's parents," she said. "John was two years younger than me and told everyone that when he grew up, he was going to marry me."

She looked at Mark and laughed quietly.

"Children are like that," he said. "He must have liked you."

"I didn't see John for many years," she said. "When I was possessed and visited Jesus, John was with him. Jesus removed seven demons from me, and I became a different woman."

"You were very fortunate that Jesus healed you," he said. "You must have had great faith."

"I traveled with Jesus for over two years," she said. "I worked with his sister to attract and minister to women."

"I am certain that he appreciated your help," Mark said. "How well did you know Salome?"

"Very well," Mary said. "When she traveled with Jesus, she stayed with me."

Mark smiled and nodded.

"I was at his crucifixion, burial, and resurrection," she said. "I was the first person to see Jesus after he was resurrected."

"He probably appeared to you because he loved you so much," Mark said. "When he told you to tell the other apostles that he was alive, he appointed you as the apostle to the apostles."

She stared at Mark in amazement.

"How did you know he told me that?" she asked.

"I was a close friend of Peter's," he said.

Mary hesitated a moment.

"I wasn't a close friend of his," she said. "I think he was envious of John and me. He thought Jesus loved us more than the other disciples."

Mary tossed her flowing long, black hair around her neck.

"I can't help but notice your hair," Mark said. "Many women have long hair, but they keep it hidden."

"I use my hair to cover my front when I walk in the bright sun," she said. "It also came in handy to dry Jesus' feet."

She looked at Mark, expecting a reaction. He disappointed her by not commenting. They continued their journey.

When they approached a great river, Mark noticed a man on a raft, ferrying people across. Mark approached him.

"We are very poor," he said. "How far down stream must we walk to find a bridge?"

"About two days," he said. "That is why I am here. This is how I make my living. Unfortunately, I can't take you across the river without some kind of pay."

Mark looked dejected. He went back and spoke with his group.

"I will take care of him," Mary said. "I will need your protection when we reach the other side."

Mark wasn't certain what she planned. Mary approached the man and pushed her hair back over her shoulders. The man stared. Mark was shocked. The man turned to Mark.

"Is she your daughter?" he asked. "Her hair is certainly beautiful."

"No," Mark said. "She is traveling with us."

The man motioned for them to board the raft. He talked with Mary as they crossed the river. When they reached the other side, Mary hugged him.

"The pleasure was mine," he said. "You and your friends come back to see me."

They waved to him as they proceeded west.

Before they reached Alexandria, Mark had learned a great deal about Mary, including her relationships with the other disciples. Levi and Philip were her close friends.

"I liked Philip because he respected me," she said. "He wasn't jealous. He knew Jesus and I were just good friends."

"When we get to Alexandria, I will introduce you to my bishop, Anianus, and my good friend, Garus," Mark said. His uncle will provide shelter for us."

Two days later, they arrived at Garus' house. A servant escorted Mark and his friends into the living room where Garus appeared.

"I have brought several of Jesus' followers from Jerusalem," Mark said. "The situation in Jerusalem is desperate. Vespasian, his son, and their troops are in northern Judea, planning their attack on Jerusalem. I have encouraged our friends to flee. Many will go to Antioch."

Garus had a slave show the men to a room, he provided each with a separate room, and he took Mark to his old room.

"No one has used your room," he said. 'You promised you would return. It is just as you left it. Welcome home, good friend."

After dinner that evening, they gathered in the living room, relaxed, and drank wine.

"This is good wine," Mary said.

She swirled the wine around in the glass.

"Are Christians being persecuted in Alexandria?" she asked.

"The situation is not good," Garus said. "We are currently at peace with the soldiers who are posted at the fortification. We hope to be able to maintain peace with them for a long time."

Mark addressed the group.

"If the situation turns worse, I want you to travel west and then sail to Gaul," Mark said. "Those in the western part of the empire are more tolerant. I have many friends in Cyrene. They will help you flee Africa."

Mary visualized the beautiful Rhone River valley. She had heard many stories of Gaul and that area. Mark saw that Mary's eyes were closed, and she was smiling. They talked late into the night.

The men found jobs and moved to a house they had rented. Mary stayed with Mark and Garus. The number of Christian faithful had greatly increased. They had built a church to honor Mark. The church was located outside the wall on the east side of the city. A large field, generally filled with cows, was located next to the church. All the farmers in the area attended the church. Garus took Mark and Mary to the edifice.

"Anianus is the bishop of this church," Garus said. "He will be pleased that you have returned to us."

"Mary and I need jobs," Mark said. "I would love to work with the priest at this church."

Garus was relieved that he wasn't interested in becoming the bishop.

"I know you will be provided a job at this church," Garus said. "Your friend, Mary, will have to talk with the bishop."

"Mary was a great friend of Jesus and knew all of the disciples," he said. "Maybe, she could teach at the school."

"I think that can be arranged," Garus said. "The men at the university are more tolerant of women who want a man's job."

"I will talk to the priest of the church," he said. "I will need a place to write. I am currently helping Mary write her gospel about Jesus."

Mark was welcomed by the staff and priests at the new large church. They were especially honored to have his help. He often helped the priests on busy Holy Days.

"I think you should know the locals refer to your church as the church with cows," the senior priest said. "It is a term of endearment to the farmers."

Mark looked at the priest and laughed.

"I can understand that," he said. "I like cows, fields, farmers, and many other of God's wonders."

The priest said. "Amen."

Pagans from all around the area of Alexandria came to the city to celebrate a pagan feast. The streets were crowded with drunken pagans. They were in high spirits when they entered the church where Mark helped the priests during the Christian Holy Day to celebrate Jesus' resurrection.

"We want to see your great Mark!" a spirited pagan yelled out. "Give us Mark or we will destroy your temple!"

Mark stood and walked to the man. They quickly seized him and bound his hands behind his back. Their quick action surprised Mark. He smiled at them.

"May God bless you," he said.

The pagans didn't listen. They placed a rope around Mark's neck and clubbed him until he fell to the floor. They dragged him outside the church and tied the other end of the rope to a donkey. It dragged Mark's body through the streets. The pagans jeered at the Christians who watched in horror.

"How do you like your cows now?" the pagan asked. "We worship good Gods, not cows. We worship the Sun God, the Moon God, the Rain God and many other Gods."

Mark remained unconscious. Eventually, the pagans took him to prison.

As Mark slept that evening, he again experienced a strange sensation. Mark knew he was about to be kill. He needed help and he wanted God's people to escape persecution. Suddenly, Mark saw the book of life. His name was listed in bolt letters. He felt like he was in the presence of something special. Mark looked toward the sky.

"My friends need God's protection," he said.

Mark felt like he was in the presence of God. A feeling of peace overtook him.

When the pagan placed a rope around Mark's neck the next morning, he didn't resist.

"I will pray for you," he said.

"You should pray for yourself," the pagan said. "I am alive, you are the one who is about to die."

Mark was martyred that day. They took his body to a large public area. They built a great fire and planned to burn his body. The Christians, who watched from afar, knelt and prayed. The pagans saw them and laughed. The wind blew strong and the fire roared with disapproval. Suddenly, sheets of rain fell from the dark sky, and the fire was extinguished. Mist from the drowned fire rose into the sky.

"God is telling us to leave him to his followers," a pagan said. "I think his God extinguished our fire."

The pagans began to flee the area. As they ran, some stumbled and fell. Many were trampled. The faithful took Mark's body to the church. They placed it in a coffin and buried it in a secret place under the building. Anianus and Garus spoke a final prayer for Mark's soul. They sealed the tomb, never revealing its location.

Mary and many church members fled to Cyrene and then, finally, to Gaul. The churches that Mark started in Africa remained strong and fought persecution. They grew and continued to be an important part of the Christian church.

ABOUT THE AUTHOR

The author served in the U.S. Navy and then went to college. After graduating with an engineering degree, he enjoyed careers (50 yrs.) as an engineer, businessman, and professor. He is now retired but writes novels.

While reading the New Testament for over sixty years and teaching Sunday School Bible classes for twenty years, John Mench Ph.D. has been conflicted by the lack of personality within the New Testament. He endeavors to add perspective to the message of the testament by creating lives for those who wrote and developed Jesus' message. He encourages you to refer to a Bible while reading this book.

Printed in the United States
By Bookmasters